Books

STAR 1

Extinction
Rebellion
Conquest
Battle Station
Empire
Annihilation
Storm Assault
The Dead Sun
Outcast
Exile
Gauntlet
Demon Star

REBEL FLEET SERIES
Rebel Fleet
Orion Fleet
Alpha Fleet
Earth Fleet

Visit BVLarson.com for more information.

Android and Aliens

(Star Runner Trilogy #3)
by
B. V. Larson

Star Runner Trilogy:
Star Runner
Fire Fight
Androids and Aliens

Illustration © Tom Edwards
TomEdwardsDesign.com

Copyright © 2022 by Iron Tower Press.

This book is a work of fiction. Names, characters, places and incidents are either products of the author's imagination or used fictitiously. Any resemblance to actual events, locales or persons, living or dead, is entirely coincidental. All rights reserved. No part of this publication can be reproduced or transmitted in any form or by any means, without permission in writing from the author.

ISBN-13: 979-8846418189
BISAC: Fiction / Science Fiction / Military

Chapter One

After chasing the alien horde away from Vindar, my crew needed a break. Even more important was the simple fact that we'd committed a considerable list of crimes in our efforts to save the Conclave. The long, slow arms of the law were catching up to us.

We made it back to Baron Trask's planet, Gladius, without much trouble. Trask gathered his fully human brothers among the Sword World planets and moved to destroy those who were Tulk-infested. Over time, he won the day.

With all that conflict going on, one would think a lowly smuggler could scoot by the androids in their patrol vessels unnoticed. But even as a struggle that amounted to a civil war between the human and Tulk-infested pirates raged, they kept a lookout for me, my crew, and our tiny ship.

Once we left the Sword Worlds, things went from worrisome to outright alarming.

"Captain, we're getting pinged again," Sosa told me as we entered Tranquility's stellar zone. She was studying a very sensitive and highly illegal set of sniffer algorithms. They were hacks, really, software tools that searched the local planetary grid for anything that was looking for us.

"The Conclave patrols are still looking for us?" I asked. "What about our latest identity edits?"

"You would think we'd be in the clear... but we aren't. Maybe we didn't get the best identity work from the pirates of the Sword Worlds."

I grumbled aloud. She was probably right. Baron Trask had offered to help us out for free—but he'd probably farmed the work to a low-bidding hacker. Who knew what new fake identity he'd bought and stapled onto my ship? For all I knew, I was Brak the Child-thief now, according to the law.

"All right... I guess we have to forget about a vacation on Tranquility."

My crew groaned aloud. Tranquility was a pleasure planet and everyone's favorite destination.

I ignored their complaints. The longer I looked at the warnings coming in from our software, the bigger my frown became. Coming to a fateful decision, I touched my microphone and addressed everyone aboard my small ship.

"Crew of the *Royal Fortune*," I said, "our plans have changed. This ship and everyone aboard are too hot to be visible right now. We're going to have to go to ground. The crew will disperse, and the ship will go into hiding."

"For how long?" Rose asked, her voice alarmed and upset. She was the sweetest member of my team and also my current bunkmate.

"Hmm..." I said, thinking it over. "Six months. Maybe a year. Until the Conclave cops forget about us."

"William, they're androids. They'll never forget."

"No, that's not exactly true. They won't forget us, but they'll lower the priority of our capture over time. They'll move on to more important targets, and we'll be able to travel around openly again."

"What about our shares?" Jort complained loudly. He was the most outspoken of my pirates, and the most laser-focused on the bottom line—his bottom line.

"You'll get your payouts—with a fifty-percent reduction. That's standard for ship maintenance and all the costs we've incurred over this last mission."

There was a lot of squawking after that, but I referred them back to their contracts. Vindar officials had paid us with tons of refined Rhodium, and we'd managed to sell off most of the stuff, but overall our paychecks had become somewhat thin.

Jort complained the loudest, but after I pointed out that he'd put a lot of holes in the hull with antipersonnel cannon ricochets, he eventually shut up.

Looking over the roster of planets where we could expect a cooler welcome, I chose Scorpii, Jort's home star system. They were half-criminal out there, as well as poor and a bit slow-witted. If a group of people could slip in and out of any system easily, it would be this one.

Jort was overjoyed about this, naturally, as it left him with no need to pay for a fare home. We dropped him off at the spaceport and saw no more of him.

"This is awful," Rose said. Her narrow shoulders sagged under the punishing gravity. "I can't believe anyone can live here. Just standing still and breathing is exhausting."

She was suffering the most due to the high gravity field, which pulled at every inch of your body at about double the normal rate. She walked in a stagger, and I cautioned her not to let her balance get off-center, or she'd fall hard. It wasn't uncommon for someone who wasn't accustomed to high gravity worlds to stumble and break bones when they hit the floor.

As quickly as she could, she found her way to a ticket booth and scanned her fake identity implants. They let her board a transport and just like that—she was gone.

Sosa sidled up to me and stood near. I glanced at her. "Where are you headed?"

She looked kind of shy. "I don't know. I... I don't really have a home. Kerson is dead and his satellite is abandoned, remember? I was planning on taking a vacation on Tranquility, but that's out of the question now."

"Right..." I said, realizing she really didn't have anywhere to go. She certainly didn't want to sit around on Scorpii. And nearby Prospero? That place was as dull as dishwater, and they hated outsiders there. "Hmm..."

Then I noticed the approach of another enigmatic figure from my small crew. He was a half-machine, half-man hybrid known as Huan. He was a bounty-hunter from the Faustian

Chain. He'd sort of attached himself to me after I'd passed up killing him and gave him a bigger mission instead.

"What about you, Huan?"

"What about me, sir?"

"I mean, what are you going to do while we all rest up between missions?"

He blinked at me with his one flesh eye. The other one was a camera, and it never blinked. "I don't understand."

"Well, we normally take breaks between missions, see? We've just finished with Vindar, and—"

Huan raised one claw-like metal hand. "But Captain, we *haven't* finished our mission. We must not rest. There is no time for such frivolities."

"Uh... what? What do you mean we haven't, 'finished?' Vindar is clean—no aliens! Even the Tulk have gone into hiding."

Huan studied me with his two very different, very disturbing eyes. "Cleansing Vindar was never my mission. Or at least, it was only a very small part of it."

Sosa and I studied him.

"What do you think our mission is, Huan?" Sosa asked reasonably.

"We must erase the Skaintz from the cosmos, of course. This requires locating and destroying every one of them."

"That's insane."

"It's a difficult task, admittedly."

I began to speak, but Sosa raised her hand before I could give him a dose of reality. "Huan, how do you think we should go about destroying all these aliens? There must be billions of them running around on a dozen different planets by now."

"Probably trillions. And there are nearly a hundred colony worlds in the Faustian Chain alone."

"Okay, okay," I said. "We're not done with the entire job. But such a struggle will likely take the rest of our lives and require the help of every human in the Conclave."

"Exactly. Under such circumstances I see no room in our mission description for hiding and creating delays."

Sosa threw up her hands. "We've already done more than our part, you crazy half-robot. Saving everyone isn't our job."

Huan studied her for a moment, then turned to me. "It seems that Sosa has resigned from our crew, Captain. We should seek new members."

"You know what?" I said, pointing a finger at him. "I know who you should serve with."

"Who?"

"That tall fellow, Lucas Droad. The guy who claimed to be a governor from the Chain."

"Droad was once the planetary governor of the colony world known as Garm."

"Whatever, whatever. That's your man. He'll never quit, and he'll never take a break. If I'd known that you were going to be this dogmatic, I would have left you on Vindar with him."

Huan thought this over for a minute, and he finally nodded. "Very well. I will take my wealth and seek Droad. I'll return to Vindar as quickly as I can."

I smiled and offered him my hand to shake, but he only studied it vaguely with his artificial eye until I dropped it.

He left us standing there in the spaceport and moved away rapidly.

Sosa laughed when he was gone. "You dodged him fast."

"He's a good guy, but he kind of grates on you after a while."

"Did you see the way he studied your hand? He reminded me of a dog wondering where his treat was."

We both laughed, and we headed for a canteen. There we enjoyed drinks and sandwiches and a good view of the blast-pans. After a few beers, I started to think maybe Sosa wouldn't be such a bad sort to be left with. She was the last of my crew, and—

"Captain?" Sosa asked me. "Is that...? Oh no... you don't think...?"

She was pointing out the window toward the spaceport fields. There, a ship was taking off.

It was a small, sleek vessel. The engines were too big for the craft, jetting out a plume of exhaust that dwarfed the ship. In a few seconds, that gush of heat and fire was only a distant spark.

Sosa and I looked at one another in astonishment. Both of us were left with our mouths hanging open.

"That was the *Royal Fortune*," Sosa said when she could breathe again. "Did Jort steal it?"

"No," I said, downing the rest of my beer. It had a bitter taste in it that I hadn't noticed before. "It was Huan… He's a zealot—and I'm an idiot. I should have seen it coming. He wanted nothing more than to go fight the aliens."

Sosa nodded slowly. "What was it he said? That he was going to go back to Vindar as quickly as possible?"

I sighed. "It looks like he meant what he said."

Chapter Two

It wasn't the first time I'd been left marooned on a backwater planet with no ship and few prospects. Fortunately, I had some cash with me this time.

Royal Fortune really had cost me in repairs—but nowhere near at levels I'd represented to my crew. My misrepresentation of the expenses had turned into wisdom now that I had fallen from grace. Perhaps this was all for the better. Maybe I'd have my vacation, and I might even find my ship again when I decided to go looking for her. After all, Huan hadn't said he was stealing it permanently—he'd only indicated a strong desire to return to the front lines out at Vindar.

"Captain, we have to stop that thief!" Sosa said.

I shrugged. The pinpoint of flame had vanished in the sky. Huan and my ship were both gone. "Are you seriously suggesting that we should report our own ship as stolen? Let's say, by some miracle, the patrolmen manage to capture *Royal Fortune*. Do you think it might show up as suspicious in some database or another?"

"Of course it will…"

"Yes. Then we'll never get the ship back."

"We should never have trusted that bounty hunter. He's half-machine and half-crazy."

I agreed with her there, but then the conversation died. We weren't in a strong position.

"Look," I said after a quiet minute had passed. "I can get another ship. That one isn't my first, and she won't be my last. I've got money and time. We might even be able to buy passage out there and recover the vessel."

Sosa didn't meet my eye. Unfortunately, I suspected she was seeing today's events in a very negative light.

Finally, she raised her head and gazed at me evenly. She lifted her hand to me, and her fingers trembled a bit. I wasn't sure if that was due to emotion or the powerful tug of Scorpii's gravity.

"Captain... I'll be leaving your service now."

"Really?" I said. "Even you, Sosa?"

She shrugged. "You said you wanted to break everyone up and lie low. This is our chance to do exactly that."

I thought it over, and I immediately understood. Moments ago, I'd been the captain of a smuggling ship. Now, I was a fugitive with a bit of cash in my pocket—and not much else.

Accordingly, I shook her hand and faked a smile. "You're right. This is exactly what I wanted. When this all blows over, we'll get our ship back and pull the old crew together. You'll still be interested in joining up again when that day comes, right?"

She studied the table between us and nodded. "I will be. I... I actually enjoyed much of my time spent with you."

Our meal ended, and I stood up to pay the check. I hugged her, and she left quickly. Was that rapid retreat due to regret, or to an urgency to escape this hot, heavy world? I wasn't sure, but I decided to believe she was full of sorrow and private yearning.

I left a pitiful tip and headed for the streets. Taking stock of things, I found I'd ended up with a spacers' bag half-full of personal belongings—almost none of which meant anything to me. My accounts—I checked them just to be sure—were entirely whole and filled with virtual cash. That was as safe as you could get when the Conclave patrolmen were looking for you.

The rest of the day was spent with my usual efforts to throw off any possible pursuers, real or imagined. I created several identities and discarded them rapidly. My best move came when I paid several parolees to take these identities and exit the star system under assumed names. Jort's people were unimaginative, so I only had to give these parolees some funds and small packets of potting soil. I claimed these packets contained a powerful hallucinogenic and gave the men instructions to smuggle them off-planet on my behalf.

One and all of these small-time criminals took the bait. Each wore a variation of my own name or some other alias that might be deemed suspicious. Believing they were transporting a tiny quantity of contraband, they took their missions seriously.

Once I was out of sight, most of them discarded the packets into handy receptacles before boarding their flights. A few kept theirs, possibly planning to partake of the mysterious substance on the trip. I had no way of knowing, nor did I care. I just wanted them to travel far and wide as red herrings to anyone who was on my trail.

It was odd doing this sort of thing out of reflex. Usually, it was an utter waste of time and resources. Upon occasion, however, I knew the practice yielded big dividends—mostly by keeping me out of prison.

Secure in my obscurity, I rented a jungle bungalow down near the beaches. This was never done by visiting tourists. As Scorpii was a high gravity world, it went without saying that the air pressure at sea level was nearly unbearable. Being from a world that also had a higher-than-average gravitational tug helped me to adapt.

I lived in my rented cabin for weeks, walking the beaches and wearing next to nothing in the way of clothing. I took frequent swims in the ocean to cool off. As a side effect, the natural buoyancy of sea water was an excellent relief from the gravity, so I spent hours snorkeling and trolling the bottom for free sources of food.

After approximately three weeks of this "vacation" I came out of the waves dripping wet and tanned the color of old bronze. To my utter surprise, a man stood on the beach just beyond the reach of the waves. He appeared to be waiting for me.

Some men might have dived back in and swam deep. Others might have attacked him. I took a different approach.

"Hullo!" I said, waving a wet arm in his direction. "We don't get many visitors out here on the beach!"

The man stood still. He didn't speak. He didn't move at all.

I approached him anyway, faking a big smile. "Are you my landlord?" I asked. "I hope there isn't any trouble with my bill, I just—"

"Captain Gorman…" the man began, and as soon as I heard him speak, I knew the truth.

He was an android. A Q-class, if I didn't miss my guess. They were the most sophisticated types, able to appear almost human in their manners and speech-patterns.

A less charitable man would have attacked for certain, now that this stranger had made several critical errors. He'd identified himself as a robot, which meant he was almost certainly connected to the Conclave government. Sure, there were crews and servants who were androids, but most of them were cops.

Worse, he'd addressed me by my real name. That was grounds for a solid killing right there. I was a fugitive and worse. I had a dozen crimes on my head, two for every day of the week except for Sundays, which I liked to take off when I could.

I stopped walking and waving. I stared at him, and he stared at me. Despite the sea breezes and the uneven sand, he still remained stock-still. It was unnerving, how motionless a robot could be.

"Who are you?" I asked him.

"I'm an inspector. An inspector general from Mutual."

"From Mutual? The planet?"

"Yes."

This was a shocker. I had no trouble imagining I'd attracted the attention of some local detective, perhaps a leadfooted gumshoe who'd been assigned to patrol this miserable planet.

But an inspector general was something different. I'd only heard of the rank, I'd never met anyone who claimed to hold it.

Just as surprising was his stated origin. Mutual was a planet at the very heart of the Conclave. All planets were equal, according to Conclave doctrine—but Mutual was much more equal than most. It was, in fact, the planet that held most of the governmental bureaucracy that ran the Conclave. It was our capital, so to speak.

"Um..." I said, dumbfounded.

I thought of a dozen lies, of course, but they all seemed doomed to failure. If this being was a Q-class from Mutual, and a government official to boot, he probably had a hundred agents lurking in the trees along the beach behind him to back him up—but then again, maybe he didn't.

"Is there anything that I can do for you, sir?" I asked.

"Yes. Yes, there is, Captain Gorman. I want you to accompany me."

"Where to?"

"Mutual, of course. I've been dispatched by the Connactic to find you and bring you in."

The Connactic? That was another shocker. Supposedly, the most gifted leader of the Conclave was the person known as the Connactic. The title denoted an all-knowing omniscience.

That wasn't the really weird thing, however. What was really caroming around in my brain were the rules of this government. There wasn't supposed to be a Connactic—not normally. Not unless there was some kind of extreme emergency going on.

After swallowing hard, I managed to utter a question. "For what? Questioning?"

The android shrugged. "We desire information, of course. But that's not the primary reason. We wish to offer you a deal."

"A deal? Seriously?"

More than anything else, this idea put me on my guard. Patrol androids from the Conclave didn't make "deals"—at least, not with the likes of me.

"Okay," I said. "But I want immunity for all my future indiscretions, and a full pardon for any I might have committed in my past."

"Really? That is quite a big ask."

"No one would come all this way to find me if they didn't want to talk to me quite badly."

I was in the territory of sheer conjecture now, but if bargaining with pirates and thieves all my life had taught me anything, it was to make your demands clear and up-front. When you were dealing with the government, that was doubly true.

The android lifted a hand to his chin. I tensed, expecting him to call in a pack of patrolmen with shock-rods—but they didn't materialize. Maybe he really was aping a human gesture that indicated he was deep in thought.

"What you suggest is within the realm of the possible. There would have to be caveats, of course. A list of acts so heinous in nature that they could not be forgiven."

"Uh... that seems fair..."

"Come then. Let us travel to Mutual. This planet is draining my batteries with the mere effort it takes to stand upright."

"Okay. After you, sir."

The android turned and walked up the beach. I followed him, and soon we came in sight of a patrol ship. It looked like a standard-issue model. I'd run from dozens of such vessels. I'd even blown a few out of space.

That was it for me. I almost halted, or turned and fled.

It was all bullshit. All this crap about the Connactic and Mutual—I'd been duped.

This guy was just a patrolman with extra software, I figured. Maybe he had a module installed for dealing with difficult types like me. They'd obviously learned to lie, and I'd been taken in. I was impressed—and also disturbed.

Instead of running, I took a few longer strides. When I was close enough, I snatched up a large stone and knocked the android's head off.

Chapter Three

Some people might choose to judge me harshly for the actions I took over the next half-hour. There were dark deeds performed, there's no denying that.

Taking the head off of a patrolman was just the beginning. It messed them up as they had a lot of sensory gear in there—but it didn't put them out of the fight. In the end, I had to open up his circuitry and shove him into the seawater. That did the trick, shorting out some of his internals.

He wasn't done even then. His eyes were still moving, inside that dangling head. His face contorted as he worked to look at me. He tried to speak, and his hands clutched at wet sand.

Fortunately, he couldn't talk. I didn't want to hear anything else he had to say. He was a liar, and an abomination, as far as I was concerned. I'd always been the type to bear a grudge against robots—especially when they looked and acted like humans.

Leaving him there in the surf, I walked to his open patrol ship and hacked my way into the pilot's capsule. The Q-type had been the only android aboard except for a few model-D jobs that didn't even wake up when I passed their charging booths.

I fiddled with the controls and gave them some emergency override commands that I'd used before. Being of small imagination, the androids never seemed to change their passwords. Maybe it would have been too difficult to disseminate the new ones if they did.

The ship roared and shuddered. Soon, it left the surface of the planet behind. No one appeared to pursue me. I allowed myself a tight smile when I left orbit.

Sure, I was in a stolen patrol ship. I knew that this solution couldn't last long. Every robot in the Conclave would soon get a priority alert. I was a hunted man again, on the run, and without any clear way to escape my fate—what else was new?

The ship rose farther and farther, skirting the larger of Scorpii's two moons. It was then that I got another shock.

Lurking out there, on the far side of the larger moon, was a fleet of vessels—an actual *fleet* of ships. After counting twenty, I stopped. There were sixty or more. There had to be.

Worse, I couldn't steer away from them. The controls were locked.

I hissed out a breath between my teeth. I hadn't been as clever as I'd thought. I'd been captured after all.

Oh sure, I tried everything. I sent out random distress messages. I faked the android's voice and demeanor. I even tried claiming I was the Connactic himself—but it was no dice. No one even bothered to answer me and my nonsense.

I hopped into an escape pod—but nothing happened. The controls were locked, the ship was locked, and I was trapped inside.

After I'd finally accepted my fate, I rubbed sand off my feet onto every surface of the cockpit that I could reach. It probably wouldn't interfere with the model-Ds that were assigned to clean things up, but I could dream.

As always, it took a damnably long time for them to get around to arresting me. Nearly an hour after I'd stolen the ship, a squad of four combat units boarded the ship. They were model-Ks, armored and armed with shredders.

I managed to take out two with a trap I'd rigged out of boredom. This consisted of a hot wire set just about kneecap level over the deck. When they came in, two abreast, the first two toasters were burned and incapacitated.

The rest slashed down the wires, and they stalked forward with even greater care than before.

All the while, they spouted their saccharine morality at me. They talked in a monotone about giving up my antisocial ways and how they wanted to help me. They always wanted to "help" people they were trying to arrest—or kill.

My second trap and my third failed. The remaining androids were too cagey, too alert to be fooled by more wires and even a minor explosive. I hoped the front man had at least suffered a bit of anxiety when his chassis was singed.

At last, they found me lounging with my dirty bare feet in the control room. I'd taken a piss on the instruments by this time—it was the little touches that could bring a man to smile after a few years of incarceration.

Of course, I expected a good beating. I deserved it. I'd more than earned a rain of blows from shock-rods at the very least.

But they didn't do any of that. They clamped onto my arms, forming perfect O's around my wrists and biceps with their plastic hands. After a few minutes of grunting and struggling, they became tired of being kicked by dirty bare feet, so they clamped onto my ankles as well.

Then, oddly, they stopped moving. They crouched there, four of them, holding me in place in the pilot's seat. I finally gave up on squirming and lay back, panting instead.

"So... what's the plan, boys?" I asked. "Are you just going to hold onto me until I starve to death?"

"We're monitoring your vital signs, sir. You're in no danger—not from yourself or others."

"Huh... that's good to know. I can't thank you guys enough."

All my irony and sarcasm were lost on them, but I didn't care.

Time passed. It felt like an hour—maybe longer. I spoke to them now and then. I raved a little.

I had to admit, if this was a new and novel form of punishment from the Conclave. It was ingenious. I was beginning to regret my choices in life, and I hadn't even been to an auto-court and sentenced by some plastic man in robes yet.

At last, I heard a new arrival. The airlock wheezed and gasped, letting a puff of space-cold air into the ship.

My eyes were puffy from my struggles, but I was able to see the control boards. Lights were flashing red, then green. The airlock was cycling.

Someone had come aboard.

I didn't bother to ask the model-K drones about it. They wouldn't tell me anything useful—if they spoke at all.

At last, I heard a softer footfall behind me. Someone had entered the cockpit—which was a tight squeeze with everyone clamping onto my extremities.

"Hey," I said. "It's about time you showed up."

"It is?" a voice asked.

I frowned. That wasn't a model-K. It wasn't how they talked. Model-Q, I figured—a sophisticated one.

"Yeah," I continued. "These guys have a firm grip on my feet and hands—but my dick is still loose and liable to make trouble. Maybe you should grab onto it."

"Heh," the other said.

My frown deepened. No android I'd ever met had a sense of humor. They never even grunted with fake laughter to make you feel better.

"Who are you?" I asked, straining to look at the figure, who was now nearby but still behind me.

"Turn the prisoner around—but keep him in his chair."

Slowly, working like a squad of synchronized swimmers, they spun me and the pilot's chair around to see who was standing in the doorway.

It was quite a shock. It was the android from the beach. I had no trouble recognizing him, as he had a split down his neck and shoulder, where I'd struck him repeatedly.

His head was back on, but it wasn't quite secured perfectly. It had been glued there, I figured. Only half of the face operated, the rest being slack and paralyzed.

The android smiled at me with half his face. "You're quite an interesting creature," he said. "More than I'd ever expected you to be, Captain Gorman."

"Thanks," I said, but I was no longer smiling. All the laughter had gone out of me. It had somehow transferred to the strange plastic being who faced me. "Um…" I said, thinking things over. "Sorry about hitting you, back on the beach. You scared me. I thought you were some kind of nutcase trying to abduct me."

The android nodded, but that only made his rubbery head and face bob grotesquely. "A very interesting case. You're a feral human, Gorman. Do you know that? We meet them now and then, but they usually aren't clever. Sociopaths. Frightened and animalistic primitives—we find plenty of those. But you are different. You're something of a throwback to a more aggressive type of human."

"That's a good thing, right?"

"In your case, on this strange and desperate day, yes. It is."

He studied me like a bug under a microscope for a moment. Then he gestured past me, toward space outside. The fleet still hung out there.

"Did you notice the squadrons we've assembled?"

"I could hardly have missed them."

"Did you know that the Conclave lacks a true fleet?"

I blinked a few times. "Uh… I thought we had cruisers."

"Have you ever seen one?"

I shook my head.

The android smiled. "What do you think would be cheaper, an imaginary fleet that everyone assumes exists, or a true mass of expensive metal and radioactives?"

It was my turn to look shocked. "You guys faked it? Seriously?"

He shrugged again, and his rubbery ears flopped a little. "Not entirely. We have some ships—but they're not impressive. Antiquated. Probably less than what the Sword Worlds could field, if they put all their strength together at once."

My jaw sagged open. My eyes were almost as wide as my gaping mouth. It all made sense to me. Why had the Conclave put up with so much from various upstart colonies? Why had they sat with their hands folded while others wrote history?

"The Sword Brothers..." I said. "Their piracy is rampant. Out on the Fringe, planets war and struggle as if the Conclave doesn't exist. Even worse... *things* lurk out there. Things from farther away."

"That's right. We lacked the strength to respond to such threats."

"Why are you telling me all this?"

The android pointed at my hands. "Are you ready yet to behave yourself? If I let you rise and sit with dignity?"

"Yes," I said quickly—a little too quickly.

The strange android smiled again with the side of his face that still operated. "All right. Release the prisoner."

Instantly, all four moving at once, the patrolmen let go of me. I sat up and rubbed at my wrists.

"Thanks. I never would have attacked you if I'd known..."

"Known that I commanded a fleet in high orbit over Scorpii?"

I shrugged. That was exactly what I meant. I'd hoped he was a lone patrolman, trusting to his luck to make the collar without a struggle.

"You are forgiven—for now. Come, let's find a more comfortable venue to discuss matters."

I followed him to the ship's tiny lounge. K-class patrolmen crowded behind me. They hadn't let go of their shredders. I could tell they were just itching to put thirty or forty low-velocity slugs into my back.

We made it to the lounge without incident, and the strange android leader allowed me to make myself a beverage. I mixed straight black coffee with a shot of *adrenol*—a mild stimulant that was legal out here on Scorpii.

Sipping the mixture, I made a face of disgust, then gulped it down. The androids watched me carefully.

The smart guy with the wrecked head spoke when I sighed in relief. "Let us start again, shall we? As I said, I'm an inspector general from Mutual. Do you believe me now?"

I shrugged. "Your claims certainly bear more weight now than they did when I first met you. Do model-Qs of your rank usually fly in patrol ships?"

The inspector shook his head. A single greasy droplet flew in my direction from his damaged neck. I was pleased to see that it didn't land in my coffee.

"No," he said. "We don't fly in patrol ships. We never leave Mutual—not normally. And my answer is 'no' to the rest of your implied question as well."

"Um... what implied question?"

"No, I'm not a model-Q. I'm something you've probably never encountered before."

Chapter Four

Being a man who's walked on fifty or more planets, I'm not easily surprised by new things. Recently, in fact, I'd confirmed that humanity had at least two other sentient alien species in our local star cluster to contend with.

I'd been under the impression for a long time now that I had the Conclave all figured out. A group of stodgy, aging dotards ran the place. Ancient crones and nearly mummified leches lurked at the core of the place, so set in their ways they wouldn't consider a new thought if it bit them in the ass.

Under that, there was a layer of plastic men. These were the ultimate bureaucrats and musclemen. Artificial and unquestioning. There were three classes of these—that I knew of, at least. Model-D androids weren't much better than robots. Barely human in shape, they were incapable of anything other than canned speech. They did menial jobs in a repetitive, incurious manner.

A serious cut above these were the model-K units. They came in a variety of types, from armed guardians to servants wearing skirts and heels. They were unimaginative, but they could talk and reason, after a fashion. They had replaced human laborers in many situations.

The smart ones, however, were the model-Q line-up. If you wanted a captain for a starship, you bought a Q. If you wanted a surgeon, it was a Q every time. They weren't quite human, and they had their specialties they liked to stick to, but they were quite capable of changing their behavior situationally.

I squinted at the thing that was staring at me with its half-wrecked head and face. "What's your name?" I asked him.

This was a question you never asked an android. They didn't have names, they had roles and tasks that defined them.

The inspector general eyed me back. "That is... a very good question. I don't have one. Not really. I had a designation, but it amounts to an account number. A login ID that is nearly random in nature."

"Okay... what are the last two characters in your number? I'll use that."

"Heh..." he said. "A nickname? I've never had one before."

There it was again. A near laugh. It kind of freaked me out. Plastic men didn't laugh. Ever.

"B-6 is the ending of my identification code," he said. "Is that what you wish to call me? I would prefer you used my title."

"Inspector general is too long. It's impersonal. If you're an entirely new kind of android... well, you deserve a name."

"Very well," B-6 mused. "You may call me B-6 if it makes you feel more comfortable."

I continued to squint at him. In part, my nonsense about wanting to give him a name was a test, a measurement of how far I could move this particular new hunk of plastic and circuitry.

"Perhaps it's now time for us to discuss the reason I've invited you onto my ship—to my fleet, in fact."

"It's *your* fleet? Isn't there an admiral involved, or something?"

B-6 shook his nasty head as much as he was able. "No. We don't really have a military here at the Conclave. Not in the traditional sense. We have a police force. It's paramilitary at best. You've met quite a number of our patrolmen and guardian units, I assume?"

"Yes. I'm intimately familiar with them."

"Of course... they are effective when it comes to arresting most smugglers like yourself. Long ago, it was determined that we didn't need a true military. The combination of an effective police force combined with convincing *talk* of a military was an excellent deterrent. Better yet, it saved the Conclave an immense amount of money."

My jaw sagged a bit again. I was astounded. Everyone had always assumed that... "But there are recruitment videos! You even advertise on social networks... I had no idea."

B-6 smiled. He seemed proud, even smug. "Yes, you see the beauty of it, don't you? It has been a highly effective social-engineering campaign."

"Propaganda, you mean."

He raised a finger between us. "We don't use that word."

"Whatever. But... what about the people who apply to work in the force? What do you tell them when they learn it's all a façade?"

He shrugged. I'd never seen an android shrug before. He was definitely more convincing than the usual models. "They don't learn the truth because they're never allowed to join. They're given a series of impossibly restrictive tests, then they're told they're not good enough to serve in the force."

"Diabolical..."

"Nonsense. Until recently, it was sheer genius. How do you think our economy has managed to sustain such a high standard of living and yet keep strict order for so many years?"

I shook my head, both bemused and slightly outraged. I was, admittedly, a con-artist, a thief, and a vagabond most of the time. But I'd never even attempted a con on such a grand scale. It would never have occurred to me.

A new thought came to my mind, and I looked up at my new plastic friend. "Who decided to do this? And why are you telling me about it?"

"The Conclave leadership made the decision, of course. They make all such decisions. As to why I'm telling you... you'll find out when we reach Mutual."

"We're going to Mutual?"

"Look outside."

I turned toward a viewscreen on the wall of the lounge. It looked like a window—but that was fake. It was a high-resolution screen.

Outside, I saw the blue-shifting stars. We were moving toward them at speed. Soon, we'd probably reach a slip-gate and be whisked away to another star system. They must have good inertial dampeners on this ship. I hadn't felt the acceleration at all.

"Why would you halt an entire fleet—even a fleet of simple patrol ships—just to pick me up from Scorpii?"

There was no answer. I craned my neck again, but B-6 had disappeared. I reflected that he wasn't all that human in his social behavior. A normal man of flesh and blood probably would have said goodbye.

Turning back to the blue-shifted stars, I watched them pass by. In turn, the crowd of Model-Ks that surrounded me studied my every fidgeting motion to make sure I didn't escape.

I made no move to do so. Not yet. This definitely wasn't the time.

About a half-hour passed before we reached the slip-gate and passed through it. I felt a slightly sick feeling—was I really headed to Mutual?

Of all the star systems I'd ever dared to visit, that one had never made the list. It was the heart of the Conclave. The place was home to every official I'd spent my entire lifetime trying to avoid—two lifetimes, if you counted the years before I died and my clone version took over. I'd never even considered setting foot on this planet.

But here I was, under arrest and traveling at physics-bending speeds into the throat of the dragon I'd always feared. It was hard to believe, and it even harder to come up with a way out of it.

During the dull journey, I was only allowed to leave the chair three times a day. Each time was for the express purpose of relieving myself. The rest of the trip—every second of it—I was forced to sit in place. I became quite sore after a while, as the human body isn't designed to sit still for days—especially mine. But the androids who were my jailors didn't even answer my complaints and suggestions. It was as if they were scripted not to listen to me at all.

So, I took my meals in the chair, I stretched in the chair, I slept in the chair, and I schemed in that same chair.

This was a tough predicament. It was one thing to avoid capture—I had a lot of experience with that—it was quite another to escape after being captured. What made things infinitely worse was the fact that they seemed to know me. They expected to be tricked and have surprises thrown at them. How could I work any magic with a pack of mute model-Ks standing around staring at me?

Oh, I tried a few moves. I did the whole "look over there" thing, embarrassing as it might seem—they didn't even turn their heads. I pretended to sleep, and when one of them was charging I lashed out at the others. They grabbed all my limbs again and pinned me until I stopped struggling, exhausted.

I spent most of my time trying to strike up a conversation. The patrolmen were doggedly impossible to reach. No number of false claims about impending ship disasters, lies about their master having called or even attempts to get them to tell me the time of day budged any of them. They stood, they stared, and they didn't say or do a damned thing that I wanted them to.

Finally, I gave up and snored until the ship shuddered, signaling our arrival.

I half-expected to meet B-6 again, but it wasn't to be. We docked at a planet that looked like an urban nightmare, and I was hustled out of the ship. I found I could hardly stand up straight after so many hours spent in a chair. After a few steps, I got my feet working again and walked with dignity.

The patrolmen took me to an airlock, then a quarantine chamber. There, I was poked and prodded. The model-Q doctors were very thorough. They didn't want a spare microbe or virus particle to get through to their shiny, perfect planet.

After the medical process, I was allowed onto a space station. It was a grand affair, perhaps the biggest I'd ever seen. For all of that, it was a dull place. There weren't a lot of regular folks around—in fact, almost everyone I saw was a model-Q or a model-K. Like all androids, they weren't much for loud talk and laughter.

Next, I was taken to a cleansing facility where I was thoroughly scrubbed by model-Ds scripted for this sole purpose. I much preferred a gentler touch when bathing—or better yet to be allowed to scrub myself, but the robots had different ideas.

Thoroughly washed and given a pair of gray coveralls to wear, I was eventually led to the umbilical station. This was an elevator of sorts that connected the space station to the ground.

There, I was finally met by the only familiar face I knew of on Mutual—B-6 himself. The damage I'd done when I'd bashed his head off back on Scorpii had been repaired. Maybe that's what he'd been up to while I was lounging in that damned chair.

"I trust you had a pleasant journey?" he asked me in a cheerful tone. It was weird, almost like he thought we were besties or something.

"It was kind of dull, but I survived it."

"Excellent. Come, let's look at the planet itself."

He led me to the edge of the elevator disk, which was plunging down a clear tube of polymer filaments toward the distant surface. Although we were traveling at around a hundred kilometers an hour, it was going to take a long time to reach the bottom from orbit.

"Behold Mutual, our most glorious planet," B-6 said, sweeping an arm over the view.

I ignored the planet, which looked exactly like every other urbanized hive I'd visited before. The Conclave was full of them. Instead, I studied B-6. He was far more interesting. He seemed prideful, in fact, about his damned planet.

That was weird, too. Model-Q types could simulate human reasoning and behavior. They had good judgement and many refined skills—but they didn't generally go around bragging about them. They didn't brag about anything. That was a purely human quality.

B-6 was breaking all the rules I'd lived with my whole life. The limitations of what an AI-based being was capable of had been clearly delineated since I was young—but this fellow didn't conform to those rules.

"B-6? Why aren't all androids as sophisticated as you are?"

He stopped talking about the view, and he turned toward me. He stared at me with those artificial eyes.

"An interesting question. I'll give you a reality-based answer. There are two reasons: one, because of expense. It takes more resources to produce a being like myself. We have to be taught and trained for years."

"You mean you go to school?"

"Something like that."

I nodded. "Hmm... and the second reason?"

He glanced at the patrolmen who stood valiantly at my side. "It's a matter of maintaining a cooperative social balance. If a being such as myself were to be given the job of a patrolman—or bathing a human like the model-Ds did in your case—that being would become bored. He might even come to be distressed by his insignificant role."

"Ah... so if you were all geniuses, you'd compete? You'd all want the glory jobs and there wouldn't be enough to go around. Therefore, you make less sophisticated models in order to keep each individual content with their slot in society."

"You catch on quickly."

I smiled at him. "It's one of my few true skills."

After that, B-6 stopped prattling on about the view. Maybe he was smart enough to realize that I didn't care. We continued our descent in silence, and after what seemed like a very long time, we reached the surface.

Chapter Five

Yawning after the long trip, I was hustled onto yet another contrivance, this time a deep-crust tram. It whizzed away, and I noted I was the only human passenger, with B-6 and his ever-present team of mute guardians as my companions.

"Um..." I said, looking around in concern. "It's getting a bit hot. Are we traveling deeper than usual into this planet?"

"Yes, but that isn't the only reason for the increased temperature. At extreme speeds, traveling through stone on magnetic rails causes friction. The atmospheric pressure is building on the external hull, and to top it all off, Mutual has a hotter core than you might be used to."

I nodded and sweated for a few more minutes, then I thought to complain again. "Don't you have air conditioners or something?"

B-6 shrugged. "We never bothered to install them. We don't often bring humans down here."

"Oh..."

At last, the long ride down to Hell ended. We stepped off the train an unknown distance beneath the planet's green surface. I felt a longing for fresh air. A light, cool rain would be even better.

I received nothing of the kind. Although the chambers we marched through weren't entirely unpleasant, they had an oppressive feeling to them. I suspected it was due to the higher pressure down here, as well as the heat. I felt slightly out of breath. It was an unpleasant sensation, but I'd experienced worse.

At last, at the end of a long, echoing corridor that was completely unadorned, we came to a plain, metal door. It opened silently at our approach, and I was ushered inside.

To my surprise, my entire entourage stayed on the far side of that door. B-6, his squad of patrolmen, they all vanished when the door shut just as silently as it had yawned open in the first place.

"Uh... hello?"

The room was lit with a flickering light. I tried not to sweat. I didn't even want to think about sweating, but it was impossible not to.

I walked into the chamber, which was featureless except for a tall metal desk that was impeccably clutter-free. I walked up to the desk and ran a finger along the edge.

"Shit..." I said, lifting a sliced-open forefinger to my frowning gaze. The edge of the desk was sharp. Really sharp. How odd...

"Mr. Gorman?" said an odd voice.

I turned, trying not to whirl around in alarm—but I failed.

There, entering the chamber behind me, was a woman. She looked remarkably like many other androids I'd met before. Another silent, all-metal door snicked shut behind her, and she walked behind the desk.

I looked around in confusion. "Um... is there anyone else coming to meet me?"

She seemed amused. Another unusual reaction for an android. But her features were too perfectly formed to be anything else.

"No, I'm the one who summoned you here to Mutual. I hope you're not disappointed."

"No, no, not at all. Can you tell me why you've brought me here?"

She cocked her head. "Haven't you guessed yet?"

"Well... I don't know. It has to be either to question me or to punish me for various misunderstandings in the past."

She smiled again. "It was for both those reasons, I suppose, and a few others."

"Can I ask your name, lady?"

"I don't have a name," she said. "I have a title. I'm the Connactic."

Struck dumb, I didn't know what to say. All of a sudden, things were becoming very clear to me—all at once.

"You're an android, right?"

"You guessed it."

"But... *you're* the Connactic? The top official in the entire Conclave?"

"Yes. There is no one else with my level of authority and capacity in the entire star cluster—at least, I don't know of another."

"But... that means humanity is ruled by the androids, not the other way around," I blurted out, and I immediately regretted my words. "No offense. I'm just taken by surprise."

"No need to apologize. You've been led to believe elderly human citizens run things here on Mutual. There's no reason why you would think anything else. In fact, I'm experiencing a surge of pride right now."

"You are?"

"Yes. I really wasn't sure how long it was going to take you to figure it out. Tell me, what tidbit of evidence tipped the balance for you?"

My mind swirled as I tried to grasp the situation and answer her intelligently. I was blown away. All my life, there had been pageants on the net showing a succession of individuals, family names of various rulers, ceremonies and dull speeches.

Had everything been a lie? Every boring detail of politics as I understood it?

Realizing she was still staring at me, expecting an answer, I worked hard to pull one out of my ass. "Well... once I came in here, it was obvious this office wasn't designed for a human, much less an elderly citizen."

"Exactly."

"So... even the desk was wrong. It has an edge on it, as sharp as a blade. No human would sit at a desk like that." I showed her my sliced finger, and she looked intrigued.

"This is excellent. Quite an achievement for my underlings."

"Um... how's that?"

She pointed a finger at me. "You. You're the variable that was overcome. You're a very cynical and cunning human, a man of the basest sort. Despite that, even *you* were fooled all the way to this very moment. That's impressive. I'll have to put a commendation into the files for both the Department of Truth and the Department of Social Stability."

"The department of what?"

The Connactic waved away my words. "Never mind. That doesn't concern you. Let's move on. I don't have time to indulge myself, to savor my successes. There are too many unresolved crises, too many failures to waste processing time on self-reinforcement."

"Uh... okay. What do you want to talk about next?"

She gazed down at that flat, brushed-chrome surface of her desk. Suddenly, it lit up and displayed a starscape. I recognized the ovoid mass of stars instantly. It was a high-resolution representation of the Conclave. The entire cluster was there, out to the fringes.

"Our home stars," I said, recognizing the chart.

"Yes," she said. She tapped a reddish star far from the center. "You were born out on Avalon, near the Fringe, yes?"

I swallowed hard. Very few people knew my home planet. I was alarmed to think this super-android was familiar with it—and my sordid past.

"Yes," I admitted.

"Fifty-six standard years ago... but chronologically, you're about thirty-nine. You were the sixth in a line of clones laid down in cold storage on Prospero."

"Uh..."

Everything she was saying was blowing my mind. I had no idea the original Gorman would have been fifty-six, but thirty-nine sounded about right. The real shocker was the idea that there had been five clone-brothers before me. What had happened to them?

I had the feeling I didn't want to know the details.

"As you can see, we've been very thorough in our pursuit of one William Gorman. We've caught you—almost—on many occasions. Always, you managed to evade our budgetary limits."

"Your what?"

She cocked her head and looked at me. "You see, we operate the Conclave in a very orderly fashion. When a fugitive is identified, a budget is drawn up for his capture. If that budget is exceeded without capture, the matter is set aside until the target rises in priority again, or is handled in some other way."

"Some other way? Like what?"

She shrugged. "Your kind often dies, eliminating the problem. You kill each other, dare too much, venture to worlds you shouldn't... in most cases, difficulties such as yourself take care of themselves."

"Huh..." I said, thinking that I had indeed done all those things on her list. So far, I'd escaped everything. "What then, made you raise the budget on me?"

"News of events on Vindar. That world has been a curiosity for a century now. It's neither part of the Conclave nor the Faustian Chain. We heard of alien activity there, and we became concerned. You took action before we did. You gathered a fleet—the only fleet humanity really has right now—and you took it out there to defeat the aliens on your own."

I puffed up with pride. "Yes. I did that. It seemed to me— to all humans—that the Conclave has been sleeping for far too long. Even now, it might be too late."

She nodded. "Budgets. Again, it was all due to our algorithms—which were laid down during the days when humans ran the cluster. We manage things from the ledger here on Mutual. We always have. It works remarkably well—but it's inflexible, and we don't adapt well."

I was kind of surprised she didn't offer any stronger defenses for her failures, but at least she was willing to admit them. It was a start.

She looked down at the starscape again. At the edge of it, a star lit up in blue. She zoomed out farther, and soon another cluster appeared. This one was far more ragged and disjointed than the Conclave, which was egg-shaped.

As I watched, the Faustian Chain transformed to a blood red.

"These are now enemy stars."

"All of them? *All* of them are lost? I'd heard that from Droad... but I'd hoped it wasn't true."

"All of them," she said. "No humans exist there independently, other than a few wild types reduced to savagery. Most are chattel. Herds for the consumption of the Skaintz swarm."

"What are we going to do about it? What can I do to help?"

The Connactic looked up and gazed at me with her insightful, artificial eyes. "We are going to strike back at the Skaintz. We're going to raise a great fleet, and we're going to destroy them all—or we'll be destroyed ourselves. Are you willing to help us, William Gorman?"

I nodded grimly. "I'll do what I can."

Chapter Six

The Connactic shipped me out to the Fringe and beyond. I was glad to see Mutual shrinking away behind me. The planet gave me a shudder just to think about it—and I've seen some pretty awful places in my time.

It wasn't just the bad, metallic, sharp-edged décor. That wasn't good, mind you, but understandable. No, what freaked me out about the place was the fact that it was run almost entirely by androids—or *artificial people*, as they liked to be called.

It just didn't seem right that humanity was ruled over by nonhumans. Sure, we'd built these robots, and they did seem to have our best interests at heart. They had a demonstrated sense of loyalty, duty, and even affection for their flesh-and-blood creators.

But it wasn't because they admired us or revered us. I got the feeling that they saw us as pets—silly animals that amused them and gave their empty existences meaning. They existed to serve and protect us. But they didn't see themselves as inferior to humans—quite the opposite. They were patronizing and essentially aliens of a different stripe.

With an effort, I did my best to put aside all my concerns and prejudices. The matter at hand was greater than any internal conflict in the Conclave. We had an existential threat attempting to invade our stars. The aliens from the Chain would destroy us all if they could, no matter if our flesh was made of meat or plastic.

Riding aboard another patrol ship, B-6 flew me from one slip-gate to the next in a seemingly endless sequence. It was quite convenient not to be dodging officials at every step of the way. As a smuggler, I was accustomed to long delays, bribes and frequent escapes at each star system.

Today, I was traveling like a king's henchman instead of a bandit. I enjoyed it, and we made good time until the last jump came—the trip to Vindar.

"Vindar?" I exclaimed. "Seriously? That's where you're taking me?"

B-6 shrugged. He'd come to trust me more these days and only posted a single rubber-fingered guard in the chamber while I talked to him.

"Where else? Without a ship, you're not much use as a scout, are you?"

"Uh… as a scout?"

"Didn't the Connactic explain the nature of your duties?"

"No, not really. She asked for my help, and I pledged it."

B-6 rolled his orbs. It was just one more in a series of human expressions he'd come to mimic almost perfectly. "I see… and she took you at your word, didn't she?"

"Naturally."

He laughed. "You see, there it is, right there. Specialization has its advantages. I'm highly intelligent, but I'm not as smart as she is. *No one* is as smart at the Connactic."

He said this last with the air of a man imparting great and certain wisdom. I had my doubts about his claims, having met some pretty cagey people and aliens, but I was also wise enough to keep quiet about all that.

"So… what's the true nature of my scouting mission? What did I sign up for?"

"A flight to the Faustian Chain, of course."

I stared at him, dumbstruck for a moment. At last, I managed a wheeze. "We're going to the Chain? Right now?"

"No, no. We're going to Vindar first, as I said. After that, you'll regain your ship and your crew. Then you'll set out on the long voyage across the desert of stars between the two clusters."

"My ship? I do think it's at Vindar, but I don't—"

B-6 raised a set of plastic fingers and waggled them. "Don't worry. We've already located it. My patrolmen have probably arrested everyone aboard by now."

"Really? Well, that's convenient." I had to smile just a bit, thinking of the renegade Huan. He deserved nothing less than captivity for stealing my ship.

"What are you going to do when you get to the Chain?" B-6 asked.

I tried not to look completely blank. "Scout around? Look at a few worlds and return when I've seen something good?"

He shook his head sternly. "No. Your mission is to find their Grand Armada. The biggest fleet the aliens have. We believe they have imminent plans to invade the Conclave in force. You will serve as our cameras and microphones."

"Um... you mean as your eyes and ears?"

"Of course."

I thought about it, and B-6 watched me closely. I tried to imagine the grotesque worlds out there, hanging in the dark. Were they full of human cattle? Or empty scorched deserts? I suspected it was going to be a mix of both.

"All right," I said. "I'll do it."

"Interesting..."

"You mean because I'm unusually committed?"

"No. I'm amused that you seem to think you have some kind of choice in the matter. Your cooperation was preordained before we sought you out. Did you think the Connactic would waste her time on a proposition? She doesn't operate that way. Her will is absolute. Her knowledge is all-powerful."

"Yeah, you mentioned that part," I said. "I just didn't know how to say it right. You've expressed my feelings on the matter with great precision."

He eyed me for a moment. Did he know I was bullshitting really hard right now? I didn't think that he did.

At last, I moved on to a new topic.

"About my ship... have you found her? What state is she in?"

He shrugged. "I gave a capture order a week ago. I've had no reports yet on the matter."

I frowned. "So... she could be damaged?"

"Possibly. She's a small, fast smuggler—illegally configured. Every patrolman in the Conclave would love to see the vessel dismantled for scrap—but fortune has smiled upon you, Gorman. We're going to give her back to you, and we're going to send you on toward the Chain."

I sighed, and I nodded. It was about what I'd figured. Vindar was a lonely star, an outpost in the great starless abyss between the two star clusters. Crossing the void to the Chain was going to be long and dull. Most likely, when we finally arrived, we'd be faced by alien horrors.

Pushing such thoughts out of my mind, I considered my more immediate problems. Huan had my ship at Vindar. Would he surrender peacefully, or would he get *Royal Fortune* destroyed?

I told myself I'd learn the truth soon enough.

Chapter Seven

Arriving at Vindar, I anxiously checked the local system scans. I didn't see any other ships. Nothing.

Instead, a large number of patrol vessels arrived together and moved into orbit over the planet. The patrolmen hailed the planetary spaceport's traffic control, telling them they were from the Conclave on official business.

After a minute or so of silence, a cautious voice came online. "Patrolmen, we welcome Conclave ships to our skies. Unfortunately, we can't offer you accommodations or fuel. We wish you well on your journey."

I was allowed onto the tiny bridge of the patrol vessel after weeks of travel. A model-Q patrol commander sat at the helm. B-6 and I were seated behind him, acting as backseat drivers.

"What do they mean they 'wish us well' on our journey?" B-6 asked me. "We've only just arrived, and Vindar is our final destination."

The patrolman turned to face us. "Unfortunately," he said, "it appears we must return to the Conclave. We are out of our jurisdiction. Without permission from traffic control we can't—"

B-6 put a hand up to stop his words. He looked at me with frustration.

"Can you explain this nonsense?" he asked me.

I pointed at the model-Q commander. "The explanation is right there. The people of Vindar know the rules. They know patrolmen always follow the rules. This is an easy way to get rid of us without offering any offense."

"Hmm… you're saying they're manipulating the scripts built into this model-Q?"

"Yes. I do it myself whenever possible."

"Disturbing and irritating. Fortunately, I'm not so easily put aside. Patrolman, hand me that com device."

Dutifully, the patrolman handed over the com set. B-6 spoke into the microphone. "Greetings, people of Vindar. I'm an official from the planet known as Mutual. Two of my ships came here a week ago in pursuit of a fugitive."

There was a delay after that. It stretched even longer than the first one. I got the feeling the shocked citizens and officials on Vindar weren't sure what to make of this intrusion.

For many years, they'd been virtually forgotten and entirely ignored by the Conclave. They existed just outside of the star cluster's borders, but had always maintained some level of good relations, if only because the Conclave was a much greater power.

We waited for a response. At last, another voice came online. It was both female, and familiar to me.

"This is Morwyn. Is the fugitive you seek a man known as Captain William Gorman? If so, you won't find him here."

I smiled. She came from an important family, and the last time people from the Conclave had ventured out here, I'd come with her. I was slightly proud to know that my well-earned reputation as a star-hopping scoundrel was still intact, even at this lonely outpost of humanity.

B-6 answered her promptly. "That is not the individual we seek. We're looking for a creature known as Huan. He might have come here with Gorman's ship, however."

Now it was my turn to look at B-6 in surprise. His words weren't exactly true. He'd bent the facts to suit the situation. No model-Q had ever done that—at least, not one that I knew of. It was further proof that he was something above and beyond a mere Q.

"We know of that creature," Morwyn said cautiously. "He's a strange beast, and I'm not surprised to learn that the Conclave is searching for him. He destroyed your patrol boats."

"What? Did you aid him in this crime? If so—"

"We did nothing. He fled in Gorman's ship when you approached. He's hiding, I believe, on the far side of the innermost planet of our star system."

"Thank you for that information, Morwyn," B-6 said smoothly. "We will pursue, and we will return after we've captured the fugitive."

"Good luck," Morwyn said, and she almost seemed to be laughing. After that, the connection was severed.

B-6 looked at me again. "What did she mean by that?"

I considered shrugging and letting him find out for himself, but I didn't feel like wasting all that time for a single small laugh. "She means you don't have a chance of catching *Royal Fortune* with patrol ships. Your ships aren't fast enough."

"That sounds like an admission of a crime, Gorman. It's illegal to build a ship that can outrun patrol vessels."

"I wouldn't be much good at gun-running if my ship could be run down by any plastic cop in a patrol boat, would I?"

Troubled, B-6 didn't argue. "Let's fly to the planet she indicated."

The patrol boat got underway, and all the others followed us.

"Uh... Inspector General, sir?"

"What is it now, Gorman?"

"Let's leave behind the rest of this posse at Vindar. One ship will be far less threatening."

"That's counterproductive. Huan must see our unstoppable power and fear reprisals."

I shook my head. "We don't want him to fear us. We want him to be curious about us. If he runs, we won't be able to catch him. Trust me on that point."

B-6 thought it over, then he finally gave the order for our single ship to fly to the innermost planet. When we drew close a few hours later, he broadcast a message.

"Criminal Huan. We know of your presence. We have brought William Gorman with us to retrieve his ship."

Huan didn't keep us waiting. Unlike the Vindari, he showed no fear of the patrol ship. He flew up proudly, emerging from the milk-and-coffee-colored clouds above the hot planet. He floated there in plain sight.

"Foolish," B-6 commented. "We could destroy him with a torpedo."

"*Royal Fortune* can outrun your torpedoes."

He glanced at me in alarm. "That is another violation, Gorman."

"I'm sure it is."

"Patrolman," Huan transmitted. "Do you really have William Gorman as your captive?"

"We do. I'm not a patrolman, however. I'm an inspector general from the Conclave."

Huan chewed that over for a moment before answering.

"Inspector," our pilot said. "We're being scanned by that vessel."

"Interesting… scanners too? Not exactly illegal, but highly unusual and provocative on a civilian vessel."

I rolled my eyes at B-6. He couldn't seem to grasp that he had thrown his lot in with a criminal who didn't care about his every rule and regulation.

"Open a visual channel," B-6 ordered. "Gorman, stand there, in front of that video pickup."

I did as he suggested, and I waved at the pinprick light that was the patrol ship's internal camera.

Once again, Huan didn't keep us waiting. "This is unfortunate," he said. "I can only assume Gorman has been compelled to help you track me down, and that the rest of his crew has submitted to you as well. I have no choice but to strike first."

The patrolman leaned forward suddenly. He turned to look at B-6. "The ship has launched a torpedo at us, sir."

"A what? Seriously? This Huan creature must be a madman!"

"Some would say that he is," I admitted. "I suggest you turn and run, sir."

B-6 looked angry. "Fire a torpedo in return!" he ordered.

The patrolman did as he was ordered. The ship shuddered and our forward screens flared bluish-white as the torpedo sped away into space.

I winced in concern. Events weren't proceeding as I'd hoped they would.

The patrolman whirled the ship around, and he put the hammer down—but it was hopeless. We'd already made tactical errors.

In his arrogance, B-6 had flown too close to *Royal Fortune*. Since we were moving at speed toward the torpedo that was coming in our direction, we couldn't outrun it. Spaceships don't stop and turn on a credit-piece. It takes time to build velocity or to reduce it through braking jets.

As a result, performing a U-turn wasn't going to work. Instead, we turned away at a wide angle and acceleration was our only option. The torpedo turned to intercept. It was going to be tight, I could tell that right off.

B-6 turned to me, and he was outright angry. That was another surprise. I hadn't seen him actually pissed off, not really, not even when I'd bashed his head off back on the beaches of Scorpii.

He pointed a finger at the tactical displays. "That ship is moving away far too quickly!" He then swung that same finger around to point at me. "I blame *you* for this, Gorman!"

"How so, Inspector? I didn't fire the torpedoes. I didn't direct our tactical approach to this planet, either."

"But you did own that ship!"

"Yes," I admitted. "It was once mine. She's quite a work of art, isn't she? Look at that acceleration curve."

"I hope you enjoy having your atoms scattered all over this lonely star system. What a way to finish a promising career."

Frowning, I looked over the data projections. That's when I realized what B-6 was talking about, and why he was angry.

We weren't going to make it. We were going to be the ones to be blown to pieces—not Huan.

Chapter Eight

"Sir? Inspector General, sir?" I said, but B-6 wasn't really listening.

"It's appalling. They said the Connactic was mad to enlist the help of vagrants and criminals—but she didn't listen."

"Sir? Do you want me to try to salvage this situation?"

He glanced at me in irritation. "You're enough of a star navigator to read numbers, aren't you? We're going to take countermeasures, and we're going to do our best to evade, but that torpedo will probably take us out."

"That's right, sir. You've got nothing to lose by letting me try to help."

Shrugging, he waved at the control panels. "Fine. Patrolman, relinquish the helm. Let this hotshot human pilot do his worst."

"No, no, sir," I said. "That's not what I meant."

"What, then?"

"Can I have the com station? I want to talk to Huan directly."

Irritably, B-6 let me take over coms. I transmitted urgent messages to Huan. A few minutes went by without response. I was beginning to sweat a little.

Finally, Huan answered. "What do you want, patrolman? I'm busy."

"Huan, it's Gorman. I want my ship back."

He blinked at me—well, his human eye did. The artificial one just focused and zoomed a bit.

"It's a bit late for that, don't you think?"

"Listen, the last time we spoke, you said you were going to take the fastest transportation you could out here to Vindar. You said you wanted to fight the Skaintz."

"That's right."

"For that reason, I accepted it when you stole my ship. You were merely doing so to get to Vindar quickly—right?"

"Yes, of course. I'm glad that you realized—"

I waved away his words. The counters were getting low. We had about four minutes to impact. "Listen, Huan. You didn't steal my ship. You're not a thief. You're a hero, a man who prioritized fighting the enemy above all else."

"Those are very kind words, Gorman—"

"I see it all clearly now. I didn't get it at first. But the Skaintz must be stopped. That's why I went to the Conclave. I talked them into gathering a fleet of ships to come out here to Vindar. Think about it, they would never send this many ships out here just to catch you. We're here to fight the Skaintz, Huan."

"That's... that's quite incredible. It's also a poor effort. Where are the Conclave cruisers? Where is the vaunted fleet that would be required for such a venture?"

"We don't have one," B-6 said, suddenly interrupting. "We never did. These patrol ships... they're all we've got."

"What? That's not credible. Every time I've heard of the Conclave fleet—"

"Every time you've *heard* of our fleet—but you've never seen it, have you? Sure, we released a few convincing graphics. Excited statements were made by paid propagandists on the grid. That's all you've seen and heard, but you were taken in."

Huan looked appalled. "But why make such a grand gesture? Why the subterfuge and base lying?"

B-6 shook his head and looked at me. "I'm disappointed, Gorman. You said this hybrid was intelligent. The answer to his questions should be obvious."

Huan looked from one of us to the other. "Surely, it can't be due to budget constraints?"

"Of course, it is. Which is cheaper and easier to build? A real grand armada, or an imaginary one?"

Huan shook his head. "Such daring. The efficacy of a virtual fleet is clear when the purpose is that of deterrence, but—"

"Um..." I said, noticing the time. "Gentlemen, I must make my final appeal. Huan, turn off that fucking torpedo, will you? It's bearing down on us even now."

The patrolman pilot began evasive actions then, throwing us off our feet. We crawled into our seats and strapped in.

"I'm horrified to learn there is no Conclave fleet. It explains so much... such as why the Fringe has been ravaged. Or why the Skaintz were allowed to invade at all..."

"Huan! Forget about that. We can explain it all later. But right now, if you don't turn off that torpedo, you'll not only be a thief, you'll be a murderer and a traitor as well!"

"What? Relax... I did that a few minutes ago. Didn't you intercept the signal? Perhaps not..."

The patrolman spoke up. "The torpedo is still bearing down on us. It's about to make contact."

"Huan, for God's sake!"

Right then, we all heard something. It wasn't an explosion, it was more of the sound a rubber ball makes when it strikes a krysteel wall.

We gritted our teeth and looked like we were meeting our death. B-6 and I did, I mean. The patrolman sat at his controls and methodically attempted to evade the incoming torpedo. As I watched, he leaned forward, then eased off the jets.

"The torpedo hit us, Inspector. It must have been defective."

"No," I said, sighing in relief. "You disabled the warhead, didn't you, Huan?"

"Yes, naturally."

This seemed to set off B-6 all over again. Apparently, he was capable of feeling anxiety and despair as well as anger. "Why didn't you destroy it? Or at least tell us the truth?"

Huan shrugged. "I wanted information. This way, I got quite a lot of it."

B-6 bitched for a while, but he eventually calmed down, and we brought the patrol ship around. I noticed that he no longer seemed interested in swooping directly toward *Royal Fortune* on an attack vector.

"Huan," he said, when he was calm and collected again. "Do you accept that we're not here to do you any harm? We're not even going to arrest you."

"Well, you did just fire a torpedo at me."

"That was in response to your attack. You attacked first!"

Huan seemed a bit put out. After ruminating for a bit, he finally relaxed. "All right. The logic of the situation is clear. The Conclave would never send out an armada of patrol ships to Vindar unless they were concerned about the Skaintz—and they also lacked the power to send a real fleet. Both these facts support everything you've been saying."

"Yes," I said, jumping back in. "Now, I have a big ask: will you return my ship to me? Will you rejoin my crew?"

"For what purpose?"

"To invade the Chain, of course. We need every ship possible to help in the war effort."

Huan stared at me with his freaky eyes for a moment. "I can't say no to such an offer. You know my scripting too well, Gorman."

I smiled, because he was right. I did know his software. He was a driven creature, and he couldn't pass up a good offer like the one I was making now—even if it wasn't entirely legit.

"By the way, Huan," I said. "One final requirement. You must forget about the Conclave's lack of cruisers. Can you do that?"

"Is that a precondition for my rejoining your crew, Captain?"

I thought that over for a moment. "Yes," I said firmly, deciding to go for broke.

He got a funny look on his face for a moment. The inorganic features, like his protruding camera eye, stopped moving... then he seemed to return to life. "It's done."

"What's done?" I asked.

He frowned. "Did you ask me to forget something?"

"Yes, I did."

"Well... I've forgotten it. All trace of the topic has been removed from my memory."

"Really? You don't even know what we discussed?"

He shook his strange head. "No. Is this condition satisfactory? I might be able to execute a retrieval script if the attempt is made quickly—"

"No, no," B-6 interrupted. "The change is exactly what we wanted. Welcome back to Captain Gorman's crew, Huan."

I gave B-6 a thoughtful look, but I didn't say anything. I figured he was pleased with things as they were now. Deciding it was for all the best, I smiled and pretended everything was okay.

Dealing with androids and half-androids was disturbing at times.

Chapter Nine

B-6 studied me for a moment after I made my fateful deal with Huan. I wondered if he wanted to blurt out the truth—to tell the crazy half-robot that we weren't necessarily flying out to the Chain to bring justice to every colony along the way. At least, not instantly.

But he didn't say anything. Just as I had kept quiet during his truth-bending, he did the same favor for me. I smiled at him.

He didn't return the smile, but he did look back at the holographic display of Huan. "I take it that we're no longer going to be firing torpedoes at one another?"

"Correct," Huan said. "Unlike Gorman, I'm a dedicated soul. A creature of enforced habits. I shall aid you in your great quest, Inspector General."

"Good. How do you wish to proceed?"

I was impressed that B-6 wasn't spouting additional requirements. He was moving with caution. It was a wise choice on his part. After all, Huan had just about blown us up minutes ago.

Huan thought for only a moment before coming up with a plan. "Jettison Captain Gorman in a life pod. Return to your fleet orbiting Vindar. I will pick him up, and I will obey his commands—whatever they might be."

B-6 frowned at this. It was obvious that Huan was being just as cautious as we were. He wasn't taking any chances—after all, I might be speaking under duress. If I was aboard *Royal Fortune* and at a safe distance, I could confide in Huan and do as I wished.

"All right," the android said at last. "I find your terms acceptable. I hope Gorman here is a man of conviction—if not honor or honesty."

I'd been insulted, but I didn't take it to heart. He might be still stinging a bit about being attacked back at Scorpii. Who knew?

Stuffing myself into a life pod, I felt a surge of relief and exhilaration as it was released from the patrol vessel and fired its tiny jets. I'd rarely been a captive, and I'd never enjoyed the experience.

Nearly an hour passed before Huan picked me up. He waited until the patrol ship retreated and nothing else came to threaten him. He scanned my tiny pod excessively, then finally pulled in close and scooped me into the hold.

"About frigging time," I complained as I climbed out. I stretched and grunted, my muscles having cramped up in places.

"I had to be sure that you weren't loaded with an explosive of some kind, Captain."

"You really think you're that important? Such a big deal a Conclave android would come all the way out here just to erase you?"

Huan studied me with his strange, disparate eyes. "You claim that creature was an android? What model?"

"I'm not sure, actually."

"Hmm... that's disturbing. He's not a model-Q, that's for certain. He's far too sophisticated and emotional. He rather reminds me of myself. Do you think he might be a hybrid?"

I blinked at that idea. "You mean, half-machine and half-man? Like you?"

"Yes, exactly."

"I'm really not sure. I've met one other like him, but she was even more advanced. She called herself the Connactic."

"What? The supreme commander of the Conclave is artificial?"

I shrugged. "Just as you are, I guess. It's all a matter of degree, I suppose. Anyone with a replacement heart, or an artificial limb is part machine, aren't they?"

Huan shook his head. "No, not really. What matters is the brain, the software. That's where the true differences lie."

"I'll take your word for it."

We climbed up to the command deck and strapped in. Huan didn't argue at all when I took the pilot's seat. It was a real pleasure to power-up *Royal Fortune* again and feel her engines throb with raw thrust.

"You have yet to admonish me," Huan said.

"For what? Stealing my ship?"

"Yes."

"Well... I should have seen it coming. I know how your mind works. I didn't give you an acceptable option. You felt you had to fly out here to join whatever crusade you could against the Skaintz. I would have done the same, but I wanted a break."

"I see... am I then, still your crewman?"

"Yes, as we agreed. But try to let me know if I'm violating some crucial boundary of yours in the future, okay?"

He cocked his head. The artificial eye studied me while the fleshly one examined the navigational panels. "Crucial boundary?"

"Yes. Let me know if you're going to act rashly in response to one of my decisions. I might be able to make it more acceptable to you."

"A reasonable suggestion. I warn you, however, that if you cause me to deviate from a path of logic and reason again, I'll take action to correct my course."

I twisted up my lips and gave him a sour glance. I'd been about to demand a solemn vow from him, a commitment to follow my orders with unquestioning loyalty.

The idea died away in my head. It wasn't even worth suggesting. Huan was his own man. He wasn't going to follow me over any cliffs. No pirate captain could expect that kind of dedication from a sophisticated crewman.

That didn't mean we couldn't work together, however. We'd been a successful team in the past. I just had to stay laser-focused on defeating the Skaintz—that's all. If I did that, Huan would be the best sidekick I'd ever had.

A few hours later we cautiously rejoined the fleet of patrol ships in orbit over Vindar. I felt kind of ill doing it.

I'd considered running off, naturally. It was my first instinct. My ship was faster than anything they had. I could probably come up with a lie for Huan that would keep him happy temporarily, and then I could escape without any chance of recapture.

But that didn't make much sense. Huan would abandon me again if I went back to the Fringe. The only reason to do such a thing would be because I didn't trust B-6... but I *did* trust him. At least, I trusted him not to arrest me again out of hand. He hadn't brought this armada of patrol boats all the way to Vindar just to capture Huan and my ship. It would have been a crazy thing to do—and B-6 wasn't crazy.

After we arrived, B-6 sent me a short, simple message. "Assemble a crew. You can't operate that ship optimally with only two men."

I agreed, but I wasn't sure exactly who he thought I was going to find out here at Vindar. The locals weren't pirates, they were mostly lame philosophers.

After thinking it over, I contacted Morwyn. Vindari traffic control had been suitably intimidated, so we had a link running to their planetary grid. It was a sign that they hoped we weren't hostile—and that they knew they couldn't do much about it if we were.

Morwyn came into view on my holoplate within moments of my channel request. She smiled, and I smiled back.

"I'm glad to see you again," she said. "I didn't know if I ever would."

Morwyn had the same bluish cast to her skin that everyone on Vindar had. She was pretty in an exotic way. Her eyes were reddish, and they seemed to gleam wetly.

"I'm glad, too. Tell me, Morwyn... are you bored on Vindar? Can it live up to all the adventures you had with me?"

She looked thoughtful. "What are you suggesting, William?"

"Dinner," I said firmly. "What do you say?"

"On Vindar, or on your ship?"

"You choose."

She thought about it. I saw her eyes slide off to one side while she considered. "All right. Come down to the capital city. You know the way. I'll meet you at the spaceport."

Smiling, I ended the call.

Huan was looking at me, and he didn't look as happy as I did.

"Another dalliance, Captain? I thought we had a mission to perform."

"Didn't you hear B-6? He ordered me to gather a crew. He said I couldn't fly this thing with just you—and he's right."

Huan chewed that over. "You're attempting to recruit Morwyn? Her skills as a crewman are barely acceptable."

I snorted. "Look, she's the only Vindari I know. How am I going to find a qualified crew on this isolated world without her help?"

Reluctantly, he acceded to my point, but he didn't seem happy. He was anxious to head out to the stars and start conquering aliens right away. It was his only motivation.

We landed at the spaceport, and I allowed Huan to stay aboard my ship while I went into town for dinner. I dearly hoped he wouldn't run off again. I'd asked him about it, and he'd assured me that he wasn't considering it—but then again, he was a shady character—almost as shady as I was.

Things went very nicely with Morwyn at dinner. She wore something gauzy and tight with a bare midriff. Every time she moved, I found myself staring.

At last, after a meal and some fine wine, I made my pitch. I asked her to join me aboard *Royal Fortune* with anyone she thought was competent and trustworthy.

She thought hard, and she asked questions. I gave her countless assurances and exaggerations. Eventually, she smiled.

"I've been terribly bored here at home since you left. My people are all so provincial. They want nothing more than to forget about the aliens and rebuild their artwork and shrines, but…"

"What?"

"It all seems so pointless. I mean, William… Vindar is still half-way between the Conclave and the Chain. The enemy is out there. What's stopping them from coming back and invading again?"

"The Conclave Fleet!"

Morwyn bit her lip. "All I see in orbit is a flock of patrol ships."

In that moment, I decided to maintain the old lie about the Conclave having a powerful fleet. It had worked for them for many years. I saw no reason to ditch a working strategy.

I threw my hands wide. "Have some faith, girl. They've got a serious fleet. You can look up pictures of it on any public grid—even here on Vindar."

She nodded thoughtfully. "All right. I guess I might as well go with you. I can't enjoy myself here, anyway. I stare at the sky every night, and I have trouble sleeping."

I patted her hand, and she put her hand on top of mine.

"What about others?" I asked.

She shook her head. "I don't know anyone who would come—except for Droad, I suppose."

"He's still here?"

"Yes. He's been trying to get the Council to build a fleet, if you can believe it."

I smiled. "I can. He's almost as driven as Huan."

The dinner was excellent, and the company even better. To summarize, I awakened the next day in Morwyn's apartment with her in bed beside me. We'd had a good deal of wine, and one thing had led to another…

There was a rapping at the door. It was an impatient sound. Grunting and yawning, I stumbled to the door and flung it wide.

Huan stood there, eyes searching me and the apartment behind me at the same time. They came to light at last on Morwyn's sleeping form. She was just beginning to stir.

"No need to apologize for this intrusion," I said as Huan walked right past me into the apartment.

"I'm making no apology. Nor do I require one—although I'm the injured party here, clearly."

"How's that?"

"You told me this fleet of tiny ships was planning to fly to the Chain. On that basis, I was duped into returning your ship to you. Now, I find the lies have expanded in nature. Did you regain your ship only to impress this hapless female and seduce her?"

"Hey, hey, come on, Huan. That kind of talk isn't cool."

Morwyn got up and eyed us both. She didn't look too happy, but she wasn't saying anything. She was listening closely. As I watched, her knuckles slid to rest on her hips. That wasn't a good sign.

"Captain," Huan said, "we agreed upon our last meeting that I would warn you when your actions might lead me to take drastic action again. Consider yourself warned."

Frowning and rubbing my head, I went to take a leak. I left the bathroom door open and yelled over my shoulder. "Don't take off, Huan. We're going to fly out of here soon. I really did ask Morwyn to rejoin the crew—what's more, she agreed."

Huan looked at her, then back at me. "That's... almost acceptable. I could question time-wasting methods, but I won't do so now."

"Gee, thanks."

Morwyn's hands had slipped from her hips and moved upward. She was now crossing her arms over her chest. Another bad sign. Dammit if Huan wasn't a cock-blocking robot. If he wasn't such a good pilot and fighter, I would have ditched him on Vindar.

"What's more," I said, stepping back to face the two of them. "I've got Droad to agree to come along, too."

"Droad?" Huan said. "You've got Droad to join us?" He sounded impressed at last.

"That's what I said."

"He agreed, William?" Morwyn asked. "When did you contact him?"

"Last night," I said, expanding upon my raft of lies. "While you were sleeping. He's eager to come."

"That's great. Droad is the real deal," she said, and her frown vanished. She began to smile. Her arms had moved away from her breasts, which left her blouse hanging open. People on Vindar were less fussy about those kinds of things.

I smiled back. We were both happy.

Now, all I had to do was deliver Droad. I sincerely hoped he was somewhere local and easy to reach.

Chapter Ten

My first move was to take another extended bathroom break. This gave me time to send out probes over the planetary grid, searching for Droad.

The truth was, I wasn't even sure he was still on Vindar. Morwyn had claimed that this was true, but hints and rumors could be old or just plain false.

Droad wasn't a man who was known for loitering. He had lived and fought in the Chain, going from world to world trying to stop the aliens from overrunning various planets.

Vindar was the fourth world that he'd fought them on—and all had been lost. Some had drowned in fusion fires that obliterated all life, others had simply been consumed by the ravenous aliens.

As I reviewed what few documents I could find on the man, I realized that Vindar was something of a triumph, from Droad's point of view. Sure, hundreds of thousands of lives and wild acres of land had been destroyed, but it hadn't been a *total* loss. Humanity still held the planet, and the aliens were gone—for now.

As to his present location, that was trickier. I finally had to contact B-6 for help.

By that time, there were polite tappings outside the bathroom door. Huan and Morwyn were becoming restless.

Both were anxious to be off, to collect Droad and join my grand, imaginary adventure.

At last, I got lucky. B-6 told me they'd lost Droad but fortunately, he hadn't lost me. My com device began to quiver, and I recognized the caller. The panel identified the caller as LD—Lucas Droad.

Beaming at my luck, I answered the call.

"Droad? Is that really you? This is such luck—"

"Shut up, Gorman. Why are you looking for me?"

"Hmm... I did a search, it's true. Are you in hiding or something?"

There was some rustling on the line. I got the feeling Droad was moving to a more private spot to discuss the matter. There were no visuals and no trace-back location, either. Just the raw audio signal. He'd always been the paranoid type—with good reason.

"State your purpose, Gorman. I'm no fool. I've seen the flock of patrol vessels in orbit. Tell me what this is about, or I'm gone."

"No, no, no!" I laughed nervously. "It's nothing like that. The Conclave isn't here to arrest you or anything. We're working together. I'm trying to put together a crew for a critical mission."

He was quiet for a second, and I had to check to make sure he hadn't disconnected—he hadn't. I let him think about it for several long seconds.

"What critical mission?"

"We're going to take it to the aliens this time. The Conclave is on board. They see the threat at last. That's why they're here."

"Gorman, that isn't how these people operate. To my knowledge, they're very unyielding and locked-in with their procedures. They're probably just trying to gather everyone who knows anything and imprison the lot of us."

I thought about the android surprise I'd run into on Mutual, and I thought Droad was closer to the mark than he realized. "Droad, if the Tulk were willing to help us, I think we can trust the Conclave to do the same."

"Why?"

I snorted. "For self-preservation, of course. No other motivation would get them to act."

"Hmm... All right. I'm going to risk it. Come alone to the location on your mapping app. Memorize it, as it won't be there for long."

By the time I had the app open, I only had seconds to observe a blue location dot before it vanished. The map pointed to the capital city of Vindar, but across town from my current location. I took note of the neighborhood and then opened the bathroom door at last.

A curious and concerned-looking pair stood in the opening. I made a show of washing my hands, turning on the fan and slamming the door behind me.

"Best not to go in there for a while."

Morwyn wrinkled her pretty nose at me. Huan studied me in silence. He had one eye on my hands and the other on my face. It was alarming when he did that. He could track two focal points at once—and he did it often.

"I've got to go out. You two stay put."

"Where are you going?" Morwyn asked.

"What of Droad?" Huan asked.

I waved away their questions. "I've got to go meet him personally. He's paranoid. He thinks all these patrol ships are in orbit to arrest him."

"I can't blame him for that," Morwyn said. "Half the people on this planet are worried about the same thing."

When I reached the door and turned to say goodbye, she threw her arms around my neck and kissed me. Again, Huan stood by quietly, watching Morwyn and I as we embraced. I suspected we were interesting zoological specimens in his eyes.

"Come back to me," she said. "Don't leave me behind with this half-robot."

I kissed her again and indulged myself with a squeeze. She didn't object.

"I'll be back—for both of you."

Then I left. I headed across the capital via a circuitous route. I checked constantly to make sure I wasn't being followed. It wouldn't do for me to show up with a plastic man on my heels. I'd lose Droad's confidence instantly.

An hour later, I was in the correct neighborhood. I didn't go directly to the address, but instead circled the building—twice. When I dared enter the lobby of the seedy hotel, I found it was full of residents of questionable character. Most were artist-caste youth, a group that I'd never found to be wealthy or interesting on any planet.

Someone cleared his throat behind me. I turned to see a tall figure. He was rangy of build, muscular but thin. He wore a hat that was pulled low over his eyes. A crooked finger was my only hint, so when he turned and vanished into a hallway I followed.

We stepped into an apartment on the ground floor. I looked around curiously. The room was as spare and unadorned as Droad himself.

"This isn't the address you gave me," I pointed out.

"Not exactly. The right building—but the wrong room number. I wanted to be sure you were alone."

I nodded. "Who do you think is after you?"

He cocked his head, and he smiled. "No one. I think someone is after *you*. I think you're a puppet on a string."

I blinked, knowing he was more right than he knew. Still, I felt I could trust B-6. Not even a plastic man would go through so much effort and expense to capture a group of minor criminals on Vindar.

"Stop worrying. The androids know."

He blinked, and it was his turn to look curious. "The androids? What do they know, and why should I care?"

I quickly explained that at the top of the Conclave there wasn't a pack of elderly figureheads. No, it was far worse. Our rulers were artificial beings.

"Most of them are just like you've seen. Slow of wit, built to tightly follow their scripts. Only the model-Q types can think at all. But there are others—more advanced models. They run things."

Droad sat on his rumpled bed. He studied his hands. "This explains a lot. All my work—I've beseeched the Conclave for help for decades, you know. They've never answered anything

I've sent. Not an official query when I was still part of the Nexus governing the Chain—and not now."

"That's all changed."

He looked up at me. "What changed their opinions? What moved them to act?"

"I don't know... I suppose the fact that the enemy invaded Vindar in strength. It had to be that."

He looked down at his big hands again. They were wrapped in ropy veins. "They've acted before. Decades ago. They destroyed Sardar."

"Right, but that's all the stuff of legend now. They're moving again—today."

"All right... but where are their cruisers? All I see is a few squadrons of small vessels."

As with Morwyn, I decided to maintain the fiction of the overwhelming Conclave fleet. "That's right. You see a vanguard in orbit. A probe. A mere scouting party. They need a fast ship with a skilled crew. And that's what we are, you see? They want my tiny ship."

"I can see that... all right. Assuming this is all true, what do you want from me?"

I pointed a finger at him. He studied my eyes, not the finger. That marked him as different than Huan. Huan would have stared at my finger with at least one eye—maybe both.

"I want *you*. I want you to join my crew."

He snorted. "For what purpose? Are there some new acts of piracy you haven't yet mastered?"

"I can't tell you what the mission will be—but we'll be pushing back against the Skaintz, I can assure you of that much."

He blinked, and he considered the offer. "With the Conclave at our backs this time instead of opposing us? That would be a change. You do impress me, Gorman. First, you brought an army of pirates from the Sword Worlds. Now, you've brought squadrons of official Conclave ships..."

After a moment's thought, he stood up decisively. "All right, I'll join you blindly—whatever this is about. You're full of shit, but you know how to get things done. In comparison,

I've been sitting here on Vindar whiling away the hours since you left."

I smiled. "That's the best vote of confidence I've gotten in a while. Let's go."

Droad stood and headed to the door in my wake. I turned, and I examined the room. "Aren't you going to gather your things?"

He shrugged. "I'm wearing them."

Nodding, I asked no more questions. We exited the room, the hotel and the neighborhood.

As we walked, Droad didn't pepper me with questions. That was a relief as I was tired of making up good-sounding answers.

Perhaps he knew I was bullshitting—but he didn't care. After all, we both knew who the real enemy was, and that was all that mattered.

A few days later, we were all assembled aboard *Royal Fortune*. Morwyn seemed disturbed by the list of those who were absent.

"What about Jort? Sosa? Rose?" she asked me. "Where did you leave them?"

I shrugged. "They left me, essentially. Don't worry about it. The four of us can fly this ship."

She didn't look happy about that answer, but she stopped complaining.

We rose up into orbit and joined the flock of patrol boats that still sat there. To my surprise, several other ships of various configurations had joined the patrol boats. There were more patrolmen as well.

"You see?" I crowed, pointing out the difference. "The horde is growing."

Morwyn laughed. "I'd hardly call it a horde. The Sword Worlds could field better."

As she was closer to the truth than she knew, I changed the subject. "We're all in for a treat," I said. "B-6 is coming aboard to meet us and discuss our mission."

"B-6?" Morwyn asked. "Oh, yes. The leader of the Conclave forces? Is he another android?"

"Yes. He's more capable than most, however."

She shrugged, unimpressed. One model-Q was no more impressive than the next to any human who'd met them.

B-6 arrived, and he walked aboard with a regal stride. He examined my tiny crew and my tiny ship. Droad was so tall he couldn't stand upright on the command deck and had to cock his head to one side.

B-6 turned to me. "Where are the rest of them?"

I shrugged. "This is Vindar. If you want me to go to the Sword Worlds, I could fill the hold with troops, shoulder-to-shoulder."

"There's no need. I do have one more man for you, however. We tried to find a berth for him on the other smugglers' ships, but they didn't want him."

"The other smugglers' ships?" Droad asked suspiciously. "Listen, B-12 or whatever it is you call yourself. What is this all about? What do you require of us?"

B-6 eyed him. "You're from the Chain, aren't you? I thought I recognized the accent."

Droad narrowed his eyes at the android, and he shook his head slowly. "Your approach to conversation is quite advanced."

"Thank you," B-6 said. "In any case, allow me to introduce the last member of your crew. Then, we'll discuss the nature of your mission."

Behind him, there was a ruckus in the passages. Our two ships were linked via a docking tube, and someone was being hustled along through that long hose of fabric and wire.

"Get your plastic hands off me, fake-man!" a familiar voice complained.

A moment later, a broad-shouldered thug appeared. Two patrolmen held onto him, struggling to keep him under control. He had a flat, ugly face, massive limbs, and a bad attitude. His wrists were manacled together, but that didn't seem to be restraining him much.

It was Jort, and every human aboard my ship stared in surprise.

Chapter Eleven

"Captain! Captain Gorman! Bash down these false men!"

B-6 eyed Jort, then turned toward me. "I understand that this gentleman is one of your crew members? Is this accurate?"

"Uh..." I said. "That depends. What's he done, exactly?"

"Captain Gorman! I will fight with you! I will tear the arms off these walking dolls. They deserve no less!"

I eyed Jort, but I didn't invite him to my side of the deck. I turned to B-6 instead. I wanted an answer first.

"He's performed no particular crimes while we've had him in custody," B-6 said.

This made me frown. "Why then are you restraining him?"

B-6 looked surprised. "Because he constantly threatens violence. If he were not restrained, we'd have to put him down."

"I see. Well... can I add him to my crew?"

"As long as you can control him, yes. Be my guest."

B-6 waved an imperious hand and Jort was shoved toward me. He was still manacled, but he turned and approached B-6 and the patrolmen, teeth bared.

"You don't frighten Jort, fake-man! You don't bleed, but you can die. I've seen it done—many times!"

"Jort," I said, putting a hand on his bicep. His muscles thrummed and strained at my touch. He was trying to break his bonds. "Perhaps we should stand down and fight at a better time. Can you take a seat over there?"

I indicated a chair in front of the weapons console. Jort puffed like a bull, but he eventually sat down and shut up.

"B-6, I thank you for returning my crewman, but I'm at a loss. Where has he been all this time? Did he follow us out here to Vindar?"

"No. We arrested him at the same time we arrested you. He was relatively easy to catch, actually, but much harder to subdue. We thought perhaps he could be of use, in case you decided to join us."

Jort's head swiveled, and he stared at me in slack-jawed amazement. "Tell me it's not true, Gorman! Tell me my captain has not sold his soul to these artificial devils!"

"It's not true, Jort. Stay quiet, and I'll explain everything in due time."

B-6 slid his eyes from me, to Jort, and back again. He knew I'd served up another falsehood, but he didn't say anything about it.

"Will you come with me to my council chambers?" B-6 asked. "Now that you have assembled your crew, I wish to discuss the nature of your mission."

"Don't trust him, Gorman!" Jort burst out. "Everything he says is evil!"

"Don't worry, Jort. I'll be right back."

I followed B-6 out, and we met together on the command deck of another patrol ship.

"What can I do for you, Inspector General?"

"You have been selected for a very special mission. We wish to do battle with the Skaintz, but we're not sure how to go about it."

"I can understand that. No one has traveled to the Chain from the Conclave for decades—right?"

"Yes, to the best of our knowledge, that is correct. There have been refugees coming the other way, in our direction, but no merchants or explorers have dared return. That's where you come in."

All of sudden the situation was clear. He didn't want me to fly to the Chain ahead of his fleet—he wanted me to scout for him. The thought of it left me cold inside.

"We need scouts," B-6 said, telling me I'd read his artificial mind correctly. "Experienced men with small, fast ships."

"Why not use a patrol vessel? Or maybe three of them?"

B-6 shrugged. "The reasons should be obvious. We don't have enough ships to defend the Conclave as it is. Nor do our ships fly especially fast. Lastly, none of us are scripted for exploration of new star systems. We're not even supposed to be flying around this far out from the Conclave."

"Ah... right. Your men aren't known for adventure or spying. All right, I'll do it."

B-6 cocked his head slightly. "Just like that? I was expecting to hear you argue for payment of some kind."

"Well... as a matter of fact, I could use some money for fuel and repairs. My crew must be compensated as well."

We haggled for less than an hour. In the end, neither was satisfied but we had reached an agreement.

"Very well," B-6 said, ushering me out. "After your tanks are full, head for the slip-gate. We're powering it up now for a series of transmissions. You'll be placed in a different location than the rest of them, a different colony. Here's a briefing stick."

He pressed a small data object into my hand. I stared down at it, then at him. "The slip-gates? But no slip-gates connect to the Chain... right?"

B-6 gave me a cold smile. "That has changed. Our technicians have been working continuously, not even bothering to charge themselves. Every one of them has a power cord dragging from one foot."

"Oh... so you've effected repairs on the gate? Isn't that dangerous? What if the enemy comes through to Vindar?"

"We're only turning on the slip-gates for a few minutes. We'll be shutting them down again the moment you've gone through."

"How... how will I get back?"

"You have one thousand hours to gather information. After that, return to the slip-gate from which you arrived and fly through. We won't wait for long. If you miss that brief window, you'll have to find your own way home."

I was stunned. I'd naturally pondered taking the generous payment he'd offered and fleeing—but perhaps B-6 knew that. He wasn't going to let me get away. He was going to watch me fly into that slip-gate and vanish on the way to the Chain....

"A thousand hours... that's about six weeks..."

"Yes."

Returning to *Royal Fortune*, I was further disillusioned. Patrol ships had pulled up, huddling around my vessel. If I tried to outrun them, they'd blow me out of the sky. I could never get far enough away in time to avoid their weapons.

Naturally, I let nothing of my sick disappointment shine through to my crewmen. I walked onto the command deck confidently, and I gave them the good news concerning our mission and the large payout. They gave me flickering smiles in return, but their greed was outweighed by very reasonable concerns.

"But William," Morwyn said, "how will we spend all this money if we're locked in some alien slaughter-pen?"

It was a good question, but I chose to evade it. I laughed. "That's not going to happen!"

"This is crazy-talk!" Jort said. "It's a trick, right? How are we going to trick them, Captain?"

"It's not a trick, Jort," Droad said. "He plans to go through with it. He plans to scout the Faustian Chain. I'm proud to be aboard such a ship, Gorman."

"Thank you, Governor Droad. Now everyone, if you'll just take your seats..."

Jort looked around slyly and grinned. He seemed to be under the impression that everyone aboard was a fool. That only *he* knew my true intentions.

We flew the ship to the slip-gate, and we headed directly for it. As we came near, it flickered into life. Even the operation of the old machine was alarming. It buzzed and cast out flares of colored plasma. Would it even work right? I had no way of knowing. I was a guinea pig and worse.

"Now is the time, Captain!" Jort said. "Free my hands! Let me help you to do a sharp maneuver. I'll run the aft guns. We might be able to take out an escort, and we'll surely be able to outrun their torpedoes."

I examined all the numbers. Jort was wrong. Even with the best of luck and skill, we were just too close to the patrol ships. They would stuff a torpedo up our tailpipes if we tried.

"Hang on, everyone. This slip-gate hasn't been used in our lifetimes."

Jort howled and banged his skull on his console. Morwyn clutched herself and her crash harness.

Droad and Huan, however, looked excited. They both leaned forward, eager to take the plunge. Droad, in particular, had eyes with a strange light in them.

I accelerated, leaving the patrol ships behind me. A plume of exhaust and plasma as long as a comet's stretched out behind us.

Then, we hit the slip-gate and vanished.

Chapter Twelve

Once inside hyperspace, we were able to relax and think for a while. It would take days to reach the Chain, even while flying at super-light speeds. The slip-gates worked by connecting two points in normal space with a tunnel containing another type of space—but it wasn't limitless. You still had to fly through the warped or folded space, to your destination—it just took days instead of years.

That was approximately the formula that the system operated with. One lightyear traveled took roughly a standard day to traverse. In a tight star cluster like the Conclave, where stars were closer together than a lightyear in many cases, it was possible to travel from world to world with relative ease and speed. This was not so while voyaging from one star cluster to the next. A thirty-lightyear trip would take a month in real time aboard our tiny ship.

The downside of a month of travel in a small ship was the possible effects of overcrowding. Fortunately, we didn't have to worry about that. My ship could support a crew of thirty. With only five aboard, we were quite comfortable. You could find someone to talk to or play chess with whenever you wanted. You could also find solitude and quiet when the time was right.

Of my crew, Droad was the most excited about the trip. After all, he was going home, and he held out hope that he could help effect a return of humanity to his home stars.

"Garm," he told me. "That's where it all started. The aliens arrived there first in a seedship."

"A what?" I asked. I was feeling a newfound interest in the topic of aliens now that we were flying into their territory.

"A seedship. A parent alien, sort of a queen, will often invade a new world by forming seedships and sending out her young daughters to colonize other planets. Each young parent can make thousands of offspring—but they require time and a great deal of food to do so."

"Food… you mean, like, humans?"

"Exactly. They eat primarily animal tissue of various kinds. Any high-calorie proteins they can capture and consume. They prefer their meals to be raw—still living, in most cases."

I suppressed a shudder. The idea of a pack of aliens chowing down on struggling human captives was both disgusting and chilling.

"You're right to be horrified," Droad said. "I was in their nests once, as a captive. It was a most dreadful experience. I managed to escape, but part of my mind still recalls the details. I've awakened bathed in sweat more than once, dreaming of the nests."

"What happened to Garm?"

"We cleansed it, in the end. We couldn't fight them off, although we fought valiantly. It was just your typical frontier planet, after all. We didn't have a large military. We did what we could, and when that wasn't enough, Nexus ships finished the job."

I shrugged. "So… what happened after that?"

"We kept finding more pockets of the aliens. They can survive almost indefinitely in space by placing themselves in suspended animation. A thousand years after they bury themselves in the ice of a comet, for example, they'll awaken and investigate when warmth and life return to the planet."

"Grim… it will be hard to ever fully stamp them out."

"That's true. But we can win in the short term. We must scour every infected world and cleanse it, then reintroduce vegetation later. That's how I see it."

I squinched my eyes with this new concern. "Complete erasure? Turning living worlds into radioactive dust?"

"Yes. Even that is only a first step. We have to keep searching for the aliens afterward, nosing into every asteroid, every bit of space debris or cold derelict craft that floats between the stars."

I shook my head. "It sounds impossible."

Droad shrugged. "We'll do it, or we'll be consumed in the end. Those are the only two endpoints I can foresee."

Hoping he was wrong, I left him to seek out Morwyn. She'd had several shocks since our love-making the night before we left Vindar, and I wanted to make amends.

I found her in an aft cabin near the engines. I was unhappy to see she wasn't bunking with me.

"I have a nicer cabin, you know," I said, standing in the doorway while she arranged her meager collection of possessions. We'd left Vindar quickly, and she hadn't been able to bring much with her.

She didn't look at me as I spoke, but I continued, undeterred.

"It's the best cabin on the ship, as a matter of fact. I am the captain, after all."

Morwyn finally turned around. I saw tears in her eyes, which were redder than usual.

"What's wrong?"

"I feel I've made a mistake. This is a suicide mission. What's more, you've clearly brought me along to serve as a bedmate. I'm feeling sad."

"What? No! Come on, this is a grand adventure for all of us!"

She finally met my eye. "A grand adventure? Are you joking? We're going to the Chain, William. The source of all the trouble. It's an entire star cluster overrun by those horrible aliens. If you listen to Huan or Droad, they'll tell you there's nothing to see there other than total devastation."

"Nah," I said, waving her worries away. "First off, you shouldn't listen to those two. They had a bad time, sure. That's why they ran out on the place." I lifted my hand and snapped my fingers as if I'd just had an insightful thought. "Wait a second, maybe that's it!"

"What?"

"The reason they play up these stories to such an extreme. Imagine that you once lost your nerve, that you feared so greatly for your life that you ran out on your own friends and family."

"That would be awful."

I snapped my fingers again. "Exactly! Such a burden of guilt and fear would be almost insurmountable. You'd pine away for the old days, you'd be filled with shame and terror. And do you know what else you'd do?"

She shook her head. I could tell by her confused expression my suggestions were working.

"You'd start to *lie*—well no, that's a rude term—you'd *exaggerate*."

"Why?"

"How could you do anything else? No one wants to be seen as a coward. So, what would a good man under such terrible circumstances do? He'd embellish, that's what. He'd expand the size, number and ferocity of these aliens until they were ten meters tall, striding over the worlds of men like twisted gods."

Her mouth was hanging open a fraction now. I could tell she *wanted* to believe.

"But Huan and Droad aren't cowards."

"No. They're not. But every one of us can be gripped by terror. Even a brave man can reach his limit. Ashamed, you would naturally want to be seen as having no choice. You'd also burn to go back home and redeem yourself."

Morwyn looked thoughtful. "Both of them are like that. They're determined to return—driven to go back to the Chain and face their fears."

I pointed at her as I spoke. She had my ideas firmly planted in her mind.

"But William, what about Vindar? We've seen these aliens. We fought them. We've seen their strength and speed. Humans aren't a match for them."

"Wrong!" I said, stepping near. "Think about Vindar. Are your people the toughest fighters in the Conclave?"

"No. Not by any measure."

"No. And yet you drove them off."

She shrugged. "We had the help of the Sword Brothers."

"Yes. And I'm sure that when the Chain was overwhelmed, after the first planets had fallen, the humans there became masterful warriors. My point is that if *your* people could beat the aliens, others might have as well."

Morwyn took a step closer to me. She lowered her voice. "But... what about Huan and Droad?"

I spread my hands with palms up. "Maybe they ran early. Maybe things aren't as hopeless as they seem."

She thought that over and nodded. "If you're right, William, I don't want you to mention any of this to Huan or Droad. It would crush them."

"Agreed," I said, almost whispering the word. Reaching back behind me, I pushed her door quietly closed. "I don't want them to overhear."

"Good thinking. Let's agree not to bring it up again."

I nodded, and by this time, we were quite close to one another. She looked thoughtful.

"Once I saw that Sosa and Rose weren't aboard... well, I thought that you brought me along just to warm your bed."

"What nonsense! I needed a competent crewmember. I needed everyone I could get. That's why you're here. I simply don't know very many people on Vindar."

She nodded, thinking that over. "What *did* happen to Rose and Sosa?"

"They left me. Rose went back home for a vacation, and she never returned. Sosa... well, she was never the loyal and committed type. She's a true pirate. Possibly, she found a better offer."

"I guess I can believe that."

Morwyn heaved a sigh, and I watched her do it. I felt compelled to act, so I gently put my arms around her and kissed her.

She was stiff at first, but she didn't protest. Soon, she melted, and we made love on her cramped bunk.

To my way of thinking, I'd neatly evaded a very dull voyage out to the Chain.

Chapter Thirteen

Thirty-two long days later, we arrived at the Faustian Chain. There wasn't much in the way of a warning, only a few flashing lights and speaking computers. We scrambled to prepare, not knowing what we'd find when we came out of the slip-gate.

When space coalesced around us, turning normal and healthy again, we ran our instruments and performed a quick scan of the neighborhood. We threw open the view portals, anxious to see where we were and how these distant stars looked.

"What a stunning view!" Morwyn exclaimed. "So many stars… they're lovely."

She was right. Even Jort was moved. His jaw hung low, and his eyes were wide and round.

The Chain was a loose cluster of some sixty stars, a whorl of sparkling suns rich in planets. It occupied a corkscrew-shaped region in space that was approximately twenty lightyears in diameter.

The visual reality of the Chain, however, was much more impactful than the description. Our own stars in the Conclave had a sort of stately beauty of their own. My home cluster was ovoid in shape and very regular. But it was, on the whole, much more boring in appearance.

"Look at the *colors*," Morwyn continued. "The nebulae are amazing. The stars seem extraordinarily bright. They shine like jewels through the spiraling dust clouds."

Droad was smiling at her praise. He felt pride in the slice of our galaxy that was his true home. Even Huan seemed to be fixated by the view.

"It is amazing and beautiful," I said. "I can only assume it's due to the formation, and the age of the stars. They're younger here, more vivacious and varied in nature. So many of our stars in the Conclave are glimmering dull-red coals. These stars are brilliant and variable."

"Uh... Captain?" Jort spoke up. "We might have a problem."

Leave it to him to get down to practical matters the soonest. "What is it, Jort?"

"I'm seeing lots of debris on track. The scanners are picking up bits of metal everywhere."

Frowning, I pulled up a screen and examined the data firsthand. The others did the same at their consoles.

"Huh..." I said, "it seems odd, but not dangerous. We're definitely in some kind of debris field. What do you make of it, Droad?"

He frowned and muttered for a moment, going over things. Suddenly, his head snapped up. "Captain Gorman, how many other ships have been sent here to scout before us?"

I blinked a few times. "B-6 didn't mention anything about other ships... not specifically."

He gave me a stern gaze. "Of course, he wouldn't. He's the most cunning of robots. I suggest we flee—immediately."

"We haven't even scanned—"

Jort interrupted. "I'm picking up motion, sir. Small, stealthy things. I don't know what they are, but they appear not to be metallic."

"Non-metallic? And yet they move in space?" I asked, baffled.

I pulled up his data, and I saw what he saw. There were indeed small objects around us. Things that were quiet and inert in space. They were smaller than life pods, but bigger than a man. The only disruption seemed to be the venting of gas from each of them. Suddenly, I had an idea strike me that I didn't like.

"They're some kind of floating mines," I said. "Something organic—almost undetectable. Huan, give me the controls. I'm taking over."

He didn't argue. I took control of *Royal Fortune*, and I didn't hesitate. I goosed her engines.

That seemed to galvanize the pods—whatever they were. They jetted closer from every direction with a sudden eagerness. Soon, we were almost englobed by them.

Fortunately, space is very large, and we were flying a rather small vessel through it. We were able to blast through the cluster of objects and evade them.

"That was very strange," Jort said as we escaped what must have been a trap. "All those little pods, seeking us. It was almost like they could see us or something."

"No," Droad said. "I think they could sense our presence somehow—but probably not with vision. This enemy is different than humanity in many respects. Even their technology is fundamentally different. They work with organic matter, displaying just as much skill as we do while working with metal and glass."

I nodded, still scanning the debris field behind us. Now that we'd put some distance between our ship and the slip-gate, we could no longer detect the pods. They were still there, of course, lurking and invisible.

"They'll go dormant again," Droad said. "Lying in wait for the next fool to use the gate."

"A mine field," I said. "That's what it is. A mine field full of living mines. I wonder how they destroy their prey."

Droad shrugged. "There are many types of explosives and corrosives. Perhaps they have a payload of one or another. They also might damage ships just by getting in the way. At high speeds, kinetics alone could destroy any ship that's moving fast."

"Let's hope we never learn the truth," I said.

"What about the metallic bits?" Jort demanded. "What's that about?"

Droad and I both looked at him. We knew, but the truth was grim. Neither of us spoke immediately.

Huan spoke up instead. "What you detected were the remains of other vessels that were sent here. I now suspect that B-6 was less than forthcoming. He's recruiting pirates and gunrunners for a deadly mission. Possibly, none have ever returned from this newly activated slip-gate."

Morwyn was clearly upset, but by now, she seemed almost resigned to whatever fate awaited her. She must be more mentally prepared to handle whatever lay in store. She'd seen a lot over the last year, flying with me and my crew.

"All right then," I said. "We can't relax quite yet. We must continue our scans. This time, Jort, I want you to reach out farther. I want to know what kind of star system we've found ourselves in."

We all worked the scanners, and we soon found the local sun and all her planets. The star was a yellow K-class. There were seven worlds circling her that we could detect. A few of them lingered in the zone where water could assume liquid form.

"Let's head toward the inner system," I said. "Use minimal power—we don't want to alert anyone who might have been notified that we slipped by their living minefield."

After discovering the minefield of organic pods, all talk of lovely stars faded away and was forgotten. We became grim-faced and determined to survive. Every tidbit of data, attractive or not, was gone over carefully—but there wasn't much to go on.

"We've got two targets that support life," Morwyn said. "One is hot and jungle-covered. A few oceans, but mostly land with high mountains. The poles have no ice at all, just steam."

Droad and Huan looked intrigued. "And the second world?" Droad asked.

"Icy, dry, flat. Almost the whole planet is tundra or an outright frosty desert. A large sea dominates the upper hemisphere."

Droad snapped his fingers at her and pointed at the scans. "We must be at Chara. There are very few systems with two inhabitable worlds in the Chain."

"Chara…" I said. "What do they call the planets?"

"The ice planet is Chara B. The other is Chara A. Almost no one lives on B, as it's too inhospitable. They have a mining crew, some tourists… that's it."

"Correction," Huan said, "it's highly likely that no humans live on either world. The aliens scoured this place decades ago."

Droad looked glum, but he didn't argue.

"We'll set course for Chara B first," I said. "The aliens are weaker on cold planets."

"Is it wise to visit either world?" Morwyn asked.

"No, it isn't," Jort said before I could reply. "It's frigging crazy!"

"We came out here to investigate," I said, "and we can't do that from a million kilometers away. We'll move to high orbit, scan carefully, and keep one foot on the thrusters in case we need to run."

No one argued or made a better suggestion, so we adjusted our course and glided toward Chara B. As we drew near, I made sure to dampen every transmission coming from our ship. We used passive sensors only, listening instead of pinging away like a warship.

When we came close enough to see the disk fill our screens, Jort became antsy. "The planet seems dead," he pointed out. "There's nothing here. Let's move on."

"We're going to glide down to one hundred thousand kilometers and do a full surface-scan. We've got to have something to show B-6 when we return."

"Why? He isn't out here risking his rubber ass in this deathtrap!"

I silenced Jort with a wave and a frown. He was the most likely of my crew to complain, but he was also the most likely to follow my orders when no one was looking. I suffered his grumbling because loyalty was a more important trait to me than peace and quiet.

We scanned the desolate world for hours, identifying six automated mines. All of them seemed to be abandoned.

"I'm reading a lot of valuable metals, here," Huan said. "Lithium, cobalt, cerium…"

"Yes…" Jort said. His big face was glued to some of the visual enhancers. Using scopes, he was able to zoom in and examine the sites through the thin atmosphere. "Loads of stuff. We could take anything we want."

He looked up at me expectantly.

"We're here to scout for aliens, Jort, not plunder abandoned mines."

"Why not do a little of both? Think of it, these mines must be broken down now, but they probably ran for years stacking up pallets of fresh ingots. Maybe they even have refined goods."

"There's no evidence of—"

"Captain?" Morwyn said. "I think I've found a battery manufacturing site."

We all moved to examine her findings. It was true. A battery factory was on the planet, which explained some of the other raw materials we were seeing.

"Refined goods, Captain! Think of the wealth!"

All of his earlier hesitation had been erased. Jort was a true pirate at heart. He had no interest in saving humanity at large, but he was willing to risk everything for a big gain.

Rather than point out his sudden eagerness for what it was, I decided to use it. "You're right. We've seen no aliens, no defenses. Let's land and collect a few samples."

Jort grinned, but it was time for the other crewmen to express reservations. They did so with doubtful looks and frowns—but no one came right out and suggested I was crazy. They might have been *thinking* it, mind you, but they didn't say it.

Chapter Fourteen

We landed at the battery plant, but I noticed my crew wasn't anxious to leave the safety of the ship.

Jort manned the antipersonnel cannon in the aft section, having moved there without saying a word. Morwyn poured over the scanning data coming in, going over every frosty millimeter of the frozen desert outside.

Huan and Droad followed me to the hold. Neither appeared to be eager to get to the planet's surface. They took their time donning environment suits and checking every seal twice.

"Come on, come on," I said, clapping my hands loudly. "We want to be off this world before dark—way before dark."

"What's this world's planetary rotation period?" Droad asked me.

I shrugged. "About forty hours. We should have at least ten good hours of light left."

Huan never wore an expression I could read on his face, but even he seemed concerned. He didn't move with his usual sense of indomitable purpose as we suited-up and faced the ramp.

Handing each man a pistol, a knife and an all-important Sardez rifle, I gave them a smile as I hit the release.

The ramp lowered, and the air was sucked out of the hold—at least most of it. Chara B had about half a standard atmosphere, and the oxygen content would only serve to prolong a man's death were he to be exposed here for long.

We walked down the ramp and our boots crunched on the crusty ground. The rocks-and-sand surface was harder than it looked, being welded together by permafrost. Even sandy spots had the consistency of dried paint rather than an attractive beach.

We looked everywhere at once for a time, even checking behind the ramp itself before venturing away from the ship. Above us, the antipersonnel cannon whirred and rotated, following us and suspiciously pointing at the buildings to the north. We trudged in that direction, as there was nowhere else to go.

"This would be an attractive spot for the enemy to ambush us—if there are any on this world," Droad said off-handedly.

"Losing your nerve, Governor?"

"I'm out here walking with you, aren't I?"

I stopped bothering him. I was accustomed to pirates—errant souls filled with greed and very few lofty ideals. As it was important to keep up morale in terrifying and unknown situations, I frequently did so by embarrassing my crewmen.

That approach wasn't entirely needed with these two, I reminded myself. Droad had an iron will, and Huan was literally half-machine. Both of them approached every situation with determination.

Shutting up, we walked toward the factory with heads swiveling at every step. The landscape was barren and flat. There were a few machines around—haulers, mostly—but they appeared to be damaged. Two of the three we saw lay on their sides. Scorch marks stained their engine compartments.

We checked them anyway, just in case they harbored fugitives or better—batteries. We were disappointed in every case. They were all empty.

"Who would attack trucks and leave them in such a condition?" Huan asked.

"Every pirate I've ever met," I answered him. "Come on."

We walked to the warehouse next. It was similarly plundered. Our hearts fell as we looked toward the dark, looming hulk which was the factory itself. If there was anything of value here—which was now highly doubtful—we would have to go inside to find it.

The factory was one of those prefab jobs they typically ran on distant colony worlds. I'd seen buildings like this one in the Conclave. They were at least a century old, relics of the early days of human expansion and colonization. Despite their age they were usually well-tooled and still functional. They never seemed to wear out completely.

"Let's have a look," I said.

I took the first step, and the others followed in my wake. Unlike Jort, they didn't grumble and complain about how dumb I was. They were both fatalistic men.

We stepped into the gloom of the largest of three yawning gates. The interior was larger than any warehouse I'd ever set foot into. It was dark inside, a stark contrast to the glaring sand and snow drifts outside. We blinked as we entered, scraping frost from our faceplates and peering around ourselves.

That was the moment the enemy had been waiting for. I should have expected it, but somehow, I didn't. The factory, the warehouse, the desolate planet and the wrecked trucks—it had all given me the impression that there was nothing to find here. I'd wrongly assumed the aliens had left for better ground.

But that wasn't the case. The enemy had waited until we stepped from bright sunlight into the dark interior of the factory to stage their ambush.

They came on with every ounce of hungry speed they could muster. If they'd been strong and hale we wouldn't have stood a chance. As it was, the three killbeasts and the single, humping, caterpillar-like shrade moved quickly—but not much quicker than a man might. They were clearly weakened, starved and half-frozen by countless years spent in this wasteland.

My team wasn't green, fortunately. We'd faced such monsters before. Immediately, we made the calculation that we couldn't escape. Running would only mean they'd chase us down and tear us apart.

Automatically choosing targets that were positionally relative to our own trio, we aimed and fired at the charging enemy. I was in the center, and I missed with my opening blast. Droad did the same.

Huan, however, wasn't easily rattled. His machine-half saved him, allowing him to squeeze off his first shot with a dead-of-center hit. The killbeast did a backflip, but it bounced back to its feet again. It was filled with a horrible vigor, and even though a fist-sized hole had been punched through its carapace, it refused to accept death for two more paces—then it dropped to the ground stone dead.

Both Droad and I did better with our second shots. We sent the killbeasts staggering, giving us enough time to nail them again. Huan helped, having finished his beast in one shot, he added two more well-placed rounds in the bodies of the enemy, bringing them down to flop and writhe on the filthy floor of the factory.

Before we could grin in triumph, however, I heard an anguished cry. Something had Droad—it had his foot.

In all the commotion, we'd forgotten about the shrade.

As cunning as any snake in a field of tall grass, the final monster had slithered close and sprung low, catching Droad and knocking him flat. Eagerly, it humped up his body and wrapped its coils around his chest. He tried to defend himself by holding his rifle between the creature and his body, but this did nothing but provide the shrade with an anvil to squeeze against him.

I heard a bone snap, and Droad called out in pain. Spittle flew from his lips as he struggled with maniacal strength. I could see clearly how he had survived deadly attacks before. He was no quitter.

"Save yourselves!" he wheezed out. "More might be coming!"

We ignored him. Huan aimed his rifle, but I batted it away. "Use your knife."

We knelt then, and we cut at the thing. It was like hacking a thick jungle vine. Rubbery flesh that didn't feel like flesh at all struggled against us. It wanted nothing more than to prey upon Droad. That was the common behavior of these vicious predators. They would gladly give their lives if they could kill just one of us. They knew they bred faster than we did, and some future horror would grow strong by ingesting our meat and finding fresh game. It was a war of attrition, one where Humanity had yet to gain the upper hand.

We worked grimly, trying not to stab Droad while we carved up the shrade, gouging its tough flesh. It was like carving into soapstone, but at last, the job was done, and the shrade relaxed in death.

Gasping and wheezing, Droad climbed to his feet. He was staggering, winded, and he had two broken ribs—but he would live.

"Can you walk?" I asked him.

"Of course."

"All right, then. I suggest you let Huan help you back to the ship. I plan to scout further."

They both looked somewhat shocked.

"What?" Huan asked. "What if there are more aliens, deeper inside? What if there are a dozen of them?"

I shook my head. "I don't think there are. I've fought these aliens in places like this before. A few holdouts are often abandoned on a forgotten planet. These creatures were left behind years ago. They were clearly awakened by our approach, but if they had any more fighters to throw at us, they would have done it by now. They like to strike with overwhelming force, and they all share a single mind when it comes to dealing with prey like us."

"What if you're wrong?"

I shrugged. "Then… I'll probably die. But I'm curious about what lies deeper within. Go back to the ship if you need to."

So saying, I walked into the factory's gloom. There were no natural light sources. No windows, no skylights. I had to use my suit lights to illuminate the way.

Glancing back, I saw the two of them were following. I was surprised—but only slightly. They were both proud, tough men. They didn't like to be shown up as cowards, even when injured.

I kept my rifle ready as I searched the passages. There was something I was hoping to find down here—and before long, I found it.

When we finally found an unplundered storehouse of battery packs, I smiled grimly. They were exactly what I was hoping for.

"Check this out," I said, slamming a pack into the back of my rifle. "A perfect fit—as if it was made for my weapon."

Droad eyed the packs, as did Huan. "I hadn't realized these packs were compatible with technology from the Conclave," Huan said.

Droad studied the packs and the rifle in his hand. "This is no coincidence. Where did you get these weapons again, Gorman?"

I told him about the Sardez system, and how it had long ago been abandoned by colonists. He'd heard the story before, but he found it more compelling now.

"I find it hard to believe that these technologies were developed in two different star clusters for such a similar purpose."

"It's virtually impossible," I agreed.

Huan studied us with his odd eyes. "You're saying that the Sardez rifles—or at least the technology to operate them—is shared by both the Chain and the Conclave? Why didn't we know this previously?"

"That's a good question," I said. "I plan to ask B-6 about it—should we ever be fortunate enough to return to the Conclave."

Stacking up around a thousand of the best battery packs we could find on an air sled, we hauled them out of the factory and back to *Royal Fortune*. Most of them were dead, but they could be recharged.

"Isn't this something akin to... looting?" Morwyn asked me as we boarded the ship and raised the ramp.

I laughed at her. "You knew who I was before you signed up with me, right?"

"This is war," Droad told her. "In a war of extinction, one uses whatever comes to hand to survive."

She didn't complain further, but she did purse her lips disapprovingly as we celebrated our loot.

I was particularly happy. I hadn't found a treasure trove of weapons—that would have been better, but power packs could be almost as valuable.

Sardez rifles fired accelerated rounds. They were essentially small-caliber railguns. They didn't have a high rate of fire, but they were extremely accurate with no drop off for over a kilometer range. Better still, the rounds hit really hard. You could take out a small vehicle with one or two shots. Essentially, they allowed regular troops to carry a rifle that hit like light artillery.

This was important when facing an enemy like the Skaintz. The aliens were so strong, so vigorous, that you had to literally blow them apart to stop them. They were like insects, or some creature made of cellulose. You didn't knock them out of a fight without doing tremendous damage.

The Sardez rifles were designed to level the playing field and give a regular human an even chance with these vicious aliens.

We took off and left Chara B within an hour of having landed. No one wanted to stay on the dead world any longer.

Leaving orbit, we moved toward Chara A next. We were feeling somewhat more confident now, as we'd seen very few dangerous aliens on Chara B. The enemy had apparently left this system for fresher worlds—or so we believed.

Chapter Fifteen

"Do we really have to go to Chara A?" Morwyn asked me as we glided toward our second port of call. She seemed to be increasingly worried as the first day wore into the second.

It was partly my fault for going so slowly. We could have blasted our way from Chara B to A in less than a day but doing so would have left a glowing streak of exhaust behind us. As it was, I used a single short burn to put us on a course to run into the path of the second world, which was orbiting toward us anyway. That way, unless someone was scanning the skies very carefully, they were unlikely to detect our approach.

I explained this to Morwyn, but she still fidgeted nervously.

"What's the matter? The first world was dead, the second will likely be the same."

She shook her head, sending her hair flying. "No. I don't think so. These aliens like the heat. They'll like this world—Chara A might be an active alien colony, a hive teeming with millions of them."

"Hmm… that's possible, but I'm not reading much radio traffic."

"They use radio signals for local communications, but they don't seem to talk that way in open space. They go silent when off-planet."

I wondered about that. It did seem to fit with their natural predatory behavior. Maybe it was we humans who'd been careless with powerful radio signals. What sense was it to fire off random messages into the void, without knowing who might be listening? Humans had been repeating this mistake for centuries now.

The closer we got to Chara A, the quieter the crew became. We all knew this planet was more likely to have alien invaders than the first one. I also sensed everyone was worried about what I would ask them to do. I hadn't yet gone so far as to suggest landing—and I figured the crew was hoping I wouldn't dare.

To be honest, I was watching and listening to every signal that came to our sensors just as intensely as everyone else. There weren't any radio signals to take note of, just a few distress beacons from derelict ships and satellite stations that had long ago been wrecked or abandoned. These relics chirped with forlorn, rhythmic loneliness. It was clear that no help had come for decades.

"It's like a graveyard," Morwyn said. "I don't like it."

None of us answered. None of us were liking it.

Jort stirred next. "Captain. Have we seen enough? I don't like this place."

"Neither do I, Jort. But I think we'd best get a little closer before running off, don't you think?"

Jort grunted and moved restlessly in his seat. He said nothing, but his displeasure was clear.

I was more impressed by the quiet demeanor of Huan and Droad. They'd been the most eager to return to this dead place. Now that I'd actually brought them here, they were oppressively silent. They offered no plans, no hopeful suggestions. I thought perhaps they were both lost in their own thoughts, reliving the horrors they'd witnessed years ago.

"I'm not seeing any threats on the scopes. The place is a tomb. Let's go closer."

Jort made a strangled sound. The rest said nothing.

We flew closer, silently, gliding toward the planet. We studied the continents, the oceans—there was life, and weather, and warmth—but not as much of it as there should have been.

"The records on Chara A say the place is a tropical paradise," I noted. "Where are the forests? The animals?"

Droad answered me first. "The Skaintz leave very little. They scour living worlds, eating everything until they finally begin to starve—then they leave, or barring that, they hibernate."

"Like those sad examples we met on Chara A, huh? I've seen that behavior before. Several of them were trapped at a remote outpost in the Oort cloud of the Sardez system. They survived—but barely. When the sun came up and someone visited, they stirred back to life again."

"Exactly. Those that still alive here are dormant, waiting. That's my best estimate. Are we going to land?"

Jort released a shocked grunt. "Are you crazy?" he demanded of Droad. "Why would you even say such a thing?"

Droad glanced at him, then looked back at me seriously. "Gorman is our captain. He's led us this far. Have faith, Jort."

"I have no faith in foolishness!" Jort said angrily.

This sort of tantrum wasn't uncommon for him. He was loyal, and he had never turned against me—but he had complained a lot along the way.

"We're going closer," I said.

I used cool jets to change our attitude, aiming downward. Rather than burning our main thrusters, steering jets released cold compressed gasses in puffs. It was a much less effective method of guiding a spaceship, but it was also much more difficult to detect.

We spiraled in from two hundred thousand kilometers range down to one hundred thousand—then fifty thousand. The crew was on edge, as was I. The planet now filled our viewscreens. Rather than lush foliage, vegetation was sparse. Even the oceans seemed to be a dirty, dishwater brown.

"Sir!" Jort called out as we dropped down near the atmosphere. "There's something... they're firing at us, Captain! We have to run!"

I looked over the data that was now pouring in from our sensors. Something had indeed been launched. A great release of energy had been reported from the far side of the planet.

Jort looked at me with wild eyes. The others studied their instruments.

"I'm seeing something..." Huan said. "Such a large explosion—I doubt it could be a missile heading for us. It's more like a battleship lift-off. Only something like a fusion warhead would show such a large blip. The whole planet probably just felt a tremor."

I examined the data myself, and I found Huan was right. A massive explosion had gone off.

"Something this huge..." I said, "it doesn't make sense. It might not be related to us at all."

This was too much for Jort. He wasn't one for logic and cold reason. He was an emotional man who operated mostly on a keen instinct for both opportunity and danger. Today, he wanted to run. On other occasions, he might have wanted to rush in and grab what he could.

Standing up, the blocky man stalked out of the command deck and down to his AP cannon in the back. There, he would sulk and curse my mother's name with great bitterness.

It was nothing new, so I ignored him. We weren't in any immediate danger—at least, none that we could detect.

"What could they be doing down there?" I asked.

Droad walked near. "May I sit at the main console, Captain?"

"By all means."

He took my place and went over the data. After a few minutes, he turned to the group, who were all watching him. We were baffled and nervous.

"I think... I think they're spawning."

"What?"

He waved his hands in the air, then rubbed at his temples. "I've heard of this, but I've never witnessed it. A planet that has been consumed, one which no longer can support their multitudes, is transformed into a launch system."

"What kind of launch system?" Morwyn asked.

"It's how they get from world to world. They launch numerous organic pods into deep space. These pods move slowly, but they gain speed with the help of solar sails and other means of propulsion. After many years, they'll reach another star system and invade it."

We stared at him in alarm. I was the first in the group to get over the shock.

"You're talking about seedships, aren't you?"

"Yes."

"Huan? Can we see these pods—can we detect them in space?"

"I will try," Huan said. "But sir… I must ask that I'm allowed to turn our sensors to active mode. We'll have to give away our presence and position."

"Nooo!" Jort shouted. His voice emanated from the console in front of us. Apparently, before he'd stomped out in disgust, he'd turned on the intercom system. He'd been listening all the while.

"It's my decision, Jort," I told him. "If you wish, I'll fire you off in a life pod."

"A life pod? A death-pod, more like! Where would I go?"

"Anywhere you want. Now, be quiet."

He grumbled about how I wasn't a smart man until I turned the volume down on the intercom, effectively muting him. I turned back to Huan.

"We'll wait until we're over the horizon, closer to the source of the explosions. Don't ping anything until I give the order."

We waited tensely until we slid around the far side of the planet. Things were grim, as we all knew the enemy was present and active below us. Had they spotted us and sent pods and missiles to intercept? We couldn't know for sure if we only used passive sensors. The enemy could be as stealthy as any human-built ship—perhaps more so.

At last, ten long minutes later, we came into view of the launch site. It was glowing hot. Surprisingly little radiation emanated from the place, however. We examined it visually. Smoke and roiling atmospheric effects had lingered.

"It looks like a big hole in the ground," Huan said. "A circular cannon ten kilometers deep—that's enough to punch through the crust of the planet to the mantle."

"Maybe they're using geothermic energy," Droad suggested. "I'm not seeing any evidence of a warhead having been deployed. What an amazing feat of engineering it would be, to build your own volcano to power a spacecraft."

I nodded. "They'll use anything to reach escape velocity. They're firing rocks and pods into space, wrecking the planet to get off it to the next star."

We felt like we were witnessing a final crime. A lovely human colony had been destroyed, and its helpless carcass was being used to infect other, unsuspecting worlds.

"Do we have a reading on the projectiles? Where are they now? Where are they heading?"

Huan shook his head. "We can't see that—not without turning the active sensors on, as I said."

Everyone looked at me. The console buzzed. Jort was making his suggestions, but I left his volume low. No one wanted to hear his thoughts, especially me in this critical moment.

After thinking it over for a few minutes, I finally came to a fateful decision.

"We have to know where those pods are going. We have to take this chance—we might be able to warn planets that are going to be invaded decades from now."

I looked at Huan. "Go active. Ping the space in front of that cannon's muzzle. Let's take a look at what they're shooting at."

Huan touched a screen, and our displays lit up with fresh data. Soon, more information poured in.

Morwyn gasped. She put her hand to her mouth. The rest of us read the screens in grim silence.

Chapter Sixteen

Pods kept popping up on our sensors—lots of them.

The aliens seemed to be using a ground-based cannon to fire the pods into space with enough force to achieve escape velocity. Once they were past the atmosphere and the tug of the planet's gravity, sails were deployed. These functioned poorly at first, slowly building up speed to guide the pods on a very long voyage into deep space.

The longer we looked, the more pods we found. They were apparently being fired with regularity toward unsuspecting worlds.

We tried to plot their destinations, but there were so many the task was difficult. Some were clearly targeting the Conclave. Six targeted Vindar—causing Morwyn to all but weep. I could understand that. Her people had suffered so much under the last invasion. To witness clear evidence that another fresh incursion was underway, well, it was enough to crush anyone's spirit.

That was the thing about these aliens—they didn't give up. They kept trying and trying until they succeeded, or they all died. There was no in-between. They reminded me of ants in that respect.

"What are we going to do, Captain?" Droad asked me. He stared at me, and his eyes were full of anger and worry. "We're witnessing an invasion of every human colony remaining, if I had to guess."

"What we going to do?" Jort demanded. He was suddenly back from sulking in the aft gun turret and looming over us. "I tell you what we *should* do. We must run to save the hair on our balls, that's what! We've got to get out of here, Captain! They must have sensed our pings. They *know* we're here. They will be coming! They will shoot those missiles at us and—"

I put up a hand. "Jort, we're fifty thousand kilometers from the planet. We have some time. Let's make it count, and then we'll run if needed. Move back to your battle station."

Jort gritted his teeth at me. He liked battle, but only when we had the clear advantage. For a few moments his whistling breath came puffing out of those clenched jaws—but then he nodded, and he wandered back into the passages and disappeared.

"Huan, take us into the middle of that swarm. Let's see if we can take them all down."

"You think we really can get them all?" Morwyn asked excitedly. "That would be such a wonderful thing. Vindar might be saved all over again."

I tossed her a nod and a smile over my shoulder. She'd always been the hopeful type, and I didn't want to ruin that. In my estimation, however, the aliens would just throw another swarm up tomorrow if we destroyed this one. That's how they operated.

"Don't bother to be stealthy, Huan," I said. "Use some of our power."

He did so, and we moved forcefully toward the flock of pods. Just as we came into range and began to fire, space around us seemed to... *warp* somehow.

"I'm getting new readings, captain," Droad said from the sensor console. "There's something out here—something we didn't see."

I had an immediate, sick feeling in my gut. My eyes crawled over the numbers for perhaps three seconds.

"Veer off!" I shouted at Huan. "Break off the attack—escape vector, and don't spare the fuel!"

Huan didn't hesitate or ask any questions. The ship swerved and shuddered as her big engines thrummed with power. *Royal Fortune* was equipped with enough thrust to move a battleship. The acceleration was crushing.

I heard a wail from the back of the ship. Perhaps Jort had failed to strap himself in properly.

"We've got tiny contacts—lots of them," Morwyn said. "What are they?"

"Missiles," I said. "Small, smart missiles. They must have scattered them out here, like dormant mines. Or maybe the pods we're after dropped them overboard when they detected us—I'm not sure of their exact nature, but we know they're deadly."

She looked at me. "But... are we going to just run, then? What about the pods? The ones heading for my home world?"

Her face was so forlorn and full of worry. She'd been on an emotional rollercoaster since we got to this accursed star system.

"Don't worry. I've a got a plan."

That was bullshit, of course. I always told my crew I had a plan, whether I did or not. It kept them calm and focused.

We pulled away from the missile flock, and it predictably trailed us. The tiny slivers of metal tried to cut the angles and catch up, but it was hopeless. Watching them, I got an idea.

"Huan, release a torpedo. Aim it for the center of those pods—proximity burst."

"I don't think we can get them all, Captain," Droad said.

"Nooo!" shouted Jort. He was listening in again. "Let me gun them down, sir! We only have two torpedoes left."

"Fire the torpedo, Huan."

He reached out his artificial arm and touched a contact. The ship shuddered, and a torpedo fell away to the aft. It ignited its engine and raced away.

What happened next was interesting. The missiles, faced with a change in the situation, wavered. I could tell they weren't sure what to do. Should they stay on target, even though we were outrunning them, or should they veer and try to intercept this new threat?

After a few seconds of fascinating indecision, they all swerved as one and went for the torpedo, which was passing them in the opposite direction. I slapped my console and smiled.

"That's our chance! Wheel around, pour on the gas again, and head for those pods. Jort, man your cannon. You'll get your chance to use it with any luck at all."

We rode out several minutes of tight maneuvering. At the last moment, the missiles realized we were again a threat, and they veered to intercept.

It was too late. The math was on our side. The missiles caught our torpedo, and they vanished when the proximity fuse went off and vaporized them.

We dashed into the swarm of pods, and we destroyed them all. I could hear Jort cackling with glee all the way from the back of the ship as he ripped into them, one after another.

"A few got away," Morwyn said worriedly.

"Yes, but maybe that's a good thing. If a small attack like that reaches Vindar, it will serve as a warning."

"But… aren't we going to go back and warn them ourselves?"

"We're going to try."

After the battle was over, I turned our ship around and headed for deep space. Any stealth we had in this star system was long gone, and we were overstaying our welcome. More pods and missiles were stirring on Chara A. I didn't want to find out what other surprises the aliens had for us.

Chapter Seventeen

After running from the inner planets, we lingered in deep space, just outside the orbit of the farthest world that drifted around Chara. It was an isolated place. A tense and lonely time.

Bound by the words of B-6, who'd promised the slip-gate would be activated again in thirty standard days, we drifted with the out-system debris.

We did our best to hide from any possible pursuit from Chara A. Using all the guile I'd developed over the years as a gunrunner, I coated the ship with ice, dampened all emissions, and did my best to make the ship look like one more tiny chunk of floating debris.

Every out-system of any planet was full of bits and pieces—usually ice and rocks. Comets came from out here, invisible and quiet even as they hurtled along, so far from the star at the center of the system that they couldn't be detected until they came closer. At that point, they would begin to melt and vent gases, leaving behind a telltale streak visible for great distances.

As long as we kept our engines cold and transmitted nothing, we were equally invisible at this range from Chara. Still, one never knew what outposts the aliens might have out here. Something small, perhaps, that listened and reported to the enemy.

So, we worried about that—and the other looming fear that grew closer to hand every passing day.

Would B-6 be true to his word? Would he light up the slip-gate again on the fortieth day? Or was I fooling myself, leading a crew of simple dupes I'd taken on this suicide mission? This was the view that Jort held firmly.

"They screwed us, I tell you. The plastic men never lie—not until I met this one. He lies all the time."

"Jort," Droad argued, "that doesn't make any sense. Why would B-6 go to such lengths if he wanted us dead and gone? Couldn't he have simply blown up our ship when we were in his grasp?"

Jort's thick finger came up, and it waggled at Droad. "Ah-ha! My opinion of you shifts. You're not so smart, because you don't understand the evil in the hearts of vindictive men—and robots."

"Explain yourself."

"Jort explains! Imagine an enemy you want to see more than dead—you want him to hurt. You want to hear him cry for his mother's milk."

Droad crossed his arms. "Go on."

"You see, if B-6 just blew us up, well, that would be nothing to him. He could do that with a flick of his rubber-parts. No, no, no, he wants us *more* than dead. He wants us to cry and beg the stars for justice."

"Jort, please stop this," Morwyn pleaded, but he didn't even look at her. His eyes were those of a zealot on a streak.

"No easy quick death for villains such as us! B-6 schemed, and he plotted. He came up with this diabolic game. First, he convinced us we're heroes—not dummies. Then, we when went on our great adventure—he laughed. This is no hero-trip. It is a one-way ticket to an alien-filled Hell!"

"Jort," I said, finally interrupting his tirade. "You don't know any of this to be true, and you're starting to frighten Morwyn."

"I'm not frightened. I'm just... concerned."

Jort finally looked at her. "That means the same thing. Look it up." Then, he turned his attention back to Droad again. "Don't you see? This way, we are doomed, but we don't know it at first. We come here, we poke around in this spooky place, and we investigate. Probably, the aliens eat us. A far worse death than blowing up nice and clean."

Droad nodded thoughtfully. "But we *did* escape the aliens."

Jort lifted that finger again. "Right! Even worse for us! Now, we're out here in deep space. Soon, we will become like half-starved lions in snowy woods. Soon, we'll return to the slip-gate, where we were promised rescue—but nothing will happen. No one will come—except maybe some other ship of fools who think they're heroes."

No one looked happy, except Jort himself, because he could tell that he was bothering us. We all knew that the slip-gate might not light up again. There were a thousand reasons for that in addition to the one Jort had invented.

Weeks went by as we waited for the slip-gate to activate again. B-6 had said it would be a thousand hours and each of those countless minutes crawled by.

I wasn't as pessimistic as Jort, but I'd come to expect no less than underhanded falsehoods from B-6. He was nothing like the do-gooder types that ran most of the Conclave. He was more like a human politician—full of platitudes and deceit.

At last, the day came. We watched until the last hour arrived, then the minutes ticked by…

When the final seconds of the long wait came and went, we stared at the instruments, barely daring to breathe.

The moment the deadline passed, Jort immediately crowed. "You see? I was right, wasn't I? Everyone called Jort a fool, but—"

"Are you crazy?" Morwyn demanded. "Do you want to be trapped in this dead star system forever?"

"Shut up, Jort," I said. "Give it a few seconds."

Ten seconds passed—then thirty. A collective groan went up from the group.

Then, suddenly, the slip-gate lit up. We all shouted with glee.

"All engines ahead, Huan," I ordered.

We lurched toward the gate, and we were all smiling big—but then, something strange happened. The slip-gate flashed, and a small object appeared in the middle of it.

"What's that?" Morwyn demanded.

"A bomb!" Jort declared. "B-6 sent it through to finish us. Do you think he was watching us secretly, all this time?"

Squinting at the readings, I frowned. "It's a ship. A small ship, like ours."

"Another scout," Droad said. "Signal them—warn them. They're flying too slowly to avoid the pods."

Gaping, we watched as space around the tiny ship stirred and came to life. A hundred pods—or perhaps a thousand—all eagerly sought that hot, metal hull. They approached from every direction like a school of pond fish rushing toward a bread crumb.

"Unknown vessel," I signaled, breaking our radio silence. "You're in danger. Use maximum thrust to escape this area."

They never called us back. Either they never heard us, or they recognized their approaching doom and were too busy for talk.

They hit their thrusters, flying wildly forward—but it was too little, too late.

The pods enveloped them. We could no longer make out the sleek sliver of titanium, but instead saw nothing. Only the bulbous and egg-shaped pods were visible as they glided close. Finally, even their engines were extinguished.

"William," Morwyn said, putting a hand on top of mine. "We've got to save them."

I didn't look at her. Instead, I studied the situation closely. At last, I came to fateful decision. "They're doomed. Jort, fire our last torpedo into that obscene lump of garbage. Blow everything apart."

He did it without even asking for confirmation. He was a man who preferred to shoot first and ask questions later.

Morwyn's hand jumped off mine as I gave this order. She didn't meet my eye when I glanced at her. She left the bridge, eyes filled with tears. It was going to be a long, lonely ride back to the Conclave, I figured.

Turning back to the situation at hand, I watched as we raced past the burning mass of pods and the demolished spacecraft in the midst of it. At least this minefield of pods was going to be out of commission for a time.

A few moments later, we raced into the slip-gate. It was about to flicker out again when we made it into the field and vanished.

Chapter Eighteen

Morwyn was cold to me on the way back. She was full of theories, suggesting that rude, crazy pilots like me had probably destroyed countless previous scouting missions before they got a chance to look at anything.

I assured her that such a case was highly unlikely, but that didn't turn her back into the girl she'd been before. She was professional, but distant. In the end, I accepted the change and moved on.

When we reached our home stars, we breathed a great sigh of relief—but it was short lived.

"Where's the fleet?" Droad asked.

"Well…" I said. "We couldn't expect B-6 just to be sitting out here for months, waiting for us to come back, could we?"

"I suppose not…"

His tone said that was exactly what he'd been expecting. I said nothing further, because I'd been expecting the same. We had both been disappointed.

There was no drifting flotilla of patrol boats at anchor, but there was a single, solitary ship. It was flown by a lonely model-Q officer with a squad of model-K guardians as a crew.

"Captain," I said, giving the bot his due. "I'm William Gorman, reporting back—"

"We know who you are, Gorman. Make your report."

Rude, but at least he wasn't wasting my time with pleasantries. "All right. We flew out there, and we found the Chara system. There were two colony worlds, both of which have been devastated. Upon visiting the innermost planet, Chara A... uh... where are you going, officer?"

The patrolman's ship was gunning his engines. They flared white, and we were left behind.

"Upon receiving useless information, my instructions are to withdraw from this system and proceed to my next rally-point."

"Useless information?!" Jort shouted over the com channel. "You're the one who's useless, plastic-boy!"

"Jort, kindly shut up. Officer, why is our information useless?"

"Every ship which has previously returned has identified Chara as the destination. They also detailed the poor status of the two colonies found there. There is no value to your intel at this juncture."

My mind whirled with questions, and my crewmen muttered angrily around me. Why, for instance, had B-6 neglected to mention these other missions? Or that he knew the jump would take us to Chara?

None of that mattered right now, so I decided to get other, more pertinent information out of the robot. "Where is your next rally-point? Where is the fleet? What could be so important that you're rushing away in the middle of my report?"

The officer didn't answer right away. Finally, the signal light lit up again. "You're cleared for a classified response, but don't relay the information you're about to receive to any other parties."

"Um... all right. Where are you going in such a hurry?"

"To Alioth. There's been a major incursion there since you left on your failed mission. All Conclave ships have been called to respond. A sizeable police-intervention is planned."

With that, the model-Q closed the com channel. That was all he would say. He didn't tell me anything else. I followed his ship, and meanwhile an argument ensued on my own command deck.

"This is our chance, Captain!" Jort pleaded. "Please, let's be done with these fools. We did what they wanted. We risked our necks, and now we're free to do as we please."

Droad and Huan took a dim view of Jort's opinions. "If you're not going to Alioth," Huan said, "I need to exit this ship at our next port of call and find other transport to get there myself."

I knew he meant it, as he'd recently stolen my ship to do just such a thing.

Droad looked at me with equal levels of concern. "Although you might think I'm pursuing Ahab's whale, I assure you that I'm no less dedicated to this cause. I too, shall be forced to leave your service if you don't follow that patrolman to Alioth."

I turned toward Morwyn next. "Morwyn, what do you want to do?"

She shrugged and cast her gaze down toward the deck. "I didn't think you cared what I thought about anything."

"I do indeed. In fact, you'll probably decide the issue."

"We're voting?" Jort blurted out.

I nodded. "After a fashion. What do you say, Morwyn?"

She looked around the group with big eyes. "I... I guess I would vote to follow the patrol ship. We've got to see what's happening at Alioth, don't we? Besides, we don't have to run from these patrolmen. They're on our side now."

Jort snorted like a draft horse. "How little you know about the synthetic men, blue lady. They will probably arrest us for flying too close to their tail fins. It will be a crime we've never heard of."

Jort had a point about the unpredictable behavior of patrolmen. They might give you a warning or a fine—or then again, they might arrest you and imprison you. Machine Law wasn't like human law, it was complex and applied seemingly at random. It was hard to know where you stood, which left outlaws like us on the edge all the time.

"Hmm... all right. We'll fly after the patrolman—or rather toward his stated destination. We'll get there before he does, given our faster engines. How can anyone claim that we're following him then?"

Everyone liked my idea—with the distinct exception of Jort—so we moved off the patrol ship's course. Planning things out on the navigational table, we calculated we could reach Alioth before the other ship did with days to spare—but not without refueling. Vindar didn't have much in the way of amenities for spacers. They didn't even have an orbital space station for visiting ships.

"First, we'll head to Scorpii," I decided in the end. "We can get all the fuel we want, along with a few other essentials."

Jort caught on immediately. "Like some more torpedoes?"

I nodded, and he grinned. *Royal Fortune* soon veered away from the patrol ship's course and flew toward Scorpii. When we were well outside of the patrol ship's scanning range, we put the pedal down and reached illegal speeds.

Many days later, we arrived at Scorpii and made certain arrangements. Then we turned toward Alioth and arrived long before the patrol ship did. Our angular course which took us through a different set of slip-gates ensured that the pilot would have no idea we'd moved ahead to intercept.

The Alioth system was oddly quiet when we arrived. It was something of a commercial hub the last time I'd been in this part of the Conclave. It was a world that was more civilized than Scorpii, but less so than Prospero. I was surprised not to be challenged by traffic control as we approached the planet.

"Full system scan," I ordered.

Huan and Morwyn immediately complied. Data began flowing in. There was some activity out near the local asteroid belt, which was thick with floating rocks and unusually close to the central star. Normally, we would have seen a fleet of miners leaching on every metal-rich rock found there—but we saw little movement.

"Let's get a close-up view of Alioth itself," I said, and I goosed the engines, putting us on a collision course with the blue-white planet.

As we drew close, we were surprised to see that a large number of transports were in orbit.

"What are those cargo ships doing here?" Jort asked.

"I don't think they're full of merchants carrying goods," Droad answered.

"What then?"

Droad and I glanced at one another. We had a dark suspicion, and as we drew closer and examined the data coming from the sensors, our suspicion was confirmed.

"They're troopships," I announced.

"Yes," Huan said. "I agree."

Jort's mouth hung open. "Troopships? The Conclave has an army?"

"Apparently, Jort," I said. "These ships are refitted freighters. See how they've got pressurized cargo bays? Normal freighters don't pump oxygen and heat into their massive holds. I think they've been modified to allow troops to survive in there."

"But…" Jort said, going over the numbers. "Ah-ha! You are all wrong! Look at that temperature, it is around zero degrees C. And that pressure—that's not good either. They must have troops who can breathe on nearly airless rocks!"

I nodded. "Yes. That's further evidence. The conclusions are unavoidable. I think they've brought in an army of model-Ks, most likely. Thousands of them."

Jort was again dumbfounded. "A huge army of plastic men? This is horrible. I hate them already. They will give us a fine for every step we take on this world."

We laughed, but there wasn't much humor in the sound. I was almost as worried about the idea of an army of guardians big enough to invade a planet as Jort was.

The truth was, I still hadn't come to terms with the idea that androids ran the Conclave. Our own star cluster was ruled over by robots, and the other had been consumed by aliens.

What chance did normal humans have in this galaxy? Our future looked bleak.

Chapter Nineteen

Alioth was an old world. A planet that had been flattened and smoothed over by billions of years of existence.

On younger worlds, there tended to be more volcanic activity, more churning of the atmosphere. Some of these younger planets also had active out-systems that could throw a comet or an asteroid toward other planets at random.

Alioth was past all that. The asteroid belt was tight and orderly, drawn close to the hot star. The planet itself had placid seas that barely rippled with waves. Even the lone moon was small and unimpressive, just enough to stir things up for an occasional tepid storm.

For all that, it was a pleasant enough place. The skies were usually sunny and blue. The air was very breathable, and the lands were covered with rolling hills and trees rather than rugged mountains.

I'd visited here a few times in the past, and I was saddened to see the place was under attack. The people of Alioth were about to bear witness to a massive conflict—but that's how war went sometimes.

"What's the population of this world?" Droad asked me.

"Less than a billion—probably half that."

"Still, that's a substantial number of people. It looks like the surface is split evenly—about half land and half sea—which leaves a lot of wild areas for aliens to breed."

I nodded. "It's probably why they chose to strike here. They're looking for a base—a foothold in the Conclave."

We studied the data closely as we came into high orbit. In case there were active anti-space defense systems, we didn't move any closer. I noticed that the Conclave forces were being circumspect as well. They were all hanging over the southern hemisphere and avoiding the north.

"They must know something we don't. Pull in above the Conclave fleet, Huan. Place them between us and the ground."

"Smart man! Smart!" Jort exclaimed.

We weren't challenged as we approached Alioth until we maneuvered near the fleet. Then, a pair of patrol vessels rose up to intercept us.

"This is a restricted area," a polite model-Q informed us. "Withdraw, or you will be fired upon."

"Hold on!" I said. "We're part of this fleet. We're scouts returning from the Faustian Chain. Let me talk to—"

"Uh… Captain?" Jort said. "I think they are going to fire. They're opening their gun ports."

"Officers!" I said. "The Connactic personally ordered me to come here and make my report to B-6!

There was a long, tense period of silence. The patrol ships drew closer as the seconds ticked by.

"Tell them again, William," Morwyn urged.

I waved for her to relax. My hand was on the controls, just in case they fired. I was reasonably certain I could outrun their missiles.

"Who dares to invoke the name of the Connactic?"

I smiled. Curiosity was the bane of all creatures, living or robotic. "This is Captain William Gorman. I spoke to the Connactic in person some months ago. She asked me to learn what I could of the enemy and relay this information back to her through B-6—he's an inspector general, if you don't—"

"We know B-6. He's commanding this mission. I will report your statements, but be forewarned, if they are in any aspect false, you will be destroyed."

Shrugging, I leaned back and knitted my fingers behind my head.

No one else in the command module seemed as cool as I was, but then, that's why they weren't in command of the ship.

Finally, a familiar voice came over the com system. "Gorman? This is B-6. Make your report and make it fast."

"Sir, my report includes a list of additional worlds that are about to be invaded by the Skaintz. If you wish me to make that list public over the common airwaves of Alioth, I will do so immediately—"

"Stop. You will speak no further. The patrol ships will escort you to the core of the fleet. After being decontaminated, you will be allowed to report to me in person."

The channel dropped before I could ask any more questions.

"Decontaminated?" Morwyn asked. "Does he think we have lice?"

"No," Droad said. "He thinks we have aliens aboard—or some other kind of unpleasant holdover brought back from the Chain."

I thought about the Tulk, who liked to live on a man's liver. Droad had a point, and I could understand why B-6 was being cautious.

We allowed ourselves to be escorted into the midst of the fleet. A half-dozen patrol ships surrounded us, gun-ports open and ready. If we made the slightest show of aggression, we would be blasted out of space.

This fact seemed to make my crew nervous, but I shrugged it off. It wasn't a new situation for me.

After an overly-long wait, I'd almost nodded off in my command chair when a pack of model-Ks came aboard. They pointed guns in our faces and were generally rude. I was escorted alone back to their patrol vessel.

"Gorman..." B-6 said after I'd been thoroughly searched and probed. "I'm surprised to see you again."

"Why? Because you thought I'd die out at the Chain? Or because you thought we'd run off once we came back?"

"Both."

I nodded. Say what you would about androids in general, there were no fleas to pick off old B-6. He was as savvy as any human commander I'd ever met.

"Well, I'm glad we surprised you." I quickly laid out the details of what we'd found at the Chara system. He listened politely.

"That's it? A series of trajectories for launched pods?"

"No, sir. We engaged these pods and destroyed a number of them." I shared with him the recordings of our combat actions.

He finally seemed impressed. "This is excellent work. I only wish you'd destroyed more of them."

I shrugged. "It was a risk-reward calculation. If we stayed, we might have destroyed more pods. On the other hand, we might have been destroyed ourselves, unable to return with a warning. Now we know what worlds have been targeted."

B-6 turned thoughtful. "Not really… we know what worlds were targeted by this particular launch on this particular day. Looking over this ground-cannon system of theirs, I'd say it takes a while for them to prepare for such launches—but probably no more than a month or two. Who knows what they targeted with their pods the last time around? Or where they'll go the next?"

I was forced to admit that we couldn't be sure of these details. It was daunting, as there might be a number of other worlds operating as seedship launchers as well. All in all, it wasn't out of the question to assume that every planet in the Conclave was already a target.

"Travelling at something close to the speed of light," I said, "it's going to take many years for these pods to reach our planets. But they will come out of the darkness at us every year in ever growing numbers."

He looked at me, and his face was frowning in concern. It was odd to see an android make that expression. I had to wonder as to the nature of his software, how sophisticated it was. Could he actually be feeling concerned? Or was he merely a trumped-up robot imitating an expression he'd seen on human brows?

Did it matter in the end? After all, humans were controlled by biological computers in their skulls we called brains. Did that somehow make us something more significant than an artificial being like B-6 or the Connactic? I wasn't sure, and I wasn't sure I wanted to know the answer, either.

"What's the gameplan?" I asked. "How do we win this?"

"Win? We're trying to survive. We're responding to each situation, seeking an optimal solution."

I shook my head ruefully. "That won't work. You can't win that way. You have to have a plan, a path to victory, and you've got to follow it."

"How can we be sure that the plan will work?"

"You can't. You try, however, and you adjust the plan when it fails. Eventually, it might succeed."

"Hmm..." the android said. "This is beyond my capacities. I will consult the Connactic."

He got up, indicating the meeting was at an end.

"Wait," I told him. "I've been an officer in colonial armies on a few occasions. I've learned that the officer in the field is always better informed than the political leaders back home."

"What is your point, Gorman? We're launching an offensive within hours. Every minute of my time you waste will cost us on the battlefield."

"I understand. But a wrong decision will cost you much more."

He shook his head. "You don't understand. I'm a sophisticated sub-leader. But I'm not the most advanced model. The Connactic, by definition, is our latest version, the most elite mind we can create."

"That includes both software and hardware?"

"Yes."

"But what about personal experience?"

He shrugged. "That's part of what we call software. A modification algorithm permits continuous learning and improving of our processes."

"But you've seen more military action than the Connactic. She's going to be worried about budgets, because that's what she knows best. She'll try to win this from the balance sheet."

"So? Is that an invalid approach?"

"In warfare, I believe it is. A half-bright commander who knows what he's doing will always win over some bean-counting genius from the home office."

B-6 frowned again. "An interesting tidbit. But it doesn't change our protocols. I will consult with the Connactic, because I don't have a clear choice to make."

"Ah-ha!" I said, pointing a finger at him. "You want certainty, but there can't be any such thing out here on the front lines. No wonder I always beat patrolmen when I come up against them. I might as well go back to my ship."

Deciding the moment was right, I staged a walkout. His eyes followed me.

"Wait, Gorman. I wish to make use of your talents. I will place you in the field after our initial landing. You will serve as an advisor."

"An advisor to whom?"

"Me, of course. I'm in command of this operation. Wait here, and I'll return after consulting with the Connactic. Don't worry, I'll relay your heretical opinions to her."

"Uh…"

He left, and I flopped into one of his uncomfortable chairs. Androids weren't much good at padding things. Their chairs *looked* comfy, but they never were.

Chapter Twenty

About ten hours later, the counter-invasion of Ailoth began. I was sorry I'd shot off my mouth so hard with B-6. The Connactic had approved of his idea of using me as a consultant on the ground—somewhere no runner in his right mind wanted to be.

The landing itself was impressive. Over a hundred transport ships had gathered, collectively holding about a million androids. It was unprecedented. They were organized into large divisions of about thirty-two thousand troops each. Every division had a more sophisticated model in charge—a man like B-6 himself.

The commanders didn't call themselves "generals", they called themselves "leads". To me, that was weird. B-6 himself was in charge of the project, so they called him a "director". I was baffled as to why they didn't use military ranks, but maybe it was because they were machines at heart. They understood order and organization, but from a more engineering perspective.

To my surprise, I was allowed to stand near B-6 on his flagship. It was more than a patrol boat, it was about the size of a destroyer from the Sword Worlds. I took the ship's existence as a good sign. At least the androids were *trying* to build a navy.

The invasion started off without a hitch. B-6 and I watched as the first big division maneuvered to land. It took three freighters to hold each division, with something over ten thousand androids packed into each one.

As I watched the three fat ships sink down into the atmosphere, I began to frown. I'd figured out their landing destination: the center of the biggest spaceport on Alioth.

"Um..." I said, "isn't that kind of an obvious place to start?"

B-6 glanced in my direction. He was going over all kinds of incoming data from a dozen screens. Somehow, he could read all of them at once and still keep up with monitored network traffic at the same time.

B-6 frowned. "Part of our agreement was that you wouldn't interrupt without vital input. Please do not distract me, this is a large operation."

"Yeah... okay."

I shut up. After all, I wasn't sure anything was going wrong. B-6 was a big cheese on Mutual, and I was basically a two-bit pirate. I told myself I should just relax.

Several minutes passed. The first of the big freighters set down in a blast pan, her massive disk-shaped feet touching down simultaneously. These android pilots had steady hands.

The other two were under a kilometer from the deck when strange, whistling shapes rose up. They were tiny slivers of metal and chemicals. Mini-missiles no more than a meter long. Each snaked up from a dozen spots in the surrounding city and the wild areas beyond. They left vapor trails that spiraled and plumed blue smoke.

"Oh, shit..." I whispered to myself.

Dozens more mini-missiles appeared—there were hundreds of them.

"Shoot them down!" B-6 ordered. An impressive array of point-defense cannons began to chatter and spray projectiles. Many of the missiles were knocked out—but not all. "Abort! Abort! Lift off again!"

The lumbering freighter gushed fire out of her jets. Massive thrust was exerted, attempting to both halt the descent and reverse it. The entire spaceport disappeared, bathed in flame and smoke.

But the missiles plunged through, and the first transport—the one that had touched down—exploded. It was a terrific blast. They must have had a lot of fuel and munitions aboard.

The explosion engulfed the second transport but didn't knock it out. It emerged from the flames like a behemoth rising out of hell. Just when it looked like it was going to escape, however, a shower of missiles struck her in the guts. She blew up as well.

The third transport, the final one to begin this dreadful descent, fared better. She took a few shots in the stern and was venting and limping by the time she reached orbit—but she escaped, losing no more than ten percent of her cargo.

"At least one of them got away," I commented, trying to put a happy spin on the disaster.

B-6 glowered at me. I hadn't thought an android was capable of such an unpleasant expression.

"You knew this was going to happen," he said.

"Nah... but I suspected it might."

"Why? Explain yourself, human."

I shrugged. "Well... these aliens are tricky. I've fought them before many times. They aren't smart in the sense of being cognitive geniuses, but they are cunning, like a lion that knows how to catch dinner."

B-6 stared for a time. "Your words are not helpful in the slightest."

"Sorry, okay, look... it's like this, B-6. You set the ships down at Mataran City, a place we know has been infected by the enemy."

"The entire planet has been overrun. There are only pockets of human resistance. Mataran City is merely one of those places."

"Right, right. You wanted to help a hold-out city under siege. I get that. It's only natural and logical to choose this place to begin—which is why the aliens knew you would land here."

B-6 looked back down at the tables depicting the tactical situation in brilliant color and detail. The entire spaceport was on fire now. In spots, it looked as if the blaze was going to spread into the city itself.

"This is a disastrous start. We've done more damage to ourselves than we have the enemy."

"Hey, hey, don't be so hard on yourself. This is your first time commanding an invasion force."

"That is irrelevant. Failure is unacceptable."

B-6 was being hard on himself, but I saw that as a good thing. If he could learn how to do something radically new, he was going to have to start doing it right now before more men were lost.

"All right," he said after going over the data. "We'll land another division to the northeast. There is a suburb there with a spaceport of sufficient size. It is only a cargo facility, but it will have to do. From that starting point, our forces can advance and relieve the city defenders."

"Uh... okay. If that's the best option."

B-6 gave me a baleful glare. "You object?"

"It's not my place to do so."

"What would you suggest instead?"

As I'd been formally asked, I extended a long arm with an index finger pointing from the end of it. I tapped at three locations. They were essentially open fields, farming areas about ten kilometers from the city limits.

"Three rural spots? So far from town?"

I nodded.

"Explain your logic, Gorman."

"Well, if you land in three locations at once, with one third of a division in each spot, you will probably get at least one of the transports down safely. I don't think the aliens can have staked out every field on the planet."

"No... but what you suggest will be inconvenient. Our forces will take many hours to organize and march on Mataran City. It will give the enemy time to prepare."

"That's true, but right now, we have no beachhead on the ground. We need a safe place of our own where we can start this invasion."

Finally, after consulting a few other androids, B-6 approved my suggestion with one big caveat: he ordered three freighters to land at each of the three locations. That meant we were committing ten percent of our total force all at once.

"Why such a big landing?" I asked him. "Can't we do better with smaller forces?"

"No. Our divisions are designed to operate in one location as a cohesive force. They won't function properly if they are scattered to three disparate spots. We will land three divisions in the city and take it over."

I was tense, and my throat felt tight as the second landing attempt proceeded. I watched as nine ships fell rapidly from the sky and set down in various fields I'd recommended almost at random. In only one case was there serious resistance. A storm of tiny missiles and a small number of enemy killbeasts rushed out to attack the landing ships as the guardians disembarked at the third isolated field.

It was a wild fight. Watching from above, I was impressed by both sides. Fleshly creatures with maximal genetic performance were met by human-like machines. Both sides seemed surprised by the other's capabilities.

The aliens came bounding close, accepting a crashing volley of accurate fire from the androids. Dozens of them never even reached the android line—but those that did performed superbly. They swept heads from necks with their horned feet, kicking high with precision.

To the surprise of the aliens, however, the artificial men didn't die. They accepted injuries that would have been catastrophic and certainly fatal to a human—but they kept on fighting.

Guns blazed. Brown leaping shapes tore apart androids. It was utter mayhem, but the androids won in the end. They were too numerous, too unstoppably methodical. They didn't feel pain, or shock. They fought until they could not function—and the aliens did the same.

Numbers were on the android side. They lost hundreds, but they destroyed every alien and continued to disembark.

I clapped B-6 on the shoulder and grinned at him. "You did it! You're down on the planet! This fight is half-over now!"

"I do not share your enthusiasm. The aliens are numerous, and in this struggle they destroyed more of my troops than I did of theirs. We precalculated a three to one loss ratio in our favor in order to be victorious."

"Oh... so you need to kill three of them for every android you lose?"

"That is correct."

"Huh... well, it's not over with yet. Any invading force is at its weakest when they are in the early days of the invasion. Your gambit paid off. You've landed three divisions out of thirty, and that might be enough to take the city."

"It had better be," he said, and he walked away. I tried to blow some more sunshine up his plastic posterior, but he refused to be mollified.

He was right, of course. The opening operation had been arrogant and disastrous. I would have landed at least ten kilometers away, in some deserted spot in the wilderness. Only after ensuring all my troops were safely on the ground and organized, would I have sought to engage the enemy.

But all that was water under the bridge now. B-6 had managed his landing. With any luck, he'd push the aliens out of the town and gain a foothold. If the aliens surrounded him and pushed him back off-planet, he could land somewhere else. That was the power that holding the high ground gave you—mobility.

Chapter Twenty-One

With three full divisions on the ground and active, we had nearly one hundred thousand troops in the field. The enemy was more numerous, but they had an entire planet to worry about. Conclave forces were only concerned with our landing zones.

Spreading out from the three landing spots to encircle Mataran City, the androids employed predictable methods. They didn't rush. They didn't move with uneven responses in any crisis. In fact, whenever anything went wrong, they all halted their advance and worked to solve the single sore point. This essentially meant that their entire army stopped advancing due to any provocation—no matter how slight.

For instance, on the day after the landing, the 2nd and 3rd divisions couldn't link up as intended. The other two points where one army touched the next were fine—but there was a lake with a large river running between the two divisions. The androids had been ordered to spread out until they were within shouting distance of one another, but they couldn't do it due to the water barrier.

One would think such a minor detail wouldn't affect their overall plans. If they simply advanced on all fronts, they'd soon contract their circle and pass the lake, allowing the plastic troops to link-up at the outskirts of the city.

But apparently, that wasn't how androids liked to do things. Instead, they were piecing together rafts and makeshift bridges, so they could link-up their front line as ordered. They wouldn't advance a single step until this was achieved.

"Hey, B," I said when I noticed this. "Are your guys lacking in imagination or what? Why don't they just advance until they link-up on the far side of the lake? You're delaying the entire operation by hours, giving the enemy more time to prepare."

B-6 blinked a lot. I think he was processing my input and trying to adapt. Finally, he turned toward me.

"That's an intelligent adjustment to the plan. I find it acceptable, if sub-optimal. I will relay the suggestion to the project leaders on the ground."

"That's very thoughtful. Will you be sending this *suggestion* as an order, or as a helpful hint?"

B-6 froze up again. "It will be an officially issued advisory."

I forced a smile. "You think they'll take the hint and run with it?"

"No. They'll ignore the suggestion unless a crisis develops. In that case, their priorities will shift and deviations will become more attractive."

"Huh…"

I wasn't impressed. These guys got things done, mind you, but it was at a glacial pace. Maybe that's why we'd seen so little action in response to problems in the Conclave.

There was always a hierarchy of needs and problems pushing against a process that was already in motion. If a problem became severe enough, it would rise to the top of the list and be addressed. Otherwise, it would never be considered until every other higher-ordered item on the list was finished.

"We're taking a big risk here," I said. "Your lack of flexibility might cause us to lose this struggle. It will certainly cause a big delay."

"A delay? I don't see it that way. Your suggestion is a delay concerning the process of linking forces and encircling Mataran City."

"Yeah, it might take a bit longer, but my way ensures you'll be gaining ground on the next step. You'll complete the overall process of taking the city faster."

B-6 thought about that. He really did. No other model of android had the capacity to do this. I watched, and I waited.

"Your thought processes are logical, but you have to realize that changing my procedures is much harder now that I'm dealing with a very high-priority project."

"Ah... I get it. You're worried about altering the plan since you've got so much on the line. The Conclave is depending on this mission—and the budget must be astronomical."

"No. No budget can be astronomical, which is a mathematical term referring to—"

"Never mind. Listen, I get your problem. You're usually able to adjust your thinking with ease, but due to the big nature of these decisions, you've frozen-up. You're intimidated by the scope of your responsibilities."

"That is... a figurative way of describing an advanced algorithm."

I almost rolled my eyes, but I managed to avoid it. Stiff-necked worriers like B-6 were commonplace. I wasn't at all surprised he was having a crisis of self-confidence. He wanted to adjust things—but he couldn't do so. If that wasn't fear of failure, I didn't know what was.

"Okay, okay," I said. "You have to weigh the importance of your responsibilities against the probability of failure. Sure, the ratio is out of balance compared to what you're used to. This is no patrol ship break down, it's a planetary invasion that could determine the fate of the entire Conclave."

"So far, your statements aren't helping my decision process."

I laughed. "Let me get to the punchline, then. The cost of failure is so great that you can't afford to strictly follow preordained protocols. No commander of a field army can afford to do that. The battlefield is ever-changing, and it requires flexibility."

"Keep on speaking," he said, and he looked at me with a surprising intensity.

"Okay. What I'm saying is that you can't let a trivial issue get in the way of your final victory. That meta goal—victory—must override your usual approach to problem-solving. The cost will be tremendous otherwise."

"This is helpful..." B-6 said. "You're saying, if I can paraphrase, that the cost of failure is so great that it balances out with the rewards of victory. Therefore, I can return to my usual algorithmic approaches rather than altering them in response to their magnified importance... Is this correct?"

"Um... I think you've got it."

B-6 nodded, and his lips twitched. A smile? Sort of... at least it was the beginnings of one. Moving to the command console, he immediately ordered his empty-headed sub-commanders to rush ahead, to contract the circle rather than try to link-up by crossing the lake.

We watched as the entire battlefield shifted. The androids, thousands upon thousands of them, changed direction and purpose almost simultaneously. I had to admit, if there was one area in which these artificial soldiers beat humans cleanly, it was in their capacity for unified action and unity of purpose.

In less than an hour, the lines converged and encircled the town. Hotspots flared up, as alien groups that had been lying in wait were met and vicious fighting broke out.

"You see that? You surprised the enemy," I said. "They weren't expecting you to switch-up your operations. They weren't ready, and you walked into their ambush points early."

It was true. The android troops, marching as one, met up with smaller pockets of aliens, mostly in wooded areas. The fighting was intense, but the androids won repeatedly, due to superior numbers and armament.

"We're ahead of schedule," B-6 said, absorbing the input from the field.

"Definitely," I agreed, smiling at the holomaps.

A hand fell on my shoulder. I startled, but when I turned I saw it was only B-6. He was looking at me strangely.

"I've made another decision. You will be the new ground commander of 2nd Division."

"Uh... what?"

"The previous commander was an individual such as myself. He perished during the earlier landing attempt. The division is undermanned and without a leader. I'd normally place the damaged division into my reserve forces—but I've changed that decision."

"Oh..." I said, mildly stunned. Was I really going to be commanding thousands of model-K guardians? The very idea seemed unthinkable.

"Do you accept this responsibility, Captain Gorman? I can't force you to do so. It is a matter of choice. You must be willing, or you will make a poor commander."

"Yeah... right. That makes sense. Listen... let me talk it over with my crewmen. I can do that, can't I? It's no secret?"

"No, it isn't. There is no one present in this star system who might object. I am in complete command of this expedition."

"Right, okay... Let me sleep on it, and I'll tell you in the morning."

B-6 withdrew his plastic hand from my shoulder and nodded. He returned to the planning tables. I knew he would stand there all night, working tirelessly and offering frequent updates to the plan.

Seeing the distinctive change that had come over him, I was left with an odd feeling in my guts. Had I somehow changed his programming forever? Had I, with a simple "no plan survives contact with the enemy" explanation that had worked on his logic circuits, managed to get him over a block in his thinking?

What if he told other androids of his caliber about it? Or worse yet, what if he shared some kind of mind-module with them? What were the implications for the future of humanity? Crap... I hoped I hadn't made these androids smarter than they already were. Humans were too far down in the pecking order as it was.

I decided right then and there that I wasn't going to share any more secrets concerning deep-thinking. There weren't going to be any more philosophies or brain-hacks coming out of my big mouth. These plastic men were going to have to figure out how to dominate the universe on their own, just like we'd done with the help of millions of years of evolution.

Chapter Twenty-Two

All my crew members were shocked—and some were horrified.

"You're going down there to march with the plastic men?" Jort asked. "Are you a dummy? Didn't you see how they fought the aliens when they first landed? They died like ants marching into flames!"

"Yes, well... hopefully with my help, they'll do better."

Droad and Huan were more thoughtful, more circumspect.

"This is an awesome responsibility, Captain Gorman," Huan said. "If there was a better commander available—but I suppose there isn't. Androids of B-6's quality aren't common. I suspect that they are created when there is a fluke in the manufacturing process. Like a flawless diamond, they must be exceedingly rare."

I supposed he was right about that. Otherwise, they would have had plenty of commanders for their divisions of model-Ks. In fact, the more I considered the idea, the more certain things made sense. For example, the androids were using very large sizes for their divisions. Why not fewer androids per unit? Perhaps it was because they suffered from a lack of top commanders.

"Captain," Droad said, speaking up next. "I think you should take the job—I feel that you must do so, in fact. We all know that a cagey human commander can outthink these artificial minds, at least in the area of tactics. The Conclave androids are basically bureaucrats. They have little to no experience with commanding armies in the field."

I looked toward Morwyn next. She nodded to me. "Do it. You have to. But what's to become of us? Should we return to Scorpii, or…?"

"Actually, I was thinking my crew should come down with me."

"What about the ship?" Jort asked suspiciously. "Only a dumb captain leaves his ship unguarded."

"Hmm…" I looked around the group and pointed at Huan. "You can stay in space and pilot the ship during the battle."

"What?" Jort objected. "Huan? Why not Jort? This man is half-plastic himself. He ran off with your ship once. Why will he not do it again?"

Huan spoke up. "Because I would never leave the scene of a battle with these aliens, Jort."

"That's right," I said. "That's it, right there. He's the best pilot we have—save for myself—and he'll be here to pick us up when this is over."

I turned to Morwyn next. "What about you, Morwyn?"

She looked alarmed. "You really want *me* to come with you? To fight with an army of androids?"

"I want you to join us. I would feel better if you were with us."

She crossed her arms. "You know I'm no soldier… You want me to be your emotional support animal, don't you? I'm not interested in that job—not this time."

I shrugged. "All right then. Have it your way. You can stay on the ship with Huan. What about you, Jort?"

"I will go where you go, Captain. I will fight at your side. I will be this animal you are looking for. When the androids turn against you, they will have to kill Jort first."

"Excellent." Lastly, I turned my eyes to Droad. "What about you, Governor?"

"I will come. I have fought these aliens on a planetary scale more than once. I've commanded armies against them—but only armies of humans. This will be different…"

"Yes, I think it will."

It was decided. Huan and Morwyn would stay aboard *Royal Fortune* after they dropped us off on the ground. Droad and Jort would accompany me—providing companionship and advice. I knew from experience that the androids didn't always make the best company, so I was glad to have some real people coming along.

The landing came at dawn. We were worried as we descended through the cloud cover, but we needn't have been concerned. Not a single mini-missile came up to greet us.

Feeling somewhat more relaxed, we landed at the camp nearest the lake. The soldiers had halted their advance in the woodlands surrounding much of the town. This concerned me immediately.

The moment I stepped off my ship's ramp, it all but lifted away under the back of my heel. I stumbled and dashed away from the jets—tossing an angry glance over my shoulder. Huan was taking no chances.

As we watched from the ground, *Royal Fortune* disappeared into the sky in a flash. It felt like we'd been marooned.

From every side, model-Ks approached. They seemed to be baffled concerning our presence.

"Civilians aren't permitted in this area," stated one of them. "For your own safety, it is strongly recommended that you leave this region and this planet entirely."

"That's not helpful, soldier," I said. "Here, scan this memory slip."

He complied, running a finger over a wisp of plastic that was smaller than my hand. B-6 had given it to me as proof of my status.

The model-K stiffened as if receiving new instructions. "This way, sir," he said, turning away and marching toward a mobile building next to a row of opaque, polycarbonate Quonset huts.

The building was on tracks, and it served as a headquarters unit while the nearby huts made for a sketchy-looking combat outpost.

"Jort, go check out the arsenal for me. Governor, I'd like you to do a quick inventory—find out what's in those buildings."

Moving to the mobile headquarters, I stepped inside alone. There I found a gaggle of model-Q officers surrounding a battle computer. They stared at me. Every one of them had to read my plastic slip—some of them twice—before they were convinced I was their new commander.

"This is most unusual," one of them said. He was just like the rest, except for the fact he had two limbs missing. His right arm and leg were gone. I was impressed that he was still able to stand and balance without aid. He was listing slightly, however.

"Are you my second in command?" I asked him.

"Presumably. Our commander died during the landing. We've now been designated as a reserve force. When losses occur in other divisions, we replenish those losses with our best operating troops."

"Hmm… that won't work for me. Cancel that order. No more troops are to be reassigned to other divisions."

"Order canceled," the crippled officer said.

At least these guys weren't going to argue with me. I kind of liked that. As a longtime pirate captain, I'd long ago grown weary of having my every order questioned.

"What are your names?" I asked the group. That was a serious mistake. Every one of them had a 'name' that was essentially a thirty-character serial number. Before half of them had recited their designations, I told them all to shut up.

"Okay…" I said. "We're going to change things up a little around here. From now on, I'm General Gorman. General is my rank, get it?" The robots looked a little disturbed, but no one said anything. I pointed at the guy with the burned off arm and leg. "You're Stumps. Colonel Stumps. From now on, you're my second in command until I find someone better."

"Did you say, colonel, sir? We utilize a complex ranking system based on hour-by-hour performance evaluations. Right now, I'm ranked #4 out of—"

"I don't care. From now on, you're Colonel Stumps. Got it?"

"Yes, sir. My response files have been updated."

Taking my time, I went through the group of officers. There were seven in all that had survived the disastrous day of the landing. I gave everyone besides Stumps the rank of major for now in addition to their own name.

"Major Cringe," I said, pointing to a female android who had hair that looked particularly fake. "You'll operate the planning table. Bring up the local situation."

She immediately moved to obey. She was quick and efficient, like all her kind. Soon, the tactical map lit up brightly. The first thing I noticed, besides the thick ring of android troops encircling Mataran City, was the total lack of movement by any of them.

"Uh… why aren't we advancing?"

"That step has not yet been sanctioned."

I frowned. This was sounding just like my previous problems with B-6 and bridging the lake. "Come on, people. You can't stop an entire military operation because one piece isn't perfectly lined up. What's wrong this time?"

Major Cringe answered, as she was the one I'd addressed most recently. "We haven't yet signaled our readiness to B-6 for the next step."

"Well then, signal him. Tell him we're ready to move out—right now."

Major Cringe stiffened up for a moment, then she unfroze again. "It is done."

Immediately, I heard a lot of commotion outside. Moving to the planning table, I saw troops converging from all directions toward the city in the center of our ring.

Had B-6 really held up his entire invasion plan for me to get situated and take command of this ragtag division of survivors? That wasn't good—he still hadn't learned how to get past thinking like a ticking clock.

Chapter Twenty-Three

One thing that was pretty cool about commanding a large group of androids was the simple fact that when they moved, they really *moved*.

What I mean by that is—instead of having to get every unit underway, each with their own individual amount of delay time—they acted as one. They all took action and began forward motion simultaneously, or very close to it.

I was expecting something more like traffic backing up at a stoplight back on Prospero. When humans did this, each human in line would wait for the car ahead of them to move and then they would move in turn.

How much faster would that process be if all of them hit the gas identically—at the same rate and at the same time? Even the car in the back of the row would be moving forward at the same rate with the same acceleration curve as the one in the front of the line.

The androids were able to do just that. Because of the synchronized nature of their minds, they could all initiate or abort a function in unison. They could all work on that function at the same time without questioning the other individuals in the group. What this meant in practice, was that once the go-signal to advance upon the outskirts of Mataran City was given, every android began marching at once, as if a switch had been flipped.

That just wasn't how humans worked, but I figured I could get used to it. In fact, my mind began coming up with new military tactics.

I couldn't have dreamed that I'd be able to surprise and dismay the enemy in the ways that were available to me now. The enemy wouldn't know which sector to defend, as they would all be under attack at once.

"Commander," Colonel Stumps, said to me, "we're getting reports of combat in Sector Three."

I moved to the planning tables again and examined them, finding that it was true.

There were flashing red areas all over the screen, which depicted where conflict was underway. Very quickly, I determined that there was a large firefight going on not too far from our position.

"Where's this battle underway?" I demanded. Colonel Stumps immediately displayed a region of red lines that lay less than a kilometer from my headquarters and my personal command, 2nd Division.

To my dismay, we were not on the front line at all. As B-6 had said, we were a reserve force and much smaller than the other two divisions that had been deployed. I think our strength was down to something like ten percent of the starting troops—the rest having been given away to the other divisions as reinforcements.

As far as I could tell, we were something like three to four thousand strong compared to 32,000 for the main divisions. The good news was that we weren't yet on the front line in combat. I immediately decided that we would have to operate as an aggressive reserve force, joining the fight when and where it was most appropriate.

Major Cringe reported in next. "General Gorman, we're encountering stiff resistance in Sector Three."

"Yes, I already know that," I said. "You told me that just a minute ago."

"Yes, sir," Major Cringe continued. She did not look flustered or concerned at all. But she did point to the map. "But you see, sir, we're actually being pushed back now."

I looked at the map, and after a while, I interpreted all the lines and splotches, greens and reds. And I realized that, yes—we were actually being forced to retreat in Sector Three.

The same story was happening in Sectors Seven and Nine. Looking around the map. I noticed something. The aliens were retreating, and they were giving ground in several spots. At the same time, they were holding in others and pushing hard in a few spots like Sector Three.

This could not be sheerly an accident. They had some kind of plan, some kind of strategy. They were trying to pull something. But what was it?

I decided it was time to consult with B-6 and get his opinion on the matter. After a fairly short wait I was in direct contact with him.

His image appeared, superimposed above the battle map, but he wasn't looking at me. I could tell his arms were moving around with dexterity, and his eyes were directed toward his own battle map. He was able to simultaneously hold a conversation with me. It was another one of those impressive things that androids can do better than humans—multitask.

"Captain Gorman," he said, "What can I do for you?"

I cleared my throat. "Actually, sir, I'm calling myself General Gorman now—since I'm a land commander." For the first time, B-6 turned his vision and glanced at me directly.

"You've given yourself a promotion?" he asked.

I shrugged. "Not exactly. What I've done is organize my own thoughts. It's not changing anything substantial on the ground. It just clarifies my role... at least for me."

B-6 turned back to the battle maps. His hands kept moving, and I suspected he was directing individual troop movements with his fingers—even as he held his conversation with me. "Is that what you wish to tell me? General Gorman?" he asked.

"No, sir. There's something wrong here. The enemy are not falling back in a uniform pattern. I suspect they're playing a trick or laying a trap."

"A trap?" B-6 said. "What kind of trap? What evidence do you have to support this?"

"I don't really have evidence, sir. I have a hunch. The aliens are not as lockstep as our android forces. But neither are they as haphazard as human forces. I suspect that there is a method to their madness of pushing in some places and falling back in others."

"What is your recommendation, General Gorman?" B-6 asked.

"I think we need to foil their plans. I think that we need to break them where they're holding firm—It's possible they're defending something vital."

B-6 didn't answer me for several seconds. The entire time, his limbs were moving around the map making adjustments. I wasn't sure if he was ignoring me and too busy to consider my thoughts and plans or if he was thinking more deeply about it. It turned out after about five seconds had passed that it was the latter case.

"All right, General Gorman. I have decided to allow you free reign in that situation after your excellent performance earlier. I see that your forces are not committed, and you've stopped reinforcing the frontlines. Take your remaining forces, and push against one of the strong points that the aliens are holding so firmly. If you succeed in learning what their plans are, report your findings."

I was a bit startled by this response, but I accepted the assignment. After all, I'd made the report, I'd run up the problem, and I did have the only reserve force that wasn't on the front line already. How else were you to easily deal with one of these situations?

I nodded, accepting my orders, and I closed the channel.

Chapter Twenty-Four

My android army seemed to take things seriously when I gave them the go-signal. I was actually pleased with the speed and direction I saw when they took to the field.

All the officers evacuated the command center and began marching alongside the mobile unit. I was a little slow to get out of the place, which was kind of like a large crawling bunker on treads. It was part trailer, but resembled a military vehicle built to traverse any kind of terrain—not just roadways.

When our vehicular headquarters lurched into motion toward Sector Three—not more than ten seconds after I ordered everybody to move out—I nearly fell over. In fact, I was the only person still in the thing as far as I could tell.

With a graceless hop, I jumped out of the door, slammed it shut behind me and trotted over to Colonel Stumps. I attempted to match my stride with his, but his locomotion was awkward and labored.

Stumps was springing forward heavily in a sort of continuous bouncing motion. No normal human could have maintained the driving pace of his hops with his one leg and one arm. A man would have gotten tired, worn out or off-balance, but the colonel, being an android, was able to maintain continuous progress without any complaint.

"Colonel Stumps," I asked him, "why is it you're still injured? Why haven't you repaired yourself?"

He turned to me. "It's quite simple. These unorthodox modifications have not interrupted my assigned function. As a commander operating in the headquarters unit, I have not been required to pick up a weapon and fire it. All replacement parts and repair efforts are distributed first to soldiers who are fighting on the front line rather than to an individual like myself who is essentially doing clerical work."

I nodded, marveling at the clear, concise reasoning and the automatic self-sacrifice. A human commander would have probably favored his own health and wellbeing over that of his troops. The androids didn't think that way—at least not the Q-level ones.

Becoming curious about the nature of his former commander, I switched to a different topic, asking him another question. "Tell me something about the commander you lost during the landing," I said. "Was he different than the rest of you officers?"

Colonel Stumps emphatically agreed. "Yes, yes, quite different. He was not a model-Q."

I would have asked him more questions to clarify the exact nature of these differences—but a firefight broke out nearby.

We had not quite made it to the Sector Three front line. In a surprising turn of events, we found that the Sector Three front line was coming to us at least as fast as we were advancing toward it.

Walking out of a clearing in the forest, I saw a shocking number of broken androids. They weren't all destroyed. Quite a few of them were crawling around partially operative, still struggling. We'd walked out into the meadow, and it was really a killing field.

Standing over them—beating them, shooting them, destroying them any way they could—were a large number of killbeasts. Their mottled gray-brown bodies churned, and long, armored limbs flailed wildly. There had to be somewhere near a thousand of the enemy in the vicinity.

Amid the fray, I was easily able to identify a number of shrades. They were muscular and serpent-like, and they rode atop the shoulders of killbeasts. The killbeasts resembled headless men with armored carapaces as tough as that of a giant beetle.

I was alarmed by the thought that I, as the commander of one of the divisions in this action, had not been forewarned that the enemy advance had gotten increasingly severe. The enemy was, in fact, colliding with us at this spot on the battle map.

No one had bothered to tell me this. Possibly it was because the androids were able to communicate over a network that was private among themselves. They did not require vocalizations between them or graphics such as the battle map. Whatever the case, I would have appreciated a warning before I walked straight into a battle.

My own faithful androids were already suffering. Dozens were broken and laying strewn all over the battlefield. The killbeasts had hit them hard and damaged a great number of the units, but for all that, my android troops were not running.

I didn't think such a thing as running in a panic could even occur to a model-K android. He was designed to fight until he could no longer operate—much like the killbeasts themselves. In any case, a large number of them were no longer able to function or at least not effectively.

This sheer tenacity to die fighting seemed to be slowing down the killbeasts somewhat. Humans tended to lie down and die much faster than these machines. Almost as if frustrated, I watched the killbeasts use their foot blades to stab, thrust, kick and slice off limbs and heads. Any body part or appendage they could find became a target as they grew frenzied and tried to end the resistance of the android troops.

When we arrived on the scene, it seemed plausible that this delay helped us not to be immediately attacked by the enemy. Jumping into action, I pulled out my own Sardez rifle, which was still slung around my back, even though none of the other officers were armed with more than a pistol.

It was time to give orders. "Major Cringe," I said, "gather the closest company of guardian troops. Form a line right here in front of me, and begin firing into those aliens. Thin their ranks down."

Major Cringe immediately stepped forward, and a company coalesced into a line within seconds. Humans could never have moved that fast. She lifted a pistol and those around her lifted rifles. Her troops began pelting the enemy aliens with heavy fire.

Now I'll say right here, one negative thing about the android army was their lack of Sardez rifles. They had weapons that were built essentially to kill humans—not Skaintz and killbeasts. This was regrettable but nothing I could fix in the short term.

I shouldered my own Sardez, and I began firing rapidly into the center of the group—disregarding any possible damage I might be doing to the androids. My reasoning was that they were already broken-up, damaged machines, and if they weren't fixing Colonel Stumps, they probably didn't have the parts to fix these guys either. Therefore, their safety was a secondary concern.

My Sardez rifle quickly became the most important weapon on the battlefield. It was essentially a light artillery piece that a single man could carry and fire. Having worked with weapons and aliens like this on battlefields before, I knew the drill.

For the most part, my rounds were aimed at their feet. When the accelerated pellets made contact with the ground, a hot mass was kicked up. This debris was pulverized—turning rock, tree stumps, dirt and everything else into an explosion of flying matter.

Everywhere I struck in the midst of the enemy lines, aliens exploded and were frequently blown apart. They soon became a chaotic mob, desperate to destroy the androids.

For perhaps ninety glorious seconds, my line of androids, led by Major Cringe and supported by my Sardez, worked over the mass of milling, confused aliens. While we rained destruction on them, more and more androids arrived. I instantly ordered them to join the fray.

All too soon, however, the Skaintz figured out that the damaged androids still on the battlefield that were so frustratingly difficult to destroy were not the real problem. The ones that were fresh and arriving at the edge of the clearing and firing into their midst…We were the real danger.

By this time, since we'd been quite successful in lashing them with devastating rifle fire, I would say their numbers had dropped from a thousand down to roughly five hundred.

The androids turned almost as one, like a flock of birds getting a signal from one of their members. The battered and damaged were left where they lay, and the aliens veered to stampede toward us. Bounding in great leaps, the killbeasts—many with an undulating shrade still riding their shoulders—made a suicidal charge.

It was their nature to overwhelm any enemy they encountered by sheer numbers, determination, and speed of attack. This time their tactics failed. They came straight at us in a wave but by the time they reached our lines, there were fewer than a hundred of them left. Within another minute's time my android troops managed to destroy them all with minimal losses.

When it was over, I clapped Colonel Stumps on the back, causing him to stumble. I almost apologized, but I figured he probably wouldn't even know why I'd bothered. I skipped it and proudly beamed a big smile instead.

I pointed at the absolute carnage on the battlefield in front of us. "Stumps! Take a look at that!" I said. "Now *that* is how you destroy an enemy formation. These aliens have met their match."

Stumps eyed me with the usual emotionless, somewhat confused expression I often got from these androids, especially when I was talking to them. No android ever seemed to properly understand me.

"What is it?" I asked him. "What's on your mind?"

"General Gorman, sir," he responded. "Your statements are in error. While we have destroyed this group of aliens, in many other places on the battlefield we're being pushed back. We have not won this war."

I grinned at him. "Not yet, Stumps. Not yet, but we will." Gathering my troops, we set out to march forward. We pressed the enemy who were not so much in retreat as simply annihilated at this particular place on the front line.

We pushed for about a kilometer until we were in the forest again, and then I noticed as I walked along that none of the androids were following me. They were all standing almost motionless at the edge of the tree line. Turning around, I walked back to Major Cringe and Colonel Stumps. I asked the major, "What's up? Why are you guys halting?"

"This is the line," she said.

"What do you mean, this is the line?"

"This is the place beyond which no android has yet gone."

I was a little confused. But I thought about it and then produced a handheld computer. Reviewing the data there, I realized that she had a point. We had advanced as far forward as any element of the android front line on any of the fronts. I found this both illuminating and irritating.

"Major Cringe, Colonel Stumps, are you guys telling me that no one is allowed to march beyond this point?" I asked them.

They glanced at one another in confusion as if they did not quite understand my question, but then they gestured toward the thinnest point in the trees. You could actually see buildings on the horizon—Mataran City was just now barely becoming visible through some of the gaps.

"It is not that we're not allowed, sir. It is that it is not yet time for that step to be taken. The advance to the city outskirts has not been triggered."

"Triggered..." I said, "is that what you call it? What is it, some kind of 'if' statement?... some kind of logical connection that's made in every one of your android brains at the same time?"

Colonel Stumps thought about this for a moment, and then he nodded. "Yes, sir. I think that is a valid description."

"So, you're saying that until every different part of our lines has moved forward to this same distance from the city outskirts, no one is allowed to advance?"

Major Cringe shook her head. She took it upon herself to answer this time. "Again, sir, it is not that we are not allowed. It is that none of us would make such a decision under these circumstances."

"Ah-ha," I said. "Now I begin to understand. It's not so much that you guys are somehow limited in your behavior, but rather that since you all think the same way, you tend to only proceed in a lockstep fashion?"

The two androids agreed with me that this was the case, and I began to understand them more intimately. This was definitely a weakness. The androids were essentially identical-minded characters, not what you wanted on an active battlefield.

The androids almost didn't have to confer with each other about decisions, since they were of the same mind. They were all going to do the same thing anyway, so they really weren't sending messages back and forth, making recommendations or generating chain-of-command decisions. Instead, they were just all acting at once upon their natural instincts and proclivities—which were essentially the same from one individual to the next. It was really weird as a human to experience this firsthand.

"All right, all right," I said. "This business of standing around in battlefields isn't going to work—not against this enemy. What we're going to have to do is break your normal rules, and I'm here to do that for you."

A ring of artificial eyes stared at me in silence.

"Because I'm a human, I do not have the same mind that all android officers have, so therefore, I'm going to behave differently than any of you would. I'm going to force you to win this battle, whether you guys want to or not."

Colonel Stumps objected. "General Gorman, we want to win this battle. It is our goal. It is our mission statement. It is imperative that we win this battle."

"Okay, okay," I said. "No offense meant, Stumps. Don't worry. I don't have any doubts about your focus or your unity of purpose. I am simply questioning your methods. As B-6 has given me the authority to command this small group from 2nd Division, I'm going to do it to the best of my ability. What's more, I'm going to trigger the advance of all android forces on this town right now."

The androids looked concerned, but they did not object immediately.

"All right," I said, turning around. "Let's march—all of you at once. Form a line. March forward."

They did as they were ordered, but they definitely looked uncomfortable. They hesitated. They took short half-steps. They swung their rifles erratically, and they looked agitated.

"What's the matter now?" I demanded. "Why aren't you guys marching as before? Are you sensing some alien formations? Are they counter-attacking again?"

"No, sir," Colonel Stumps said. "We are breaking with behavioral norms. This puts every android into an error state, so while we are still functioning, we're proceeding with increased caution and transmitting warning messages to our superiors."

I looked at the two of them, and I blinked a few times. "Transmitting warning messages?"

Moments later, my communications headset began talking to me. It was B-6, and he seemed as agitated as the rest of the androids on this planet.

"General Gorman," he said, "what do you think you're doing?"

"B-6, good to hear from you, sir. I'm doing exactly what you asked me to do. I'm winning this battle."

"Gorman, a significant portion of my entire army is currently deployed on this planet, and what you're doing, as far as I can tell, is putting it at risk."

"With all due respect, sir," I said, "do you want me to be your general? Do you want me to lead your armies to victory? Or, do you want me to be one more android who doesn't know what he's doing? Because I've got plenty of those down here. You're welcome to replace me with any one of them."

B-6 was quiet for a while. I knew by now that he was thinking it all over carefully.

Finally, he responded. "Gorman, you are hereby authorized to proceed. Consider yourself an experiment with an undetermined outcome."

I thought about that and nodded to myself. It was a pretty big risk, a generous level of trust that B-6 had just given to me. I couldn't ask for more.

"Thank you, sir," I said. "That's all." I closed the channel before he could give me any more restrictions.

Marching forward and pressing the line deeper, we quickly emerged from the last of the trees and approached the outskirts of Mataran City itself. All around me, for kilometers on both sides, I saw androids in the gathering darkness of the evening. More and more of their lines marched forward just as we had.

I knew that at two points besides Sector Three, the enemy aliens had managed to counter-attack and push back the android lines. But they'd been defeated here and in the majority of firefights. I decided it was best to simply ignore the pockets of aliens that were pressing outward and instead advance, attacking the enemy at the city outskirts.

Darkness fell as we marched into quiet streets. They weren't actually empty, but they seemed devoid of normal life. There were no pets, humans, or even living trees to speak of.

There was carnage, however. Bodies were everywhere. There was also a lot of twisted wreckage. Crashed vehicles littered the streets. Barricades made of furniture, fencing materials and bricks from buildings formed defensive lines now and then, but they were all broken and the defenders were absent. At every one of these barriers, the citizens of Mataran City had already perished. They'd been overwhelmed by the aliens and destroyed.

As I walked through the unnatural stillness of this city of the dead, I became increasingly somber and remorseful. If we hadn't wasted our time, we could have possibly saved some of these people. I took a large amount of video material of all these tragedies. I wasn't able to find a single living animal or person in the city—other than the few aliens that we found and destroyed, and there weren't many of those.

It was clear to me now as I marched around the dark echoing streets that the aliens had perhaps been trying to escape our encirclement. They'd already done their worst deeds here—devouring and butchering the city. Perhaps the three different places they'd pressed outward were attempts to escape our ring of marching plastic men rather than an attempt to actually defeat us in battle.

Whatever the case, the city was a total loss, and all we had managed to do was kill a few thousand aliens before the battle was over.

During all the excitement, I'd forgotten about Lucas Droad and Jort. I'd been caught up in the battle. I contacted the mobile headquarters, and I asked them to join me in the heart of the town.

When I realized that the city was pretty much empty and devoured, I slowed down our advance and Jort caught up with me.

"Captain Gorman, Captain Gorman," he said. "There you are! Always, you have been one step ahead of me! It's been crazy-time trying to follow you."

"Sorry, Jort," I said. "A battle is a battle. It waits for no one."

Jort nodded enthusiastically. "I understand, Captain. I understand. You are a smart man. You are a fast man. You marched ahead to make these plastic fools work hard and fight hard."

Lucas Droad found us next. We were in the center of town by this time. It was a scene of carnage that was made both better and worse by the fact that most of the bodies had been consumed by the aliens. There were remnants, however. Bloody clothes, shoes, occasional fingers, discarded bones... It was disgusting and Jort, Droad, and I were the only ones forced to smell it.

"This brings back memories," Droad said, "... unwanted memories. It seems the Chain has not suffered alone. This is exactly how things went back in my home colonies. I am saddened in the extreme to see this playing out all over again in the Conclave."

"No!" Jort exclaimed. "You're wrong! The plastic men will stop them. I have seen them fight. I have seen them fight while our man here, Gorman, gives them orders. These plastic fools, I think they are better than regular human fighters—they have no fear. They don't stop until they are torn apart. They are the perfect antidote to the poison of these aliens."

Droad smiled grimly at him. "I hope you're right, Jort. I hope you're right."

I gave orders for the town to be searched for survivors, but I already knew there wouldn't be any. These aliens were very thorough.

Most upsetting to me was evidence indicating the slaughter could have been reduced. A few of the inhabitants could have been saved if we'd only moved more quickly, but no. B-6 and his men had circled around the city, joined forces, formed a perfect line and marched slowly into the dying city. That, combined with some counterattack efforts made by the aliens had given them enough time to kill everyone in the town.

There were occasional signs of fresher blood—not just dried stains. I found it all upsetting, but I had to remind myself that the androids had done pretty damned well. They had defeated the aliens, they had won the day. Sure, we were too late, but perhaps the next time we'd do a better job.

By the time we three humans and thousands of androids had returned to the troop ships, I was bone-tired. Even Jort had stopped his continuous talking. As I walked toward the massive ramps—each the size of a city block—alongside my android army, B-6 contacted me at last.

"You achieved victory," he said to me.

I laughed. It was a bitter and hollow sound. "Victory?" I asked. "Not really. Yes, we destroyed a few of the enemy, and we took the town, but all the people are dead."

B-6 thought that over. "That is still a victory," he said. "The aliens killed here are not going anywhere else. We took back the city."

"I disagree," I said. "The Connactic should know that this was a failure. Taking the city is not good enough if all the people are dead."

"An interesting disharmony of thought," B-6 said. "It seems pointless to belabor the discussion as we are not going to agree. There is definitely room for improvement, and you definitely helped us achieve our goals in this part of the campaign."

"Good," I said. "I'm glad I could be of some help. Now, I suggest we quickly move on to the next concentration of human life on this planet. If we move faster this time…"

"No," B-6 said, interrupting me. "No, I don't think we're going to do it that way. For one thing, there are precious few humans left—this city was the last. What we have to do now, is finish destroying the aliens."

"Okay," I said. "Can I help you with that endeavor?"

"Yes. I want you to take direct command of the next action. You are going to invade a nest."

I glanced at Jort and then Droad. "Do either of you gentlemen wish to accompany me this time out? You, Jort. You were complaining about having been left behind before..."

Jort looked alarmed. He thought about it, swallowed hard and then nodded. "Yes sir, Captain Gorman. Yes, I will go with you. You are a smart man. You won the day. I want to see aliens die—lots of aliens."

"Okay," I said, and I turned to Droad. "What of you, Governor Droad?"

He looked thoughtful for a moment. "I've actually invaded many nests, many times," he said. "I think I can help you to do it right."

"Excellent," B-6 said. "All three of you will serve as commanders. Now, return to your ship. The campaign will move on to the second continent, the one to the north."

Chapter Twenty-Five

A day or two later, I found myself landing on the northern continent of Ailoth. This section of land was raw and wild. There were no real cities here, just a few outposts. With Jort and Droad at my side, I was again given command of a division of android troops. Unfortunately, there were no replacement soldiers—only a few thousand were in fighting shape.

The Conclave army had no facilities to build new androids, only repair old ones, so I was given no reinforcements. Altogether, I had less than three thousand troops. The good news was that my seven officers had all survived the previous battle. They'd escaped harm largely because we'd missed the heavy combat at the end.

In any case, it didn't take us long to find a nest in the north. It was in a mine—of all things, a lowly copper mine buried in the slopes of some worn-down mountains. Using LiDAR and various other forms of sensory equipment, we managed to find the fresh tunnels underneath the mine that shouldn't have been there.

These tunnels wormed down deeper to the enemy nest. Below the original mine we could make out cavernous larvae chambers. Here, the aliens were still in their hungry, youthful stage and not yet differentiated into one of the myriad forms of the enemy. It all reminded me of looking at some kind of an oversized alien ant farm. But... these creatures, I had to remind myself, were far more advanced, intelligent and deadly than any form of ant I'd ever run into.

"You want to know what I'm thinking, Captain Gorman?" Jort asked me as we landed and disembarked on the broad ramps of the transport ship.

"Sure, Jort," I said. "Tell me what's on your mind."

"I'm wondering where all the people are."

I shrugged. "What do you mean? We're just out in the countryside looking for nests. This is a pretty large planet. It never was thickly inhabited. You can't expect there to be cities everywhere, and these aliens have done well to hide themselves in the most remote locations."

"All of that's true, sir," Jort said. "All of that is true. But it's strangely empty in this part of the planet."

He was right, of course. The quiet was bothering me, too. We'd arrived before dawn, and when we'd landed on the northern continent, I was alarmed by what I noticed. There were no lights anywhere, few obvious signs of life of any kind. Only the quiet forests stood as mute witnesses to the invasion.

"Hmm," I said, thinking it over. "Well, perhaps the local towns are trying to hide from the aliens. Maybe they don't want to give away where they are by burning the midnight oil—or maybe they've simply lost power."

Droad spoke up next. "Jort has a point. When we invaded the southern continent, that city had lights, *some* signs of human activity. The bodies we discovered when we walked into that town were fresh. Here, I'm not getting the sense that there's much left..."

"It's thinly inhabited, yes, but there must be someone alive," I insisted. Thinking it over, I decided that after I organized my unit I would ask B-6 about it.

As my group was rather small compared to a full division, I was given the task of scouting the first nest we'd found. A full division was supposed to land later in the day to deploy a full complement of 30,000 androids. These would organize and destroy any strong resistance that we weren't able to handle.

I could tell that circumstantially this was an odd decision made by B-6. Why not simply land a full division and get it over with? Why couldn't B-6 get ready as quickly as possible, march in, and kill everything?

Well, perhaps it was because he wanted to do it on the cheap. Perhaps B-6 figured he had an expendable unit—one led by a gullible man of flesh and blood such as myself—who could be thrown away. My ragtag army wasn't much better than I was, being a broken pack of half-wrecked robots that the Conclave didn't need any more.

B-6 was cagey. Of that much I was very certain. I suspected that he would rather let the rest of my division fail and die than damage a fresh one. There were other possible reasons, of course. It could be that B-6 wanted to observe me in action in a different sort of situation. Invading a nest required different tactics than did retaking a town. There would be no human civilians running around, just the aliens in their domain. When pitted against androids who were invading—in this case led by a human—the results of the experiment could be illuminating. Would I win, or would I lose?

B-6, I suspected, was performing an experiment. He wanted to know how a nest invasion would go before he committed more valuable troops. He was performing this experiment with an utter disregard for my life or the existence of his most damaged division.

That only made sense according to his way of evaluating things. Androids weren't known for their compassion. They knew enough to follow a success with another similar success, but that didn't mean that they rewarded individuals for good behavior or even good service. They only concern themselves with efficiency as an overall strategy. The aliens and the androids were similar in this way. They both just wanted to get things done, budget allowing.

After trudging up a wicked slope, we reached an opening carved into the side of a large hill. It yawned like a mouth and led into a pitch-black mine.

As we three humans—Jort, Droad and I—advanced toward the entrance, we became increasingly concerned.

"How come no aliens are coming out to shoot at us?" Jort demanded. "Where'd they go?"

"Jort's right," Droad, said. "It does seem unusual. Something's wrong here."

Thinking it over, I decided I agreed with them. Rather than marching my column of troops into the open mouth of the great mine, I called upon Colonel Stumps.

He came hopping up to me with surprising alacrity, even though he was going uphill. I looked him over. "Stumps, who would you say is the most expendable individual here?"

Stumps did not think it over for more than half a second. "That would be me, sir," he said. "I'm the most expendable because I'm damaged."

I nodded. I'd known it was the correct answer before I'd asked. I'd wanted to see if he would admit it, or if he would attempt to preserve himself the way a human might.

"All right," I said. "I want you to lead an expeditionary force into that mine. You will take one hundred troops. You will not be the first one in there, but you won't be the last either. Your mission is to proceed into the nest, make contact with the enemy, and then return with a report of what you find."

Colonel Stumps stared at me for a while. "Am I going in now, sir?" That was his only question. I wouldn't say that he was eager to go in there and die, but I would definitely say that he was not at all concerned about the prospect of his own destruction. I found that interesting by itself, and I nodded.

"Go, Stumps. Go, and good luck to you."

He hopped away, furiously pumping his single leg and waving his single arm. He soon gathered exactly one hundred guardian-level androids. Together, the group marched up the rest of the slope and disappeared into the yawning mouth of the mine. While this was going on, Major Cringe came up to stand near me.

"Sir?" she said.

"What is it, Cringe?"

"Sir, if Colonel Stumps does not return, who will take his place?"

I looked at her, interested in her thought processes.

"Do you want it to be you?" I asked her. Cringe looked down for a moment as if considering this question very carefully.

"I would not say that this is a desire of mine, but I am curious about your judgment in the situation."

"Thank you, Major," I said. "If Stumps doesn't make it out of there alive, you will become Colonel Cringe."

"Very good, sir," she said. "May I ask one more question?"

"Of course."

"Why me?"

I smiled. "Because you had the presence of mind to ask the question. These other five officers didn't say a word."

She glanced around at them and then looked back at me, and she nodded.

"Very well, sir," she said, and she walked away. She began inspecting the remaining troops who were straggling up the mountainside. They gathered around and formed ranks in case we needed to go in with more force than just one hundred men—which I suspected we would.

Before I could even get worried about whether Stumps would come back out, or what might be happening down there, we were attacked.

It made perfect sense to me, in retrospect, that the enemy were not quietly dozing inside that copper mine. Nor were they completely taken by surprise and befuddled by our presence so near their important nest. Instead, they were planning a counterattack all along, and they'd spent the time we'd given them since landing to get their forces in position to jump us.

That's how these aliens thought, I realized—they very rarely defended anything. They attacked, they attacked, and then they attacked some more. That's how they defended in the end. If their attacks killed everyone in our military, there would be no need for a defensive strategy.

"Dark things!" Jort shouted. He was pointing high into the sky. "Dark little things—flying toward us, sir!"

Turning around, I lifted my rifle all in one motion. I stared off to the south where Jort was pointing to a wooded area in the mountains that was somewhat higher than the nest entrance itself.

The enemy's flying form was called a "culus" and there were few things more terrible than seeing thousands of them coming your way.

A cloud of flapping alien creatures rose up over the mountaintop and swooped down upon us. It was like a vast flock of gigantic, ugly birds, but these birds were the size of farm dogs. Birds without feathers that had leathery, gargoyle-like wings instead. They came on as might an invasion of demons.

"Major Cringe, have your men pick targets. Fire into the mass of beasts when it comes within range."

She relayed the orders, and my three thousand-odd troops shouldered their rifles as one. Not one of them fired prematurely, another benefit of android troops over humans. The enemy was not yet in effective range for their rifles, so no one panicked and wasted ammo.

This was not true for me, however. Having the only Sardez out here besides Jort and Droad, I adjusted my sights and loaded a special round that was developed to cast tiny flechettes in a wide spray in the enemy's path. I ordered Jort and Droad both to do the same.

Cursing and rattling ammo out of their pouches, they thumbed the rounds into their respective breeches. They stood to either side of me, and we all lifted our Sardez rifles at once. Three shots cracked the still, mountain air almost as one.

Holes were punched in the approaching flock—not huge holes, mind you, but holes nonetheless. These quickly closed-up as the enemy brought their ranks back together again. We fired again, all three of us releasing a second volley, and it was only then that the aliens reacted in a coordinated fashion. Their tight cloud became more a flat disk. Still, we continued to fire, dropping hundreds of them.

As they drew closer, the androids joined in, but now that they were not so densely concentrated, our shots did not do anywhere near as much damage. The android guns used normal munitions that didn't spread out and punch large holes in the enemy air formation. All they were able to do was get lucky now and then and knock one out of the sky.

I began to feel good about this attack, as we were definitely winning the fight. The enemy was losing thousands of flapping little monsters per minute, and by the time the survivors got to us, we should be able to make quick work of them.

That was when a cold finger of dread ran down my spine. I stopped firing and wheeled around, eyes sweeping the landscape. Droad saw this and turned with me.

"You guys are missing all the fun," Jort shouted over his shoulder, firing again and again at the attacking culus swarm.

Droad's eyes met mine. "Do you see them?" he said.

"No," I said, "but they must be downslope somewhere."

He nodded, and he pointed down low toward the base of the mountain that was serving these aliens as their nest. There, I spotted stealthy movement.

It was as if the rocks themselves were in motion. Shadows under the trees shifted as if there were a wind moving the branches around—but there was no wind, or at least not enough to explain that massive, rolling, humping knot of shadows.

"Killbeasts..." I said. "Major Cringe!"

She came rushing to me in an instant. Her eyes were fixed on my face.

"It's time to change targets, Major. Take two thirds of your men, wheel them around, and attack downhill into those trees immediately."

Again, unlike a human commander, she did not question my orders. She did not say, "But sir, we're not yet done shooting down all the culus swarms." She simply charged away, dividing her forces into three and having her sub-officers work to obey her. Very quickly two thousand troops, two thirds of my force, turned, reloaded, and advanced to different firing positions. Aiming downslope instead of up, they made ready to shoot into the shadows under the trees.

Realizing they'd been spotted, the boiling mass of killbeasts broke free from cover and charged us. There were thousands of them. How many thousands I wasn't sure, but it had to be close to ten.

My heart sank as I realized that while I had believed that going into the nest was almost certainly a death sentence, I had also falsely believed that waiting out here on the slopes outside the nest while sending scouts inside was a safe move. This was quite clearly not the case.

"Sir, sir, *sir*!" Jort shouted. He was thumping me on the shoulder with his massive hand. "Sir, those bird things—they're almost here."

"Jort, you stay focused on them. Put your back to ours. Kill every alien that flaps closer. Put them all down with your android troops in front of you.

His eyes were wide, almost bulging. "What are you going to do, Captain?"

I pointed downslope at the charging mass of killbeasts. "I'm going to kill all of those things."

Jort's jaw sagged. He looked horrified. "We're trapped," he said. "We're stuck on this mountain. We're all gonna die right here."

I nodded. "Yes, that's quite possibly true, but if you don't start firing your weapon and killing every one of those bird-things you can, then it most certainly *will* be true. Pull it together. Keep fighting."

Jort swallowed hard, turned around, and he did as I'd ordered. Oh sure, he cursed, he complained, and he raged at the advancing enemy—but he kept on firing.

When the culus flock landed among my troops on the upper slope, they revealed that each concealed a shrade. Every culus had a snake-like shrade tucked under its belly, and together, the alien teams fought to rip my men apart. They only stopped when they were destroyed.

Turning back to the downslope situation, I saw that the battle was playing out quite a bit differently. This enemy force was coming toward us, but they had not yet reached close-range.

I was alarmed to see they were carrying rifles just as we were. Were they Conclave rifles? I suspected that they were. They cracked, snapped, and whined exactly like the weapons my androids were using. Had they been taken from fallen androids? Or had they been taken from the dead colonists?

I didn't know, and honestly, it didn't matter. What I *did* know was that we had to kill thousands of them before they killed all of us, or this battle was going to be my last.

So, we fought. We fought hard. The battle seemed to go on for an hour, but in reality, it was no more than fifteen to twenty minutes.

The short version of the story was that they overwhelmed us. They came in ravening hordes and destroyed countless androids all around us.

Eventually, it came down to me, Droad and Jort. We all stood back-to-back, firing our Sardez rifles. We killed more than our weight in aliens every minute.

Things seemed beyond hopeless, but we did not despair. We were angry, desperate, and mean. We had vastly superior weaponry. We were in a good defensive position, having placed ourselves in a cluster of boulders, and we were quite determined to literally fight to the death—as we had no other choice.

All around us, thousands of androids were systematically destroyed. Parts of them still crawled and writhed, wriggling and moving erratically. Their dying servomotors whined and sparked. The weirdly-colored yellow-orange oils they seemed to use for blood dribbled and oozed everywhere.

For some odd reason, the aliens did not charge in to end the fight. Instead, they circled around us without going for the final kill. They could have sent in the snake-like shrades—slithering through the boulders. They could have flown in a couple of fresh, flapping culus monsters to dive down from the skies and rip our faces off. Or simpler still, a hundred or so killbeasts could have charged our little circle of boulders and killed us before we could have killed more than half a dozen of them.

But they didn't do it. Instead, they moved to where we could not get our sights lined up with them, and they went quiet. We still knew they were out there of course, moving around, shuffling, muttering to each other in their weird languages of clicks, squeaks and chirps—but they did not attack.

Hours passed. The aliens kept their distance, rarely giving us a chance to shoot at them. We spent our time huddling among our cluster of boulders, lamenting our fate. Eventually, the day began to fade into night.

"They're waiting for darkness," Droad said.

"Do they really need the cover of night?" Jort demanded. His eyes had never been so wide, so alarmed, so full of the knowledge of his impending death. "I'm almost out of ammo. Why don't they end this?"

"I don't know, Jort," I said wearily. "Maybe they're getting out the steak sauce."

"That's it!" Droad said suddenly.

We turned to him, and his eyes gleamed wetly in the dying light of the day. They seemed to be lit by an internal madness.

"That's definitely it," he continued, staring into the gathering dusk without seeing it or us. "I doubt they've had many humans to eat here at this isolated nest."

"What?" I said. "Are you serious?"

"Absolutely. You see, these aliens have a hierarchy of their own, and unlike the androids, they have emotions and preferences and… tastes."

"Tastes?" Jort demanded. "That's a bad word. That's a *terrible* word. Why would you use that word, Mr. Governor? What's wrong with you?"

Droad smiled grimly. "What's wrong with me? I said I've experienced these aliens before—on several occasions. I've been inside their nests. I've watched them feast. Their most advanced forms are true horrors."

Jort and I exchanged glances. We weren't happy to listen to Droad, but we couldn't help ourselves.

"The queens are gigantic monstrosities," he continued. "They sit upon thrones of spit and slime hardened into a structure that looks like running wax. They like to taste many different meats, rare and unusual meats—and I mean *living* flesh, mind you. They prefer to keep their food alive to truly enjoy it. Because of this, I think they mean to capture us, to take us into their nest and consume us."

I looked around, horrified. I could not deny the logic of his words. It made too much sense. Why had they destroyed and dismembered every plastic man on the side of this mountain but left the three of us alone, despite the fact we had more dangerous weapons? Why had they encircled us but not advanced to make the final kill?

"They must want to capture us alive... What are we going to do?" I asked Droad. "What *should* we do? Should we kill ourselves?"

Droad nodded thoughtfully. "That is a very rational option."

"No, it isn't!" Jort said. "It's not rational at all. It's *insane*. Jort isn't killing himself. I'm killing these aliens. I'm gonna make them tear us apart."

"We shall see," Droad said.

Listening closely in case they were sneaking near, we hunkered low with the barrels of our rifles stuck out at three random angles. We sighted on everything that moved, shuffled, or flapped around on the mountain outside our shelter. Now and then we cracked off a shot. Occasionally, we got lucky and nailed something, but usually we missed.

The enemy was still out there, and they had us surrounded, but they weren't coming close. They weren't giving us easy shots, either.

Over time, the sun dropped behind the mountain range and disappeared. Darkness fell, and the glorious stars of the Conclave wheeled up into the sky overhead.

Still, we lay in our rocks, hiding—hoping against hope that the monsters would go away, even though we knew in our hearts that they would not.

Naturally, we frequently attempted to contact B-6. We requested rescues from the ships that waited in the skies, but none of our long-range communications equipment was functioning after the battle. None of the androids who knew how to use the equipment had survived anyway, and so we crouched, and we waited, and we listened, and we prayed that we would somehow make it to see the dawn.

Chapter Twenty-Six

Long before the sun rose again over Ailoth, the stalemate changed. We three humans in our tiny cluster of boulders, surrounded by countless alien predators that slunk and slithered and crawled around us did nothing unexpected—but those who hunted us did.

"Captain Gorman?" Jort whispered. "Captain Gorman, look. Look!" He pointed desperately into the dark. I squinted and peered. My eyes were blurry, sore, and tired, but I saw *something*—something dark, something that humped and slid over the ground.

I fired at it as did Jort. A moment later, Droad joined in. The shrade was hit more than once. Big chunks of it were blown apart, but it seemed to be doing something odd. It wasn't really attacking, but instead almost seemed to be suckling upon a rounded rock near the center of our position.

At last, it slumped down in death, curling up like a leech that had been plucked from a human body. It left behind a chunk of itself—a scrap of meat, a dark blob like a slug that had adhered to the boulder where it had died.

"We should destroy that," Jort said. "We should shoot at it until there's nothing left but a smear."

"No," Droad said. "Leave it alone. I think I know what it is. Let's just wait."

So, we slumped back into our makeshift fortress. We waited several long minutes.

Then, a strange, wheezing voice began to speak. At first the words were whistling and incomprehensible, but after a minute or so, we were able to understand them.

"Meat..." it said. "Meat, listen to me..."

Disgusted and worried, Jort and I exchanged glances. I looked at Governor Droad, and I noticed he didn't look surprised. He had those crazy, wet, staring eyes again.

"Is this what you were expecting?" I asked him.

He nodded grimly. "Yes, I've seen them form mouths before in order to communicate with us. They have an organic form of technology for the most part. They grow the things they need rather than building them out of inanimate metal, plastic and steel."

"Okay," I said, nodding. "What shall we say to it?"

"I'll speak for us," Droad said. He turned toward the blubbering thing on the rock, and he called out to it. "Who is it?"

"I am the parent of this colony," the weird, floppy mouth said. "I command all the armies in this region. I am sovereign on this mountain. The slope is an extension of my body, and the nest beneath the ground is my womb."

"I see," Droad said. "You are the parent of this nest. We are honored to speak to you."

"You are *not* honored," the mouth corrected him sharply. "You cannot be honored because your kind is so lowly, so meaningless, that you are not worthy of any form of honor."

Droad was not irritated by the alien's arrogance. He took it all in stride. He shrugged and continued to talk to it.

"Be that as it may," he said, "what can we do for you, queen of the mountain?"

"You have only one logical purpose. That is to provide sustenance. We wish to taste your succulent flesh. We will not be denied in this desire."

"Well, then," Droad said, "if you wish to kill and eat us, you certainly have enough servants here to achieve your aims. I don't know what we can do for you."

"You can submit," the voice said. "You can give yourselves freely to the rightful ruler of this territory."

"Why would we do that?" Droad asked in quite a reasonable tone.

"Because it is correct that you would do so. You have hurt me greatly. You have hurt my servants. You have hurt my children. You have killed thousands. This misbehavior has damaged my internal peace. My plans of conquest have been delayed—but not thwarted. Never think that you have won, human. You've only prolonged the inevitable."

"All right," Droad said. "We accept all of what you say, but you still have to answer my question. Why should I help you in any way?"

"If you will not act out of a sense of justice," the alien said, "if you will not submit to right the wrongs you have performed, there is no point to this conversation."

Just outside our range of vision, we heard a tremendous amount of rustling as the carapaces of the killbeasts slid over rocks. They were out there slinking and hunkering—probably crawling on their thorny bellies to get into position for a final charge that would overwhelm us.

"Hold on, hold on," Droad said. "You haven't given us any incentive to cooperate with you."

"What?" Jort said. "Are you crazy? You sound like a crazy man. You talk like a crazy man. You *are* a crazy man. Jort will not submit. Jort will give these animals nothing but teeth and bullets."

"Shut up, Jort," I said, laying a hand on his shoulder, which trembled and shivered like that of a horse under my grip. "I think I understand the governor's plan. Let him talk."

Droad, after glancing at the two of us, continued to speak.

"Alien Queen," he said. "You have already told us that we are honorless and unworthy. Therefore, you know that we are creatures that will not submit, at least, not due to our own sense of justice. You knew this before you started this conversation. Therefore, you must have something else in mind. What do you offer us in return for submission?"

There was a pause in the conversation then. Perhaps the alien was doing some hard thinking. Perhaps she—for I assumed it was a she, although the voice itself was somewhat androgenous in nature—perhaps she was conferring with other aliens. I really didn't know.

"We could overwhelm you easily, and we will," the mouth said. It slobbered and wheezed as it spoke. "But when the killing is over, and it is time to have our tasting, your bodies will be cooling, lifeless, and low in flavor."

"All right," Droad said, thinking that over. "So, you want us to be consumed alive? Why should we concede to that?"

"You will be harvested regularly and fractionally consumed. You will submit in order to continue living."

"Ah," Droad said. "Now I understand the nature of your offer. You're offering us life, but as sources of meat for the long term. Unfortunately, our bodies cannot give meat continuously. We can't grow more meat and then give again—not easily. We aren't designed in such a manner."

"That's a pity," the mouth said, "but I understood this about you already. I am not ignorant. I have sat upon this world for months now. I have examined your species, and I have tasted you. Your kind is flavorful—rich in the extreme…. You are so unlike the countless beasts of this planet. You are apex predators, being at the top of the local food chain. Your meat therefore contains within it hints of all the other meats that you have consumed. It is always the case that the most flavorful meat is that which has consumed countless other varieties of sustenance."

"I see…" Droad said. "So, we taste better than say, a squirrel? Or something else from these woods?"

"Absolutely," the voice said. "You are an incomparable delicacy compared to the fodder that I've been forced to feast upon for weeks now."

To me this conversation was grim indeed. It did seem that the aliens had already won this continent just as they had won the southern one. Perhaps we'd arrived too late to begin with.

How could it be that B-6 hadn't known this? He'd told me we were coming here to rescue the world—to fight with the aliens, to drive them off, to save all those who lived here. But it wasn't true. It *couldn't* be true.

The colonists here had already been beaten before we landed, or they were in the process of dying out. Perhaps there were some that still clung to life, but this creature seemed to be saying the northern continent had been devoid of humanity for weeks.

These facts were incongruent with what B-6 had told me, but I quickly decided that it didn't really matter if B-6 had lied or not. Right now, we were negotiating the details of our own consumption—discussing just how and when and why we were going to end up as dinner for these aliens. It didn't much matter right now what B-6 had said or hadn't said.

B-6 had also said he'd be bringing a full division to land here, and he hadn't shown up with that either. Regardless of what his game was, we had to do what we could to survive.

Droad looked at me. I could tell he was thinking hard, just as I was, but probably upon different rivers of thought.

"Queen of the mountain," he said at last, "I might have a solution—a solution that will be acceptable to both of us."

"What is this solution?" the blubbery lips demanded.

"Instead of consuming us outright, instead of eating the meat from our bones immediately, you could merely drain our blood—a minute amount from each of us. We could replace this blood each day and therefore keep our sweet flavors in your digestive tract for much longer."

"This is an interesting proposal," said the mouth. "You are offering to become a beverage, rather than a meal? Hmm… a highly flavorful beverage, but in very short supply. I'm not sure that I could contain my lust for the taste. We Skaintz like to eat in quantity as well as quality."

"I understand," Droad said. "Perhaps our blood could be sprinkled over other meats—the standard fare that you've been consuming, to add flavor to each bite."

"Ahh," said the alien. "Now that is a concept worthy of consideration!"

During this conversation, Jort had become increasingly agitated. At this point, he couldn't take it any longer. He stood up, leveled his Sardez rifle, and pointed it directly at the blob of meat that was speaking on the rock. A moment later, the rifle cracked, but he did not strike the mouth on the stone, because I had shoved the barrel of his weapon aside.

Instead, the shot flew off into the trees at the bottom of the mountain, setting one of the charred trunks alight in an explosion of splinters and licking flame. The trees had not fared well during this battle, and the stray shot had in fact succeeded in rekindling fires that had died out earlier.

"Sit your ass down, Jort," I ordered.

"Captain, Droad is trying to turn us into milk cows—blood cows, even. He is crazy. He is as bad as that thing on the rock. He is as mad as that creature that crouches down in the bottom of this nest." He was pointing, gesturing, shoving his finger wildly toward the entrance to the tunnel. "I'm not going to do any of this."

"Jort," I said, "you will follow orders. We are trying to survive. There is such a thing as stalling. There is such a thing as buying time. Do you want to die now? Or do you want to die later?"

Jort swallowed hard. He looked at me. His eyes rolled around in his head.

The aliens were out there moving around in the darkness. We could feel it. We could see it. We could hear it. Finally, with a grunt of frustration, he sat back down and crouched among the boulders, muttering to himself.

I turned and tapped Droad again, suggesting he continue his negotiations. He was after all, an excellent negotiator. Who could become governor of a Colony world without having mastered such skills?

"I'm sorry for that interruption," Droad said.

"Your apology is both pointless and irritating," the voice said. "I will ask further questions. I require further details. How much flavor enhancer can the three of you produce per day?"

Droad and the alien then fell into a very strange conversation. It was somewhat medical in nature, where he discussed the amount of blood that could be safely drawn from a human being with a healthy spleen—which all of us presumably still had.

He also made a large point of selling the alien on the idea of making further captures to increase the size of its herd. I marveled as I listened. He seemed to be describing animal husbandry to a neophyte that had never considered the idea.

The alien for its part seemed fascinated. She *wanted* this to work. She was bored with herbivore meats and whatever leaves and grubs and insects and other random things her servants managed to bring her each day. The idea of having the fine sweet taste of a human's blood dribbled over all these other horrendous offerings, like a glaze on a desert, was really fascinating to her.

In the end, we struck a bargain. We would lay aside our rifles, we would march down into the nest, and we would be drained there of a minute amount of blood every day.

Most importantly, we would survive.

Out of the three of us, Jort had the hardest time with this negotiated settlement. He was an emotional man, and who knew? Perhaps in the end, his natural inclination to go out standing on his own two feet and killing everything that came at him until he no longer could fight… perhaps that was the better way.

For my own part, I have to admit, I'm something more akin to a rodent than a fighting dog. Mind you, I'm a savage, smart, sneaky rodent—but a rodent nonetheless. After all, I had survived being frozen as a clone and been awakened by robots determined to dismantle me. I didn't die easily.

As we entered the tunnels, surrounded by strange shapes and stinks, a sense of doom came over us all. Still, I talked in a cheerful manner, hoping to uplift the sagging spirits of my companions.

"I've dealt with quite a number of unsavory aliens in the past, and I plan to deal with more of them in the future," I boasted. "Maybe, just maybe, if we allow ourselves to be captured, and we performed our jobs as milk cows—or blood cows, as Jort would prefer to say—B-6 might someday show up to conquer this side of the planet."

"You think that could really happen?" Jort asked. His eyes were hungry for hope.

"Yes. Definitely. I'm counting on it, in fact. We'll know our freedom again, Jort."

Jort talked about what he would do on that bright day, while Droad brooded silently in his own thoughts.

For my part, I tried to scheme, but I didn't have much luck. We were captives, and I didn't think much of our chances.

Chapter Twenty-Seven

I've had a lot of bad experiences in my life, but my time spent in the alien nest had to be about rock bottom. It started off bad, and it got worse as the hours wore on.

Jort was the first problem, right up front. He didn't want to go into that nest, and I really couldn't blame him. Who could?

"Captain Gorman, sir? I can't do it. I'm not that kind of man."

I nodded. By this time, the aliens had already removed our rifles from us, so I said I understood if he wanted to take a knife and charge at the killbeasts—maybe getting one or two of them. I told him I would respect him for it and not to even think about the fact that Droad and I would probably die soon afterwards. His eyes bulged a little as he thought this over.

"Why would you die?" he asked.

"Well, we made a deal, and the deal was that the alien queen is to get three humans to provide enough blood to sprinkle over her meals. If it's only two... well, that means we started off by breaking our word with her immediately. Who knows how she'll react? But still, as I say, I respect your personal freedom and your dignity. If you need to die now instead of later... okay. I'm okay with it."

Jort stared at the ground and shuffled from foot to foot, steaming and raging.

Behind us, the killbeasts prodded us with their horny arms and legs. Up close they were even more grotesque and weird looking than they were from a distance. They were kind of like praying mantises that walked on their hind legs—bony, gray-brown limbs sheathed in chitin. We were in the hands of gigantic social insects, and we all knew it.

Finally, Jort stopped staring at his shoes and grunted a curse or two. "I'll go with you," he said. "I will go into the nest. I will suffer, and I will dream only of my death. Nothing else will cross my mind."

"Good," Droad said. He seemed a bit annoyed with Jort's emotional outbursts. He himself had obviously been in situations like this and probably worse.

"Look, Jort," he said, with a new thought. "Our situation is not all that grim. The androids are retaking this world. They will, at some point, come here and rescue us. On many of the worlds where I have witnessed invasions, there is no hope for people like us—but we may yet see the light of the sun again."

Jort looked at him. "Great," he said.

And so, we were marched down under the ground into the tunnels. At first, the dirt was relatively clean apart from weird tracks, marks, little turnings on the walls, and scratches on the stones. There were some railroad tracks half-buried in the dirt. They probably had once been used to shuttle down mining carts and bring out ore from the copper mine, but none of that was operating now. No one was mining any metal these days. The mine had just provided the Skaintz with an easy starter tunnel—something for them to quickly infest and live in.

As we went deeper down to the bottom of the old mine, into the newly driven tunnels, things changed. The walls, instead of being tooled and lined with metals and struts and concrete shells to hold them up, became weird and almost intestinal in appearance. They were smooth and slick in places—even moist, as if we were in the entrails of some gigantic beast instead of an artificially constructed and dug copper mine.

It was on the third level, at the bottom of the deepest tunnels, that we came out into a large chamber. It was very dark, and we weren't allowed to shine any lights. We barely had enough of a glimmer from our equipment to see by. Apparently, the aliens could see in the dark, or else they had some sensory apparatus like sonar to penetrate the blackness.

Using nothing but glowing screens from some of our gear that we'd been allowed to retain, we were able to make our way without stumbling and tripping in the dark. When we came out into the final chamber from an adjoining tunnel, we immediately got a sense of its immense size. You could tell the walls were no longer near and close, but rather distant.

There was an echoing effect, a light breeze. That breeze brought us a mix of many fetid odors. The unpleasant scents were accompanied by a lot of strange, scratching sounds—the sounds made by limbs sheathed in chitin as they moved over dirt and stone.

Our final destination was a pit of sorts. It was full of bones and half-eaten, half-rotting carcasses. It was disgusting beyond belief. The stench alone was overwhelming. There were no flies, fortunately, but the sickly-sweet smell of rotting meat was overpowering.

"We should have just died," Jort said. "This place… this is worse than death. I did not want to end my days as a saltshaker for some giant ant creature. We are buried and forgotten."

"You promised you would shut up," Droad reminded him.

"Yes… I'm sorry. I can't stand this place."

We were forced to climb down into the slimy pit, a place that turned out to be the source of the worst of the offensive smells. We crouched down there in misery.

Hours crept by—it was hard to know exactly how many. The batteries on our various instruments and devices were dying down. There was no hope of communicating through all the layers of rock and stone and metal that made up the mine itself. No signal could penetrate this giant wall of earth that surrounded us.

Finally, there was rustling and unusual activity above the pit, which was about three meters in depth.

"What's happening?" Jort asked. "What are they doing? Are they going to eat us now?"

"Is that really your fondest wish?" Droad asked.

"No," Jort admitted, "no, but *something* must happen. I can't stand it any longer."

As if to answer Jort's plea, made to the alien gods that owned this nest, a familiar alien voice began to speak again. They had been building a mouth, I suspected. They'd grown it on the side of a stone perhaps as they had outside on the surface of this world.

"Creatures," the voice said, "it is time to perform your promised duties."

"What must we do?" I asked.

"Fine meats will be cast into the pit. You will open your veins, and you will cast your flavorful essence upon the meats. They will then be taken to the queen for consumption."

"All right," I said. Let's do it."

"This is crazy," Jort said.

We sat there, crouching together shoulder-to-shoulder, squatting on the bottom of that vile hole. Somehow, it was comforting to physically sit close to another human. Normally, I would never have allowed such close contact with other men, but when you're in true terror and fear for your life, in a disgusting place of alien feasting, your only thoughts are about survival.

Just then, without warning, something large and wet slapped down in front of us. We recoiled from it as it was a little bit splashy. Gore flipped up into our faces. After a moment we reached out, gingerly, tenderly running our hands over the carcass. It was still warm.

"If I had to guess," Droad said, "I'd say it's some kind of a goat."

"A skinned goat," Jort said. "Do you think they skinned it alive? What monsters!"

I wasn't so sure. I suspected it was some kind of alien meat—neither goat nor skinned, but I didn't care to enlighten anyone. "All right," I said. "Who's going to go first?"

"What?" Jort said. "Aren't we all going to do it?"

"No," I said. "That doesn't make any sense. Why should all three of us cut ourselves at once? One of us will do each of these meals, and then someone else will do the next. We'll take turns," I said.

"Ugh," Jort said, "this is so disgusting."

Droad produced a knife and without any arguments stabbed the back of his hand. He turned it to allow the blood to dribble off his thumb onto the meat. He ran it back and forth drizzling it, flavoring the meal for the aliens. When he was finished, the meat was taken by killbeasts and moved up out of the pit.

A grotesque cacophony of sound began after that. We could hear snorting and wet gargling noises and munching, tearing, ripping sounds. I could only imagine what kind of mouthparts were working over that piece of meat. We weren't able to see the queen in the dark, but we could hear and imagine her, and the images were quite horrific.

At last, the strange noises of consumption ended. We relaxed, leaning back against the grimy walls of the pit. We were thinking that for now this horrible experience was over—but it wasn't so. Another large chunk of meat slapped down into the pit. We all looked at it. We stared aghast in the final glimmer of our instruments.

"She's not done eating yet," Droad observed.

"More," the mouth on the rock said. "More flavor this time. I prefer my meat to be well seasoned."

"Seasoned…?" Jort said, and he crossed his thick arms indignantly. "Well, I'm not going next."

"It's your turn, Gorman," Droad said. "This was your idea in the first place."

I could not argue with him. I stabbed my hand, I sprinkled the blood, and I did so liberally. We used what bandages we had with us to patch ourselves up, and we waited while the alien again consumed an entire carcass.

When it was over, we expected another carcass to be thrown down into the pit, wondering how much this thing could eat—but that didn't happen. The parent was finally sated, and she moved away. We could hear her bulk as she dragged herself across the floor of the tunnel.

After that, the mouth they had grown to speak to us fell silent. All we heard was the strange, chittering and gibbering of the aliens themselves. No one addressed us, and there was no more comprehensible speech. We were left to sit slumped at the bottom of the feeding pit, hoping against hope that all these horrors would end soon.

What seemed like days passed. We thought it was days, but it was hard to tell. Our electronic devices had lost their battery power. We had taken to stealing slices of raw meat from the most savory chunks that fell into the pit. None of these tasted right, because they weren't goats after all, but at least they weren't human.

On what I estimated would have been perhaps the third day, the parent demanded even more flavor and cast down several pieces of meat at once instead of the usual one.

"I do not understand," I said, addressing the mouth after it had made its demands to us. "Why so much meat?"

"Because I have brought my sisters," the alien said. "I have bragged to them in neighboring nests. They've been invited to come and indulge in the flavors you have provided for us. They wish to know your flavor just as I have."

"But we are drained," I said. "Our arrangement was that—"

She stopped me then with what sounded like a screech. Was it a screech of rage? I thought that it was.

"Silence!" the mouth said. "You will be obedient, and you will provide flavor for my guests, or I will take one of you, slay it and consume it!"

"To do that," I said, "would mean an end to these fine meals. It would be foolish—"

"You dare call me a fool? You... you who lives in my food dish to serve me? You will not call me a fool!"

"I'm sorry," I said. "I'm tired, and I know not what I'm saying, but we must be given proper food, drink and rest, or we will not survive for much longer. And then there will be no more flavor enhancement."

"Such weaklings," the alien complained. "I don't know how your species has given us so much grief. If it weren't for your machines, you would be helpless."

"That's probably true," I agreed, "but for now, if you wish to continue enjoying these fine flavors you must provide aid to us."

"All right," she said. "I will do so, but first you shall heavily flavor three carcasses."

The three of us cut ourselves and sprinkled our own life blood liberally, which did seem to be coming out more slowly with each passing day and hour.

We sat back somewhat exhausted and thirsty. We drank water that they provided in gourds. The water wasn't fresh. The meat stank. Everything was gruesome.

After that, the meat was hauled away, and we were entertained by the sounds of three aliens eating in stereo all around us. It was almost more than the mind could take. I began to think that Jort had been right in the first place, and I should have accepted death when it was offered. A clean death was to be envied compared to this unending torture.

In the end, this alien was probably going to eat us anyway. All we had done was prolong our suffering. I almost despaired, but what kept me going were the other two. They seemed to believe in me. At least Jort did.

Droad... It was hard to tell with him. I didn't know what he believed. He was just a grim, wild-eyed survivor-type. He focused on each hour passing, each meal, each swallow of water. He didn't want to die. I could tell that much. He must have loved life dearly in order to put up with something like this for a second time. After all, he was the only one of us who'd known what he was getting into.

Because he had been in an alien nest before, I knew he was more experienced than I was with these aliens and their ways.

"Droad," I whispered to him when the feast was done, and the aliens had retreated. "Droad, we've got to get out of here. We can't wait any longer. We're going to have to do something."

"What would you suggest?" Droad asked me.

"I don't know. Maybe we can figure out a way to kill this creature. Perhaps, if we leaped up and surprised her—

Droad laughed. It was the first laugh I had heard from him since we had come to this world.

"We're too weak now. If you were going to try anything like that—any wild antics—you should have done it when we first arrived."

"All right, all right," I said. "Something else, then. What else can we do?"

Droad shrugged. "I guess we could poison her."

"Poison her how?"

Droad sighed. He dug in his pockets and pulled out various electronic devices—tapping on one. "These things contain batteries. There are harsh chemicals in here. Picked apart and secreted in the food, they might make this monster ill."

"Yes!" I said, thinking it over. "A sick alien is unlikely to want to eat us as quickly."

"That is undeniably true."

Soon, we put the plan into motion. We sacrificed every battery, every chemical that was in our survival kits except for a few light sources. We used things meant for medical purposes or to spill dye into water—anything we could think of. Not knowing what would affect the alien, all of it was gathered to carefully inject into the next piece of meat that fell down into the pit.

By the time the next chunk of flesh was thrown down, we'd amassed quite an amount of toxin. Probably, we overdid it with all three of us working on putting anything we could find that might be harmful into the meat.

Once we'd done our worst, we sprinkled it with blood. All three of us worked to slather the meat more heavily than ever before.

Jort went further, coughing, hawking and spitting on top of it. I didn't know if that would help, but I didn't think it could hurt, so I let him do it.

Finally, the meat was hauled away again, and the alien began feasting.

"Mmm, good... This is good. It is unusual," she said. "What did you do that was so different for this meat?"

"Nothing," I said. "Nothing at all. Perhaps this meat comes from a different species."

"No, not a different species. Strange..."

"I believe I struck an artery by accident," Droad said suddenly, adding into my lie. "I bled much more profusely than I planned to."

"Ah," the alien said, "that would explain much. Fresh lifeblood—a dangerous if tasty mishap. Have a care in the future. Too much flavor at once could endanger my pleasure."

After that, the alien smacked and chewed and scratched and swallowed in the dark. Eventually it finished the meal, grunting and burbling in satisfaction.

Jort, Droad and I all sat quietly in the gloom together, wondering what we had done, wondering if it would have any effect on this beast at all.

We were excited, and we were worried—but most of all, we were hopeful.

Chapter Twenty-Eight

After attempting to poison the parent, we were more nervous than ever. Especially because nothing was happening. In fact, she'd enjoyed her meal more than ever.

Some hours later, we'd finally reached our breaking point. We had grown so tired of existing in grime and filth, despairing and grumbling, that we had taken an immense risk.

Like anyone who attempts to slay their sovereign, we were worried that we were mad for even having plotted this coup. We feared we were going to be ripped apart when our attempted assassination was discovered.

Hours went by, several long hours.

"It's been too long," Jort said, whispering to me in the dark. "Definitely too long. The parent should have been back here. It should have been eating again. Why isn't it eating?"

"You know why it's not eating, Jort," Droad told him. "Let us pray that it never eats again."

Jort stood up in the darkness. "You mean you think we killed it? That's a crazy thought."

We didn't answer, but Jort began to stumble around the pit, running his leathery hands over the rough, crusty walls. "If we killed it, then they'll know. They'll figure it out. They are not dumb. These guys aren't really ants—they're much smarter than that. They're smart aliens. They have spaceships and stuff. Very smart. We were dumb."

"Maybe," Droad said. "Maybe you're right. Maybe in the end, we'll wish we hadn't done any of this—but we did do it. So now we must wait."

Jort was not a man who enjoyed waiting. I can tell you that after having associated with him for quite a while. He grumbled and complained and squirmed. He seemed less at ease than ever before. He'd seemed happier when we were sprinkling our blood upon various hunks of alien meat in the darkness. I figured the complete uncertainty of our current situation—that's what was getting to him now.

Time passed. It felt like many hours since the last feeding—more than we were used to. It's so hard to measure time when you're sitting in the dark, squatting without a single electronic device to give you a hint, but it didn't really matter. It had been a long time—too long. Suddenly, we heard a sound. It was a sound we had not heard before. It was a very loud sound—loud like an explosion.

"What's that?" Jort shouted. "The walls, the dirt and the earth are shaking!"

He was right. We could hear it, the crumbling and sifting of dirt. We could hear loud reports one after another, and then the ribbed ceiling began raining little flecks of sand and stones down on our heads.

"This whole thing is going to collapse!" Jort shouted.

"It would be a blessing if it did," I answered.

"What a bad ending. What a stupid finish," Jort complained. "I knew we should have died up there in the sunshine, in the light, in the open air. We should have died like brave warriors. That would be better than being crushed by stones in this stinking hole."

"Shut up," Droad said. "Something's happening."

We listened tensely, crouched in our now-familiar hole. It was quiet for a while in the nest. Sure, there were some rustling sounds. The Skaintz were on the move. They were moving with greater speed and purpose than before. I got the feeling they were racing out of the nest—hundreds of them going right around the feeding pit on both sides.

Then the loud thumping sounds came again—about six of them in a row.

Thump, thump, thump, thump, thump, thump.

"Those are explosions," I said, "far above."

"These aliens don't use explosives," Droad said. "At least, not often. Guns and missiles, yes. But not bombs. I bet it's B-6. The androids... they're bombing the nest."

"Oh Lord," Jort said. "Oh, sweet, dear Lord above. You must save us. Take us out of this food pit. Let us go!" He was standing now and throwing his arms wide—beseeching the sky, which was doing nothing but drifting sand down into his face.

It was then that we heard a strange, shrill, warbling voice. It was a different voice than we had heard before. The voice came from the mouth on the stone. I could tell that much, but it sounded weak, raspy and different.

"You have done this," it said. "You are bad-food. You are evil!"

Droad gripped my arm. He stood up, and I stood up with him. Jort was still beseeching the sky, but Droad and I, we were on the move. We had already isolated a spot on the side of the food pit which had, through random chance, caught a number of thick bones and formed a crude ladder. It was the only spot through which we figured we could escape, should we ever get the chance.

Outside the food pit, in the larger cavern around us, it was much quieter now. Almost no Skaintz' seemed to be around. They'd all rushed out of the nest, probably to defend it.

As we began to climb, the voice which came from the mouth on the rock began to speak again.

"You have sickened me," it said. "I was not sure at first, but now I know. You flavored the meat so well, I could not detect the poisons."

"Jort, come on," I said. "This is our chance."

He stopped doing his prayer act in the middle of the food pit—opening his eyes and looking startled.

"Where are we going?" he asked me.

"You are going nowhere," the strange voice said in its weak, raspy tones. "You are evil, and you must die. When I recover, I will eat every scrap of you. I will feast upon your flesh while you are still alive. All three of you will die today!"

I was up to the top of the pit by this time. I reached down to help Droad, who'd given me a leg up, and pulled him out of the hole. Jort climbed like a monkey. He needed no aid from either of us. His big shoulders still had a lot of strength in them. This planet was low gravity by his standards, and he was able to almost hurl himself up out of the ground with the power of his legs alone.

We all stood on the floor of the cavern, breathing hard and coughing.

More distant reports sounded above us. Something was striking the nest yet again. The walls shook and chunks fell from the ceiling.

"I will taste your succulent meats, and I will drink your sweet blood. Your juices will flow like wine in my mouth." The raspy voice kept on talking, kept on prattling, kept on telling us all the horrible things it was going do to us when it got the chance.

Jort found it first. He took a rock, and he struck the mouth over and over again. He crushed it to a pulp, grinding it into a bloody mess. After that, we heard no more of the parent and its threats.

"Where do you think the parent-thing is?" Jort asked.

"I don't know," I said. "Let's get out of here."

Escaping the nest was easier said than done. We had saved a couple of low-level light sources. They were items that used chemical light rather than battery-driven light as our batteries had already run out. Emitting a wan glow from our handheld lights, we followed this glimmer of hope, walking around the cavern like blind mice seeking to escape the farmer's wife.

We found the tunnel that led out of the great chamber, and that led us to what could only be the throne of the parent. The throne was a monstrous thing—a pile of bones and furs and chunks of stone. All of it was held together with wax-like resins. These had been poured over the throne to keep it together.

Crouching on that throne was a being of unrelenting horror. It reminded me of an octopus, but an octopus with chitin-sheathed limbs that resembled the arms of a crab or some kind of nightmarish insect.

I was about to suggest to the others that we sneak on past this thing, which was slumped and probably dying on its throne, when Jort took it upon himself to charge at it. He used the same stone he'd used to smash the speaking mouth. He used it on the parent with a similarly effective result.

The giant alien woke up to some extent, flailing away with its large, powerful limbs, but it was too weak, and Jort was too strong. His sense of outrage superseded any fear and disgust he felt for this alien monstrosity. He jumped up on the throne, and I didn't try to stop him. I let him vent his rage and frustration upon the monster because, in the end, that was really for the best.

He beat it and struck it over and over again, cracking its exoskeleton and smashing the soft parts inside. Soon, it was reduced to the same sort of pulpy mess as the talking mouth.

"I think we need to get out of here now," Droad said in a reasonable tone.

I had to agree with him. We began to race up out of the nest. In a way, once we found the exit tunnel, it was rather easy to figure out which way to go because the right direction was always upward. At every ramp, hole, and opening in the ceiling we climbed up.

Several times, we met up with confused creatures. Not all of them were violent in nature. Frequently we met some kind of table-like worker-beasts. These possessed a single powerful arm that could pluck at things.

One of these tried to grab me and put me on its back. We kicked the alien worker over on its side, and its legs flailed in the air like a turtle left to die in the sun.

Climbing up and up, higher and higher, we saw very few of the killbeasts. The warrior-types were doubtlessly streaming out onto the mountainside and fighting for the safety of their nest.

Eventually, we saw sunlight ahead of us. It was hard to believe, but we'd actually made it to within sight of the surface.

"What are those things?" Jort said, pointing over my shoulder. "There are creatures coming this way—coming toward us!"

Quickly, we hugged up against a wall in a curved alcove we'd found in the side of the tunnel. We slid inside of it, pulling a dead worker creature over us for cover. Hiding there, we waited.

The creatures came closer. We crouched low, suspecting an army of killbeasts was about to walk by any moment.

But when the invaders drew near, we realized they were not aliens, but androids instead.

Never in my life had I been so glad to see a guardian-class android. They were artificial machines but still a thousand times preferable to any of these bug-like aliens.

We jumped out, lifting our hands over our heads. We flagged them down, and they turned their weapons upon us. After staring for a moment, their pattern recognition software figured out who we were, and they lowered their guns.

"Human civilians," said a squad leader. "Please proceed out of the nest. It is scheduled for demolition in eighteen minutes time."

We took his word seriously. Running again as best we could with cramped, sore legs, we raced for the exit. We were half-starved from lack of blood and proper nourishment—but minutes later we stumbled out of the nest and into the sunlight.

More and more plastic men marched past us, but they gave us very little attention. To them, we were just civilian survivors. We probably looked the part as well, wearing ragged clothes. I was bloody, grimy and gaunt. We must have looked like wraiths from a crypt.

At last, we ran out into the sunlight, whooping and blinking. The androids had arrived at last. They were several days late, but it didn't matter. We were happy and beaming and just glad to be alive. It was sheer joy just to be outside for one minute. Just to breathe fresh air rather than the stink of the animal den that we had escaped.

We talked to every android we could find once we were outside, but none of them seemed to be able to help us. When we asked for them to communicate to B-6, the universal response was that such a thing was impossible. We'd been classified as civilians not combatants, and so none of them would listen.

Eventually, I found a Q-class officer. I managed to get his attention and convince him that I was worthy of a moment of his time. He scanned the three of us, checking our retinas and other biometrics against the database that the Conclave held. We were identified, and B-6 was informed.

Less than ten minutes later, I climbed aboard a massive transport. Thousands of androids had deployed into the nest, searching, taking samples—and I hoped, looking for survivors. As the great ship began to lift off, the androids withdrew from the nest and blew it up, sealing the entrance forever along with any aliens that may still have been left inside.

Chapter Twenty-Nine

Even after we were rescued from the nest, we were not immediately back to being our regular selves. I now understood much better what was always wrong with Droad—how he seemed a little off somehow, a little morose, a little distant. It's because he had spent too much time in places like that nest, sitting in a food dish waiting to die.

As was my normal response to tragedies and bad predicaments in general, I did my best to bounce back, to enliven everything for everyone else. I laughed as I clapped my hands on Droad's back and Jort's as well.

"Can you believe we got out of there?" I asked them. "We are serious escape artists. We have to be some of the luckiest men alive in the Conclave today. Droad looked at me. He didn't say much, but he did manage a frosty smile.

Jort on the other hand was more convinced. He chuckled and said, "I guess you're right, but I would prefer the luck of the man who had never been in a food dish. I would trade places with him right now. I would erase these memories from my mind forever."

"Yes, I guess so, Jort," I said. "I get it. You had your cage rattled, but you lived. You survived. You're not a weaker man because of it. You're a stronger man. You're going to recover, and you're going to live, and you're going to kill these aliens. You'll do this so it will never happen to anyone else.

Jort thought that over for a minute or two. Finally, he nodded. "Yes. You're right. I must not be gloomy. I must not think of the nightmares, the nest. Instead, I will think only of revenge and the destruction of these aliens. How can we do it? It helps me understand Huan better. He's a madman, half-man, half-machine but entirely insane. And that's because he was in places like that, isn't it?"

"I think so," Droad said. "I think so." Jort fixated on Droad next. "And you," he said, "Always a strange one, but now I see things differently. Now I see that you are strange only for being as normal as you are. How much time did you spend in something like that food dish before, Governor?"

Droad shrugged. "Time is difficult to measure in such places. If I had to give it a guess, I would say two or three weeks.

"Oh," Jort cried, slapping himself dramatically on the forehead. "Weeks, you spent. Weeks in Hell and Purgatory. In the worst, most vile, despicable place in the Conclave, or... wait, for you it's the Chain. This becomes even more hopeless and even more grim." He was half talking to himself as well as talking to us at the same time. He was now staring at the ground and shaking his head, marveling at the idea that Droad had suffered these things before and was still standing before him.

He pointed a big fat finger at Droad and looked up, peering at him. "Gorman is wrong," he said. "It is not Jort who is lucky. It is not Gorman, who is lucky. It is this one. It is the Governor Droad. You are the luckiest man I've ever known. No man could get through weeks in those nests not only living at the end, but also still at least partly sane."

Droad finally laughed—a real laugh this time. "I think you're right," he said, "I don't think any of us are completely sane any longer, but we're mostly sane which is pretty damn good. It's close enough. I'll take it."

I smiled watching the two of them reconnect. They seemed like they had bonded somewhat over their experiences in the nest and now they were coming out of the foggy state of reliving the trauma of the nests, and that was a good thing.

"All right then… " I said, clapping them both on their backs again. "Let's go. We'll fix the Conclave and eradicate these monsters. Let's keep the place safe so that people like Morwyn and a million others don't have to go through what we did or worse.

With new purpose, the three of us marched through the transport ship to the bridge. We were allowed on the command deck but with frequent looks of concern and surprise coming from the various guardians. They did not stop us because technically I was still a commander of a division. And because I had that rank and status, I was, to some degree, above them in the chain of command. It was because of this that no one questioned us. Even the model-Qs on the command deck stayed clear of us. There were quite a number of them—about thirty operated the transport ship. In the middle of all of them was B-6.

He was set in a strange pose again, where he was in the middle of a hologram depiction of the tactical situation of the entire planet and much of the star system. In fact, his arms were held out to either side, his eyes darted randomly, seemingly over the landscape of a dozen different worlds all at once. He reached out with plastic fingers and brushed a world. It would zoom into focus, and then he would put it away again.

As this was going on, I wondered what he was looking for, or exactly what planet was he looking at. I thought I recognized the general shape of the primary continent on Tranquility. It was the planet that was known for leisure in the Conclave, and that gave me a pang, a pang of worry and fear. I was fearful for all those vacationers on that fine world—one of our best, one of our finest in the entire Conclave. Could it be true? Could that planet be on the list right now as well as these others? The idea sickened me, but I forced a smile, marched ahead and waited until B-6 took notice of us.

For a time he ignored us. He worked his controls. He worked his hands in opposite directions with exaggerated movement. Both hands had fingers extended, making strange gestures. He made pinching motions with his forefinger and thumb on one hand, and at the same moment, he was making spreading motions with all five of his fingers on the other. Zooming in, zooming out, spinning a planet, picking a spot, tapping it twice and bringing up the details.

I could tell that visually he was working with a sophisticated interface—scanning, looking, controlling. I was a little concerned that he wasn't just looking at the planet we were orbiting right now. Instead his vistas had been cast much further afield, all over the Conclave. Were there invasions everywhere? I shuddered to think it.

At last after several minutes passed, during which Jort had become fidgety even though he had stayed silent thus far. Droad had stood like a statue. His eyes moved alone, looking from place to place, calculating, estimating. He too was figuring out the meaning of the visuals we were seeing from all over the Conclave. Finally B-6 turned his head and looked directly at me. "Now," he said, "what can I do for you, General Gorman?"

I smiled at him and raised a hand in basic greeting. "I have to tell you that we are very glad to be here and to be alive. In fact, I want to thank you for coming to rescue us. Sure, it took you a long time. Sure, you did not manage to get here when you said you would, but at the end you showed up and that's what really matters." It was a backhanded compliment, but B-6 took this in stride.

"I had many other strategic matters to attend to," he explained.

"I understand," I said. "I fully understand this is a war, and a war on many fronts. I can only imagine that other events, other places were prioritized more highly than we three humans stuck in an alien nest."

B-6 shrugged. "Actually, we had accounted you as dead. We lost contact with the unit commanders, and once all of your soldiers were dead, we no longer received any updates from the field in this region. Therefore, when we were about to land, it had been determined that you were no longer present for a rescue, that your entire command had been destroyed. It was decided that we should move on to the next target on the priority list."

"What?" Jort said, unable to contain himself. "You abandoned us? You didn't even check?" B-6 glanced at him, then glanced back to me.

"So, B-6," I said, deciding to switch the topic, "what is the agenda for today? Have we won this planet? Have we won this particular battle?"

"Yes," he said. "We have eradicated the majority of the enemy. We have saved all of the humans that were here or at least those that we were aware of, and now we are proceeding to the moment of cleansing."

"Cleansing?" I asked.

"Yes."

"Well, how exactly are we going to do that?" I asked.

"With a bombardment of select radiation isotopes," he said. "We will burn the enemy that we find, and leave the rest in place. In other words, the buildings, the structures, the plants, they will survive, but we will have to reintroduce fauna."

"That sounds quite drastic," I said.

"Yes, it is. It will be an unfortunate loss to the ecosystem. But there are other worlds willing to donate animals, bacteria and everything else that will be removed."

"But, it won't actually be the same animal types as the originals," I said.

"Yes, correct." B-6 made an irritated gesture. "That's true, but we must do what we can that will get this planet up and operating with human life within three years."

"Three years, Hmm?" I said. "Well I guess that's pretty good." Jort and Droad both looked somewhat surprised, but they didn't argue about it.

Two more days passed. While we were in orbit, we watched the bombardment first hand. It was not a series of hot explosions with mushroom clouds or that sort of thing. It was more a sprinkling of radiation that was as if the protective magnetosphere and atmosphere had been stripped away, giving the straight cosmic rays a way to beam down directly onto the surface.

Virtually all animal life and much of the plant life perished during those long hours. We watched as the planet browned and dimmed, turning less green, less vibrant. It was a grim thing to watch. As it turned out, the androids were forced to apply more radiation than they first expected would be necessary.

This was primarily because the aliens could endure it more than B-6 had suspected they might. Worse, once they figured out what was going on, the aliens dug deeply into the mountain sides, hiding underground. Their various nests had to be blown open and thoroughly excised. I realized as the process went on, that I was not really seeing or watching the cleansing of a world. It wasn't like witnessing a surgical miracle to fix a sick planet, but rather I was watching a world die.

Normally, a man like me would look for a way out of the situation, for a way to run off to a safe place and find what happiness and solace I could. Watching the demise of a whole world below, I was not able to suspend my disbelief. I was grimly compelled to entertain the idea that this was going to happen over and over again all across the Conclave. In fact it had to be exactly this that had happened to the Chain itself.

Decades ago the adverts were doing their best but I wasn't sure that any human would survive it.

The aliens were like a cancer, and sometimes the cure for such things was even worse than the disease itself. I decided then and there that although B-6 and the Connactic were trying their best, they really weren't well equipped to solve these problems for us. They were too inflexible of mind, too limited in their toolset. There had to be another way.

As the third day dawned, I coldly watched the transport ships leave orbit to work their destructive solutions elsewhere. We were left in their wake over a nearly dead world. I went to see B-6 again by myself.

"Inspector General, sir?" I said, gaining his attention. He looked up with a glance, and then turned his strange artificial eyes back to working his screens.

"What is it, Gorman?" he asked.

"What's our next move, sir? I asked him.

"We are headed to the next world. Xerxes, it is called. The ongoing process there is much like what we've seen here, but in an earlier stage. We should be more viable this encounter."

I nodded without believing him.

"I think I need to work on another approach," I said. This got his full attention. His fingers almost stopped twitching, and his both his eyes rose up and locked with mine.

"Another approach? You have a suggestion for me then?"

"I think I do," I said, "but I'm going to require my own personal freedom, and I'm going to require getting my ship and crew back in order to pursue it." B-6 continued to stare at me for a moment.

"Would you care to elaborate on these plans?"

I shrugged. "Not really. Some of them might involve elements which would run contrary to the rules of the Conclave, and therefore I need the freedom to operate independently."

B-6 stared at me for several more seconds before turning his eyes back to his screens and beginning to manipulate them again.

"This is interesting," he said. "You have given me quite a conundrum, a puzzle, as it were. I know you're effective. I know that you are dedicated to this cause, and yet you speak of doing something outside of Conclave norms. I am therefore drawn to respond in two opposing ways at once. Part of me wants to know what you are talking about, but another part of me must not know—if it would, as you say, raise your odds of success."

"It would," I affirmed. "What I'm asking for, I guess, sir," I said, "is that you trust me. You trusted me before when you made me a general of one of your divisions, and I think I performed relatively well."

B-6 nodded in agreement. "That's true. Your performance was approximately 36% better than my artificial commanders."

"36% Hmm?" I said, wondering exactly how he had tabulated that, but not being interested enough to ask him. "Well, then what do you say?"

"I will have to refer and confer with the Connactic over this."

"The Connactic?" I asked. "So you're not really able to make independent decisions? I thought that you were in command out here on this expedition."

"I am."

"No," I challenged. "No, you are not in command. Command means that there is a considerable degree of independence, at least within your operational sphere of possibilities. Your mission as I understand it, is to eradicate these aliens, to defend the Conclave."

"That is true," B-6 said.

"Well then, this is definitely something that directly involves your success in your stated mission, and therefore, I would suggest that you will allow me the freedom to go without any questions. I'll report back within a month as to whether my plans are viable."

"Interesting," B-6 said. His hands were twitching again. His eyes were moving, but I knew he wasn't ignoring me this time. "All right," he said. "You have convinced me, and you have convinced the limitations of my scripting—both at the same time. That is a sure indicator of the dire nature of the threat to the Conclave. Rules are being bent from every angle. It's quite disturbing. All right, Gorman. You are Captain Gorman once again. You are a general no longer. You will be given back your ship and your crew, and you'll be sent on your way. I will expect a report and hopefully some superior approach to completing my mission upon your return."

"Thank you, sir," I told B-6. "Thank you very much." Then I turned, and I left his office before he could change his mind.

Chapter Thirty

It took me a few weeks and a lot of intense conversations. There was some arm twisting involved as well, but in the end, I managed to get my crew back together aboard *Royal Fortune*.

The truth is, it was quite a relief after commanding armies that consisted of thousands of androids, crawling around inside alien nests, and expecting a horrible death at any moment. One could call these kinds of things adventure, but it wasn't the sort of adventure that I really enjoyed. Being on my own ship, on my own command deck, and with my hands on the helm... Now that, to me, was living.

"Oh, Captain Gorman," Jort said, "This is so good. Back on board our own ship, flying in space with no plastic men behind us. This is wonderful. I feel so good. Where are we going to go first, sir? Maybe to Tranquility or Scorpii? I know it's my home planet. But there are some good women there. You really should try them. They can squeeze... "

"Jort," I said. "We don't need any details. Listen, group. It's time to talk about our destination."

Morwyn, Huan, Droad, they all gathered around. Even Rose was with us again. She decided to rejoin when she had heard about a Conclave planet being destroyed. Realizing she wasn't safe on her own home world of Prospero, she changed her mind about retiring from my tiny pirate crew.

All of them looked at me, hopeful and expectant. Jort especially was beaming. He was certain that we'd be going somewhere fun, maybe to take a vacation from all these difficult times. He was of course, severely mistaken. Out of the whole group, only Droad seemed to know the truth, or at least he had an inkling of it. He was grim faced and smiling. There was not one hopeful bone in his body today.

"All right. Here's the deal," I told my crew. "We're going to the Sword Worlds. I've looked into it, and Baron Trask is officially being made into a duke. This elevation in status involves a loud ceremony, and I plan to attend."

They all looked dumbfounded at this news. Of all the destinations they figured I might have listed, this one was pretty far down the list. Jort recovered first.

"Okay," he said. "Okay, I think I get it. A loud ceremony—that means a party. A pirate party! I bet you those guys really know how to put on a good show, good eats, lots of women, lots of wine… Yes, it's a little crazy, but I think we could have fun there."

I nodded, and I smiled accepting Jort's enthusiasm. The rest of the group—the women in particular—were frowning. Rose spoke up first.

"Do we really have to go there? She asked. "Do we really have to go to that horrible planet with those horrible people? I thought we'd seen the last of them. Just the way that Trask and his men look at me… I don't feel safe there. I really don't, William."

Morwyn fidgeted as well. "I'm not certain I want to go to the Sword Worlds either, Captain," she said. "Last time I went there, we were attacked."

"Yes, yes," I admitted. "This is true, but things are different now. Trask is my greatest ally among the Sword World pirates, and now he is rising in status. This will make us much more safe than the last time we were there."

Jort laughed at this. "Maybe," he said, "and maybe not. The pirates, they're unpredictable." I frowned at him, wishing he'd stop freaking out the women.

Droad leaned in close next. "I think I understand the nature of your mission, Gorman," he said. "You plan to go there to gain the support of the mercenaries. Am I right?"

"Yes," I said. "Of course. Why else would I go to such a hive of ill repute?"

"This is good news," Huan said speaking up. "At last. I was worried I was going to have to ask to leave your service again, sir, but if this is truly your mission, if this is truly related to driving the enemy from the Chain, then I can join you."

"Oh, you and that Chain," Jort said. "All those stars are dead. Why do you even concern yourself? We must save the ones we have left."

Huan did not seem to be offended. "I do not intend to rescue the people of the Chain," he said. "The planets of the Faustian Chain—every colony as far as we know—are indeed dead, gone and destroyed, but in order to save ourselves from suffering the same fate, we must destroy the aliens that have hatched there. They are sending countless seedships toward the Conclave."

Jort made a farting sound with his mouth, and walked away. He did not think much of our chances of going out to the Chain and pushing back on so many millions, probably billions, maybe even trillions of enemy aliens.

"We can't dismiss the whole thought out of hand, Jort," I told him. "These aliens... they're all offense as far as I can tell. They take each planet, consume it, and then fly to the next. Each planet they have consumed has essentially been turned into an empty vessel, just a leftover shell that serves the one and only purpose of infecting the next star in the Chain. As far as I know, that's how they've crossed the cosmos. In order to survive such an onslaught, we have to do two things. Destroy the seedships as they come in and keep destroying them. At the same time, we need to go out to where the seedships are coming from and destroy those nests as well."

"Why's that?" Jort asked. "Why don't we just sit here and play goalie. I know that B-6 is planning to put a patrol ship permanently in orbit over every colony world in the Conclave. If these patrol ships shoot down every incoming seedship, we've got nothing to worry about."

"Not so," Droad said, coming into the conversation. "That is a losing strategy. The patrol ships will eventually be overwhelmed or the aliens will adapt and sneak around them—something will happen in some way. If you seek only to defend, your enemy will eventually figure a way around your defenses. This is one of the central principles of warfare."

"I agree with Droad," Huan said, "and I also agree with Gorman. We must take the fight to the enemy. And as far as I can tell, one of the few groups of people we have any influence with might successfully go on offense with us against the aliens. It would have to be Baron Trask and his Sword Brothers."

"There is another way," Morwyn said. We all looked at her, and she did not look happy. "The Tulk," she said. "They know how to fight these aliens better than us, being aliens themselves. They were hunted and rooted out of their home worlds long before we ever got here and started colonizing these planets. Perhaps we should go back to the Tulk and ask for their advice."

"Crazy talk," Jort said. "This is crazy talk. A Tulk cannot be trusted any more than the Skaintz. They're all aliens, and they all want to take over our planets."

Morwyn nodded. She could not deny the truth of Jort's words. "Yes, but the Skaintz are far worse. We should work with the Tulk again as we did before."

"You're only saying this because your father was consumed by a Tulk," Jort accused.

"That's not true," Morwyn said, but I could tell that Jort's words had hurt her, that they had affected her, and she was upset. This gave me pause. Was it true? Was Morwyn actually working with the Tulk on some level after her father had been taken by one? I wasn't completely sure. I slammed my hands together making a loud popping noise.

"All right then. It's been decided. We're going to go see Baron Trask. We're going to watch him being raised up to the rank of duke."

The group grumbled , many of them quietly pointing out that I had stuck to my decision from the first place, and the whole conversation had meant nothing, but I didn't care. As the captain of the *Royal Fortune*, my crew could either serve me and aid me on any given mission, or they could get off of my ship and find their own way across the stars.

It took us eight days to get to the Sword Worlds. We had fun, and we showed one another clips of the fighting on the colony world that had been destroyed, but we weren't really happy. All of us felt that a dark pall was still hanging over us.

When we arrived at Gladius, we were immediately met by aggressive gunboats and questioned. After a time the Sword Brothers accepted my identity and the identity of my ship and we were allowed to pass unharmed. Several hours after that, we reached orbit and parked our ship over Gladius.

Sensors actively pinged my vessel continuously. Dozens of missile batteries, ground based laser platforms and even some space-based defensive systems all targeted my ship. I maintained a relaxed and easygoing atmosphere the whole time this alarming procedure was carried out.

In time the Sword Brothers became convinced that I was indeed who I said I was, and Lord Trask contacted me directly. The pirate's big, ugly head filled the holoplate. Hairy, beetle-browed and frowning, the pirate looked around my crew warily. He pointed a big, fat finger in my direction and scowled.

"Gorman," he said. "Captain William Gorman, or at least his clone, why would you be here again after I've suffered so many losses already at your hands?"

"What?" I asked. ...suffered at my hands!" I was already noting that I liked my last visit better. Back then, the pirates had seen me as a possible source of employment, not as a possible threat.

"Don't play innocent with me, Gorman," Trask said, "and don't come back here offering more trinkets and rifles. I've got enough. What I need now is good men with a steady hand to defend these planets of mine."

"Hmm," I said, thinking over his words. "Do I surmise correctly then that Gladius has been attacked?"

"Not just Gladius, two other planets as well. Seedships came. We blasted them from the sky, but somehow, some living strand, some scrap of alien DNA managed to get to the surface. It managed to nest, although it took months to do so. Only just recently did we manage to burn it out. It's possible more are still out there in the wild on our planets. It's too grim to think about."

"I'm sorry for your losses, sir," I said, "but how exactly am I to blame for this?"

"These aliens were discovered by you, Gorman. You shall forever be associated with them. When they arise, I shall think of you and no one else. Nothing will ever change my mind about all this."

"Very well, then," I said, throwing up my hands. "I can see and hear that you want nothing to do with us. You don't want to hear our proposals. You are not interested in your own welfare or the welfare of the Conclave. Therefore, I shall seek counsel with someone else."

"What are you talking about?"

"Don't worry about it," I told him. "It means nothing to you. I'm going on to the next Sword World. Sure, I had come here to watch your elevation ceremony. I was proud to know a real duke of the Sword Brothers, but if I'm not wanted, I shall be on my way."

"Shut up, Gorman," Trask said. "You're not allowed to leave. You will attend me at my elevation, and you will enjoy yourself too. My hospitality will be better than anything you've ever seen among the Sword Brothers."

I found this rather easy to believe, as I'd never seen much in the way of hospitality at any Sword Brothers world. There were nine of these planets. Each was named after a different kind of sword. All of them were packed with vicious, selfish pirates, each of whom had a poor reputation among his neighbors. Less than half an hour later *Royal Fortune*'s jets were singing as we plunged down through the atmosphere and made a gentle, precise landing on a blast pad near Baron Trask's headquarters.

Chapter Thirty-One

The hospitality of true pirates is always a risky thing to experience. My crew was on edge, but they did their best to present a united front of calm confidence. This was after a stern lecture by me, of course, as to the appropriate behavior one should exhibit when dealing with people like Lord Trask.

The Sword Brothers were different than any other group of humans that I personally was aware of. By comparison, the Conclave crowd living under android rule was very weak, mild and timid. They followed rules, and they followed them exactly as they were written.

This is the polar opposite of people like the Sword Brothers. These people were raiders, mercenaries, killers, robbers, and thieves, but despite all that, they had their own sense of honor that was framed around their own interpretation of right and wrong.

Socially, they had a hierarchy that was built on ranks of nobility. This in turn had evolved into their own unique culture. They had no king, probably because that rank could never be agreed upon or held for long by any single individual. The higher you climbed within the hierarchy, the more pressure there was upon the person holding that rank from all the others below him. So, from the lowest recruit on up to barons such as

Trask, there was constant strife and an ongoing struggle for supremacy.

One of the most surprising things about Baron Trask was simply that he had lasted as long as he had in his position. He had easily spent 20 years as a baron and now was soon to become a count. He had never been deposed. I knew that his success and longevity was not actually due to being the best commander, nor the most loved. Rather, it was due to the very shrewd set of rules he lived by.

For example, he liked to strike first and to strike last. When a rival presented himself or herself, he would find a way to get that rival killed or to murder them personally. Either through a duel or a suicide mission, something of that nature. By constantly weeding out those who might rise up to challenge his supremacy, he maintained his position while simultaneously looking for opportunities to step up one more rung on the ladder.

One might wonder how a person such as myself could trust and deal with an individual like Baron Trask. The answer was twofold. First of all, my occupation was that of a gun runner. This made me someone who Trask needed, and it kept me breathing in some circumstances all by itself.

The second answer was more subtle. By understanding Trask and his motivations, I was able to keep myself and my crew from becoming his victims.

"Why do we always come here in the end?" Rose asked me. "These people are so unpleasant. I really hate them."

"You shouldn't," I told her. "We come here because we need them, because we need hard fighting men, men who are willing to die. There are limitations to what artificial androids can do successfully. These limitations have been exceeded by the Sword Brothers. For that reason, Rose, we need them."

I had not told Rose or anyone else in the crew that the Conclave did not have enough ships to launch a serious fleet toward the Chain. This sort of news would be devastating to my crew, and very demoralizing if it got out to other humans. Besides the negative effects of the knowledge, I also decided to keep this information secret just because I liked to keep secrets. Information that was not commonly known was a trade good that could be used at opportune moments. Thus far, the moment to share the information hadn't come.

Our ship landed with a gush of flame and exhaust. We lowered the ramp and stepped out on the blast pad. It was still hot. We could feel the heat coming up off the ceramic tile of the landing area right through our boots.

Walking unescorted, we made our way to Trask's fortress. It had grown in size since the last time I'd been here. It was no longer a squatty building constructed of random blocks of stone, perhaps three stories high. Now it was at least eight stories, and it was a rather dark and menacing hulk with outbuildings as well. In the distance were barracks—large affairs—while around the entire base of Trask's stronghold, a town had sprung up.

We could hear music playing. We could hear traffic, even the sounds of children playing in the distance. There were commoners and plenty of them on Gladius—not everyone was a mercenary or a pirate. If I had to estimate, I'd say only maybe one in ten of the humans on this planet served directly as a Sword Brother. They were the most important citizens, however, being the people who brought home spoils from raids and the cash from mercenary deployments.

One could compare the operation of the town to that of a fishing village. Not everyone in the village was a fisherman, but the fishermen were the heart of it. Those who brought back sustenance from the sea, shared their harvest and supported everyone else. And so, in a Sword Brothers town, every kid wanted to go off into space and be one of the heroes. Every adult either feared such a fate or had already experienced it and was lucky enough to retire alive.

My eyes swung back to the hulking, rambling house of Lord Trask. It was surrounded by twitchy missile launchers, beam turrets, and all kinds of defensive hardware aimed at the sky. Every member of the Sword Brother nobility feared a lightning attack upon his base. Naturally, he also dreamed of performing just such an attack upon victims on other worlds.

Passing by a dozen automated and deadly defensive systems, we were finally greeted by human guardians at the entrance. The doorway was low and dark and wide like the mouth of a great cavern. The massive stone doors that led into Trask's Hall were ominous all by themselves.

A series of recruits wearing blue and silver—the colors of House Trask—stood to either side. They challenged us, identified us, and then let us pass by. I noticed that several of them held Sardez rifles, the very weapons that I'd worked so hard to bring home to Trask and with which I'd bought both his cooperation and friendship.

Once inside the stronghold, we were escorted by an elderly chamberlain into a great hall. This was reached by going deeper, rather than upward to the higher stories. We were underground, I realized, and I wondered how deep Trask's domicile might now go. It did not surprise me that there were large vaults underground. It was always safer to be in a bunker than it was to be up on top of a tower. Hunted men such as Trask who live by their wits always seem to know this.

"There you are, Gorman!" Trask boomed, coming forward with his arms thrown wide.

I swaggered forward to greet him. I dodged the hug and shook his hand. He laughed, and he gave a hug to each of the women. Rose and Morwyn forced themselves to smile as he touched them, just as I had instructed them to.

"I think I know all these people," Trask said, "except for this freakish machine-man over here." He pointed at Huan. "I remember you having such a servant last time we met on Vindar, but I don't think I ever took his measure personally."

I introduced Huan and Trask. Then we all moved to a large table. We dined there and were fed a truly fine meal, much better than the last time I'd visited Gladius.

"Lord Trask," I said, "you seem to be doing very well for yourself."

"Thank you for noticing, Gorman. I *am* doing well. So well, in fact, that I have no need of your guns or trinkets or grim tidings from other worlds."

I glanced towards Droad who glanced back at me. Perhaps Trask didn't know why we were here, or perhaps he had just assumed that I had come for the same reasons that I had come on previous occasions. At least this time he wasn't constantly talking about me being merely a clone of a better man.

The evening went on rather smoothly after that. We continued to eat, we drank wine, and after a while even the women started smiling real smiles. It was a somewhat festive occasion.

"Trask," I said, "have we somehow stepped into a night of unusual celebration? I don't remember every evening being a party like this one."

"You're right, Gorman. Tonight, is a special night. Tonight, is the last evening that I will be called Baron on Gladius. Tomorrow, I'm ascending to the rank of count. I shall be Count Trask after this. Several new ships have come to my banner, and there is an opening, as you may know, after the Vindar campaign."

I nodded, knowing that one of the counts had been injured during that battle and dropped a rank by losing too many assets, soldiers, ships, and the like. Apparently, Trask had been busy capitalizing on this gain and making it official.

"That's very interesting," Droad said, joining the conversation. He'd been quiet for most of the night, but he was obviously listening and picking up on everything about these people and their culture. "How exactly is a rise in the rank of governance secured—other than by killing your rival, I mean?"

Trask laughed, and he took the comment in the best light possible. "We're not as crazy as we may seem from the outside," he said. "We don't shuffle ranks at the top very often. Normally, it is done because of a large loss on the part of one leader or another. Conversely, it might be a large gain on the part of a lower ranked individual. In this case both happened. Even so, it has taken nearly a year for me to secure what has already been somewhat accepted and understood—that I'm rising in rank and Count Drago is dropping."

"So, none of these stations are determined by birth?"

"No, we don't use a system of hereditary rule. We are a meritocracy. Essentially, if you're the best killer, the best looter, the best mercenary, if you don't lose too much, and you manage instead to gather a lot of wealth, to make good deals… well, more troops will come to your banner, and over time, your position as a higher-ranked individual will be secured. Also, at times, there are retirements at the top that are not violent in nature. Sometimes a man simply grows too old and feeble to hold his position, and with no heirs to pass it on down the line to, it is left to the lower-ranking barons, knights and others to take the rank and fill the empty slot."

"Very interesting," Droad said. "So that's it then? Tomorrow you're just going to have a ceremony and be pronounced a count?"

"Not exactly..." Trask admitted. "There's a little bit more to it than that. Since Drago is still alive, and he still commands a relatively large force, he has opted to fight a duel with me. This is all largely ceremonial nonsense, of course. It's for show really, to give the troops something to go home and talk about—a morale-building event, if you will."

"I see," Droad said. He slid his eyes to me, then back to Trask. I could tell he wasn't quite sure what to think, but he was definitely intrigued.

I, for my own part, was alarmed. Trask was acting very confidently, and he was talking down a duel with Count Drago, a man who could not possibly favor him in any way, shape or form. From where I stood, this looked like a nasty fight was in store, and he was talking as if it was all mere formality.

I had seen Trask duel before, and it had been a vicious and very personal affair. He had in fact, cheated on that occasion, using a poisonous dagger. No one who had witnessed the struggle would be willing to admit that of course, but we knew it all the same. I had to wonder what my eyes would be seeing when the strange ceremony was held the next day.

Before the night was out, Trask formally invited us all to attend his inauguration, his ascendancy to a new rank, and we naturally agreed. We were sent off to private apartments where we slept as soundly as we could—well knowing that we were in the very heart of a pirate's den.

No one molested us as we were under Trask's protection. That right there is an example of the importance of choosing a powerful lord among the Sword Brothers to be your patron. Some of the lower-ranked types, the less savory people among the populace, did not have such a firm grip upon either their natural emotions and appetites or those of their men. We might have been robbed or attacked in some fashion during the night were it not for Trask's aura of goodwill and raw power.

When the morning came, after we had a brief breakfast, we were summoned outside to a courtyard. The yard was several floors up from where we had slept. We found ourselves in an arena of sorts. There were seats behind high walls and two openings at either end of the field of honor. The open area in the center was covered in lumpy sand.

On our side, the side that faced to the west, a throne could be seen. It was built with the same dark stone as the rest of the building—but no one sat on it. On the opposite side of the arena was a throne facing east of the same exact appearance. It also stood empty.

We sat next to the throne on our side, wearing cloaks of blue and silver that showed we were there as guests of Trask's house. Our seats looked down into the arena without obstruction.

Another group of important-looking people sat opposite us. They wore red and gold which I assumed identified them as Drago's entourage.

With us were Trask's knight-captains, which now numbered seven rather than the three that had followed him the last time I'd been here. A similarly-sized flock sat on the opposite side of the arena.

Plenty of other men and women were in attendance, about a hundred on each side. It wasn't a tremendous crowd, but it was similar to what you might see at a sporting event in any small village on a colony world.

My eyes fell again to the flat field of sand between us. I eyed the arena from a tactical standpoint. The walls were approximately four meters high all the way around. It was clear there would be no escape for the contestants once the two barred gates were lowered at either side.

We attempted to engage Trask's knight-captains in conversation, but they were reluctant to talk about the event itself. They discussed instead the victory over the Tulk that they had recently achieved and the Skaintz of Vindar. They talked about their ships, about their men, about their wealth and about their own prowess.

At last, a horn blew a single long note. Two figures stepped out into the sunlight, one from either end of the arena. One wore blue and silver. He was clearly Trask. The other, in red and gold, must have been Count Drago. He appeared to be a young man, younger than Trask at least. He was also tall, slender, and quick of movement.

The two men did not charge one another, grunting furiously and madly trading blows. I'd half expected something like that, but it was much more ceremonial. Instead, they stepped forward to the center of the arena, faced one another and nodded. This was a demonstration of mutual respect and honor for one another.

Each of them then drew a blade, a blade of simple metal. There didn't seem to be any energies powering either weapon. With these weapons held in their right hands, they then reached with their left and touched a bracelet.

A coating like gelatinous water grew up from each of these bracers to cover their hands and then up their arms, over their entire bodies. I realized it must be some kind of a forcefield. When they moved, the forcefields moved as well.

Flowing and translucent, the fields looked almost as if each man was encased in a bubble of man-shaped water that had somehow adhered to his body. The force fields were not very thick, perhaps only a few centimeters in depth.

I had to wonder if the field covered their eyes and somehow occluded their vision. Perhaps that was part of the contest, that in using such a defensive system, you were challenged to find your opponent through that wavering, underwater look, by which each man was handicapped. Either that, or possibly their eyes were not buried in the force field like the rest of their bodies. Whatever the case, I couldn't tell from the stands, and I didn't bother giving it more thought.

I turned to one of the knight-captains, a woman Astrid who I'd met on previous campaigns with Lord Trask. "What's the deal?" I asked her. "Is this a fight to the death?"

"Probably not," she said. "They must simply score on each other. Once blood has been spilled, honor will be satisfied."

"Hmm," I said. "Well then, why have a fight at all?"

"It's tradition," Astrid explained. "Even when there is a fairly uncontested transferal of power, those who are losing rank must at least put on a show of having defended it. That way, they can keep the loyalty of the men that they retain."

"I see," I said, and I did see. Sword Brothers were all about risking their lives at the command of their lord. It was very important that the followers of any given leader believe in him—that they believe he was tough enough to hold the rank he had somehow gained in the past. I could understand how a ritual combat like this could be used by both participants to demonstrate to their followers that they were still worthy to lead.

The two men, now shielded and armed, stood stock-still for a moment until at last that single horn blew again. When that one note was heard, they went into motion. They stalked each other, circling and then suddenly stepping close, slashing with their blades. Sparks flew as their blades clashed.

The two swords were of medium weight. They were lightly curved and designed like saber. I thought that a heavier weapon, like a broad sword, might do better. To get through a forcefield you needed to hit hard—hard enough to cleave limbs.

I supposed these dueling swords could do the job. They were thin, light, and quick. Deadly enough when thrust through a man's guts.

The swords rang against each other, steel on steel. Now and then one dipped past the guard of either man to score a flash of orange light when it toughed his shielding. The crowded cheered at these moments, but still, nothing penetrated the shielding for nearly a full minute of dueling.

The crowd in the meantime slammed their hands together and made videos with announcements to broadcast live. I presumed the spectacle was entertaining to anyone who was interested across the entire planet.

"It's a show," Morwyn said, leaning to me and whispering into my ear. "It's a show for the entire world. Everyone must be watching this on their local grid."

"Yes," I agreed. "It's a show, all right. It's a good one too, but how are they going to conclude it?"

Morwyn shrugged not knowing the answer, so we turned our attention back to the fight, which had heated up to some degree.

Both men were now in a clinch, each trying to grab the wrist of the other. When the shields touched, they produced a fierce orange-yellow glow, with sparks that flew outward in a spray. Apparently, the two force fields were not in harmony when they got too close.

Each man held the wrist of the other, each trying to bring his blade around to bear. Neither could manage it, and they finally shoved each other away and circled again. They were panting now, winded.

"It's a very even contest," Huan said. "I wonder who will win."

I glanced at him, but I didn't say anything, because I had my own feelings on who would win. Trask had been far too confident the evening before. If there was any chance he was going to lose this, he would have been sweating and scheming. Instead, he had partied like he hadn't a care in the world. This told me everything I needed to know about how this contest was going to go.

The men came together for a third time. Both were sweating and filthy now, and they seemed very winded. Fortunately, the weather was not too hot, but you can only struggle for so long in a physical contest like this without becoming exhausted.

Almost too tired to hold their blades up, they now used two hands on their sabers. They swung them with wild overhand chops rather than movements of finesse. The sabers clashed more brightly against their shielding as the men continued to tire, leaving long streaks of sparks.

They parried wildly and staggered more often as their fatigue grew. Soon, they were unable to lift their blades to parry one another's strokes. At one point, seeming to need the support, they even leaned into each other, grappling heavily in a great shower of glowing light and running, colorful plasmas.

With a hoarse bellow, Drago shoved Trask off him with both hands, nearly dropping his weapon. In return, Trask stood there reeling and chuckling like a lecher.

Then Baron Trask found new energy and stepped forward, sweeping the legs out from under his opponent. Drago went down on his back roaring in fury. Trask strode forward with a victorious shout, lifting his blade, but to everyone's surprise, Drago had managed to raise the tip of his sword and pressed it up, under the older pirate's great paunch.

Through some trick of physics, the point slowly penetrated Trask's belly as he advanced, and he was lanced at least lightly in the guts. A gasp went up from the crowd.

"First touch!" a man in red and gold shouted from the stands opposite us.

"First touch!" agreed another, nodding vigorously.

"No, no," someone howled from our side. Boos erupted all around us.

Trask sensed disaster. He rammed his boot down on his opponent's gauntlet, and he leaned down on the hilt of his sword.

Drago's arm was hopelessly pinned under Trask's ample weight, but Trask didn't halt the fight. He thrust his sword down hard and long into the other man's chest. It sunk down slowly over a period of perhaps ten seconds. Finally, the tip penetrated the wavering shield, piercing it.

Drago frantically grabbed at the blade, trying to shove it aside, but he was unable to with Trask leaning with all his bulk down upon it. At last, there was a crunching sound as Trask's sword pierced his breastbone, his heart and probably his spine. Gasps went up from the crowd on both sides.

Trask cheered and lifted his fists tiredly above him, shutting off his shield. He shook his clasped fists over his ugly and disheveled head.

"Trask wins!" he shouted. "Trask wins! Long live Count Trask!"

The boos from the far side of the arena grew deafening. The men took to their feet, and they shook their fists in anger rather than congratulations. Alarmed, all of us in the blue and silver on our side of the arena stood up as one and stared darkly across at our counterparts.

"This could go very badly," I observed. Droad nodded in understanding.

I knew it all might turn into a wide-open melee between two different groups in two different camps. Each was feeling wronged by the other.

"Wasn't Trask supposed to stop at first touch?" Morwyn asked me, whispering in my ear.

"Did he just cheat?" Rose asked.

"Yes," I said. "He did cheat. Let us pray that he is successful in pressing his claim. Otherwise, we might be in the middle of a war zone."

Chapter Thirty-Two

Trask's duel had ended in dishonor and humiliation, but Trask himself was unrepentant. Sure, he had broken the rules, and he had abused his opponent. After making the mistake of allowing himself to be touched first, he should have been declared the loser. But instead, he had forced the issue by killing the helpless man.

That was Trask in a nutshell. He hadn't gotten to be a top-level pirate by playing the nice guy. He had declared himself a count, and that was that.

The following day an even larger ceremony was held. This time, only Trask's trusted advisors and loyal followers were allowed to attend. Neutral visitors such as ourselves were included because we weren't likely to challenge his new rank—but we were nervous.

Trask even went as far as putting the emblem of the office upon his own neck. It was a heavy gold chain with a locket of depleted uranium. My crew and I sat in the crowd, our spines bolt upright and as mute as statues. We all sat silently and stared. No one smiled. No one clapped. We held perfectly still, until others in the room, who knew the rules of the game better than we did, began to signal their approval. At that moment, we all began to clap as one. I had instructed my crew to do this, and they followed the instructions closely. When you clap for a tyrant, you start early, and you end late.

Once the ceremony and the feasting were over with, we were allowed to talk to Trask in person. He requested that I attend with my lady friend. This of course, presented me with a problem because I had two of them. One was Rose, my former girlfriend and longtime companion, and the other was Morwyn, another more recent girlfriend, who had also broken up with me.

Hmm. Which one of these two should I choose to take to the meeting? After all, they were both attractive and interesting.

I ended up choosing Rose—not because she was smarter, but because she was more elegant thoughtful. Morwyn, being of Vindar, had an exotic bluish cast to her complexion which Trask would probably like, but I held firm.

Accordingly, I took Rose to the dinner meeting with Trask and about twenty of his advisors around a long table in an even longer hall. We ate, and we drank, all without bothering to test our food for poison. I was hopelessly under Trask's power. If he wanted to kill me, he would kill me, and acting frightened of the possibility wasn't going to reduce the odds of something bad happening anyway. So, we dined, we smiled, and we talked.

Finally, we got around to business as the meal was cleaned up, and we were down to a couple of final after-dinner drinks. Trask, as was usually the case, did not have a female consort of his own present at the table. He did often have women around, but he did not generally bring them into negotiations and conversations. He ruled alone, as far as I knew, and had no children. If he did, he had kept them secret from us.

This was a common practice among the Sword Brothers. They made an effort to hide those they cared about, so they could not be used as leverage against them. Very often, these various knights and barons actually had spouses and children. But advertising who these individuals were could only serve as a possible future weakness. Therefore, the relationships were never openly displayed in front of outsiders.

I wasn't exactly an outsider. Trask and I had campaigned together more than once, and we had done business on several occasions but all the same, I was no Sword Brother. I could never be fully trusted.

Be that as it may, Rose sat next to me, and she smiled and was as charming as she could be. She played the part exceptionally well and avoided saying anything embarrassing. This made me realize I had actually made the right choice.

Morwyn was probably a little smarter than Rose, a little more savvy, a little more discerning of details under the surface, but that wasn't always a good thing. If she were to bring up a topic that Trask did not want to talk about, especially one she was emotionally invested in, then all her other positive traits would be erased in that single moment. Rose was much less risky of a companion in this delicate social landscape.

"Captain Gorman," Trask said, interrupting my thoughts. "At long last I have time for you. I'm very glad you came and attended my ascendancy."

"I take it then, Count Trask," I said, "that you're finally willing to talk business?"

"Yes, but let me ask you first, what did you think of the entire process?"

I halted, frozen for just a moment—my face was blank. Naturally, I thought it had been a sick travesty. I knew that essentially, Count Trask had embarrassed himself in front of the nobility of his own planet. I'm not sure that he cared, but he definitely had not followed the rules, and he hadn't behaved in what anyone would consider an honorable fashion. But I knew this was not what Trask wanted to hear.

At the same time, I did not want to purely simper and cringe in his presence. If Trask saw me as too weak, too supportive, or too obsequious, then he would lose respect for me. Therefore, I had to strike a delicate middle ground. Accordingly, I shrugged as I spoke, to appear as nonchalant as possible.

"The internal affairs of the planet Gladius have little to do with me. I have no more of an opinion about how you run your court than I do about how the Connactic runs the Conclave."

Trask frowned for a moment because I had mentioned the Connactic. The ruler of the Conclave was rarely brought up in open conversation.

"That's an interesting answer," he said. "You speak as if the Connactic is more than a figurehead, more than a myth."

"She is," I said, and I allowed myself a small smile.

My attempt to alter the direction of the conversation had succeeded. Trask had taken the bait. Now he was interested in the Connactic, and no longer trying to determine whether or not I thought he'd embarrassed himself on the field of honor during the duel. The situation was exactly as I wanted it.

"You know something of the Connactic?"

"I do," I said. "I know quite a bit about her. In fact, I met with her rather recently—in person."

Trask scoffed, laughing while his ample belly shook. "Come on, Gorman. You're a bullshitter, but even you can't get away with such a boast."

I shook my head. "I'm not boasting. I'm telling you the flat and honest truth." I then began to tell him a story. It was somewhat edited, but essentially, I discussed how I had been run down and captured by the Connactic, then dragooned into doing a scouting mission all the way out to the Faustian Chain.

As I spoke, he became increasingly alarmed and concerned. When I explained that there had been a recent invasion of a true Conclave planet by these aliens, his interest was at its peak.

"So, the rumors about Ailoth true?" he demanded.

"Yes, Count. It's absolutely true. I was there fighting on Ailoth. A month before that I witnessed enemy alien seedships being launched. I can easily imagine most of them are headed for the last remaining human worlds—the Sword Worlds included."

"This is grim news, Gorman. What's the Conclave going to do about it?"

"Well," I said, "For starters, they've set up a rather large army of over a million guardians with over a hundred ships to transport them. They're carrying these large divisions of troops to any infected planet and eradicating the aliens on the ground."

"Huh…"

Trask picked up a knife and a pear and began slicing into it. The man seemed to enjoy eating more than he had the last time I'd met up with him. Perhaps it was an affectation of wealth and age.

I let him think about this new information for a minute. At last, he waved the knife in my face. "It would seem that in the case of Ailoth, the Conclave failed to act quickly enough."

"Agreed," I said. "Their new plan is to put a patrol ship at every planet in the Conclave at all times, specifically searching for seedships."

"Patrolmen waiting around for more seedships to invade… I don't like the sound of that. How are we going to smuggle anything or land any mercenaries if they're watching every planet for a hundred light years around?"

"I didn't say *every* planet would be watched, I said that the Conclave worlds would be. Out on the Fringe, or even farther out in the case of a planet like Vindar… Well, they probably won't get any protection at all."

"Oh, that would include the Sword Worlds."

"Yes."

"We shall have to maintain our own vigilance, then."

"Yes, I would recommend it."

"Hmm, this is strange. You're describing a system of careful defense, but how long can such an approach be successful? You can't win a long war with defense alone."

I pointed a finger at him. "That's exactly what I told the Connactic and her inspector general. We must go on the offensive. It's important to defend, but eventually some of these seedships will slip through. When they do, we have a good chance of losing the planet they land upon. The enemy might even figure a way to get around our patrol ships. They'll change their tactics, and we'll be helpless to stop them. If we sit on our hands long enough, we'll all be wiped out eventually."

Count Trask was squinting at me now. He was thinking hard. "What about their cruisers?" he said. "If you know this much, perhaps you know what their counter-strike plan is. Will the Connactic send her fleet to the Chain to shut down these worlds that are generating an endless stream of invasion pods?"

"Possibly. At least they're awake and doing something—but as we know, the Conclave is always slow to act. They prefer half-measures to decisive action."

"Yes," Trask said. "You describe their mode of operation perfectly. Where does that leave us—you and me, I mean? Why are you here? You aren't just selling guns. Not this time."

"No," I said. "I'm not. I'm now selling survival. I'm here to sell you on the idea that some level of cooperation is needed by all humans in order to defeat this enemy."

He was squinting again, and he did this for several long quiet seconds. Finally, he laughed and slammed his big hands on the table.

"I get it," he said. "This is a fool's trap, isn't it? You were sent here by the Connactic to talk me into another suicidal run, exactly as my late benefactor Count Drago performed when he invaded Vindar and lost his army. It's the very reason I've become a count on Gladius. You seriously think I'm going to fall for the same trap? That I'm going to spend my soldiers, my ships, my blood, and my treasure vainly trying to save the Conclave's ass? I don't think so."

I shrugged as if unconcerned. "What do you think will happen," I asked him, "if a serious invasion does reach the Sword Worlds?"

"I don't know," he said. "I guess we'll do what we already did with the Tulk. We drove them off. We'll do the same with the Skaintz."

"I wouldn't call that a plan," I said, "but at least you're thinking about it. I would say, however, that the Tulk and the Skaintz are not comparable. If the Tulk had taken over a planet or two of yours, the Conclave would not have acted. In fact, the Tulk did so, and as you remember, the Conclave did not come here. They did not seek to burn out your planets. They did not seek to crush your fleets with their cruisers. None of that happened."

Suddenly, Trask stood tall. He knocked over a goblet of wine, and then he picked up the empty goblet, and he threw it at me. I dodged as it flashed past my right ear.

"A threat? An open threat?" he shouted. "I heard it, Gorman! Don't try to take it back. You came here under the banner of the Conclave and the Connactic, and now you are telling me that if I don't do what they want that they're going to come here and burn my planet out. Just the same as they did Ailoth—and to the Sardez before that."

For my part, I did not stand up, shout, or point my finger back at him in a rage. I reacted calmly. You had to handle a wild man like Trask quite carefully.

"I said no such thing," I replied.

Rose took that moment to put a small hand on top of my wrist. "Perhaps we should leave, William," she said.

"No, no. Don't worry if Count Trask seems emotional. He's got a good reason to be."

Trask eyed Rose and then me. He finally sat again, forcing himself to calm down.

"All right," he said. "Let's try to proceed in a more civilized fashion. You're telling me the Conclave has no intention of defending the Sword Worlds. You're also telling me that if we get infected, we might be treated as a cancer by the Conclave, rather than being ignored and allowed to do as we wish out here on the Fringe. They will see our plight as a threat to them."

"I said none of those things, but they do follow logically, don't they?"

Trask nodded. "All right, fine. You've laid out the problem. You've described the situation. Now, what do you propose that we should do about it? And don't tell me that we should fly to the Chain and do all the work the Conclave is unwilling to do."

"No, sir," I said. "I don't think any such suggestion would be appropriate. Here's what I propose... I think you should come with me, Trask, and meet the Connactic. Perhaps the two of you can work out a mutually beneficial arrangement."

Trask blinked several times. He seemed stunned.

"Me, meet the Connactic? Are you kidding? Her plastic men wouldn't allow me within one hundred light years of her palace."

"Not so," I said. "If you were to come in a more neutral capacity, perhaps aboard my ship as a guest, I'm sure that the Connactic…"

"Come on, Gorman! Do you expect me to leave behind my retinue, my guardian—all of my wealth and starships and thousands of troops—to merely walk into the lair of the Connactic?"

"You would be treated as a diplomatic envoy. Sometimes people have to take risks in order to make deals. The Conclave people have never come here and attempted to arrest you, have they?"

"That's because they've been well-bribed all the way along."

"All right then. What that sounds like to me is that you have already been dealing with the Conclave in a rather indirect and unofficial manner. Perhaps it's time that the Sword Worlds and the Conclave come to a more mutually beneficial understanding, a more formal arrangement."

Count Trask's eyes lit up. "Are you talking about official recognition? Legitimacy? That's madness, Gorman. It could never be achieved. They pretend we don't even exist."

"Yes, that's right," I said, "but what if one man—you in particular—were able to elevate the status of all the Sword Worlds? Which one of your pirate brothers here has ever done anything so impressive? Who among you has ever shown themselves to be a more legitimate leader? This opportunity, in fact, lies at a whole new, and higher, level than ever seen before now."

"Huh." Trask took his time in thinking it over. "No one can boast of such an achievement… None here, at least."

"That's right," I said. "That's why I came to you with this proposal. I know you're an ambitious man. I know you're a capable man. I know you are a man of vision, and I'm here to help you."

Trask sat back and considered my suggestion. I could tell his mind was whirling. It seemed like perfect timing to make this offer to him now. He had just bumbled in front of his entire planet. His ascendency to count was clearly less than legitimate. Any man in that position would be seeking a way to regain some respect and prestige. I was offering him just such an opportunity.

He stood up again, and he bowed to Rose and nodded to me. It looked as if he were about to take his leave, and possibly think about my offer over the evening. That's what I would have done if the situation had been reversed—but he didn't take that measured approach.

"Captain Gorman, I accept your offer. Tomorrow I will board your ship with a single bodyguard, and we will fly to meet your Connactic. If this turns out to be some kind of trick, some way to get me arrested and slowly strangulated in the Connactic's royal palace—with my corpse placed on display to be laughed at and spat upon—know that I will curse you and haunt you for the rest of eternity."

I nodded, accepting his threat and his curse. "I would expect nothing less, Count Trask."

Then I stood up. Rose did the same a moment later, looking a little weak in the knees. Her eyes flicked back and forth between Trask and I, but she kept her apprehension subtle.

I reached out a hand across the table. After a moment's hesitation, Count Trask took it, and we shook hands.

With a nod we both retired, and the dinner was over.

Chapter Thirty-Three

Trask decided to accompany us back to the Conclave. He did not bring any ships, none of his destroyers, no escorts or fat bellied transports full of pirates. None of these things would have been accepted inside the Conclave itself, of course, and he knew that. He traveled as a civilian passenger aboard *Royal Fortune*.

For me, this was quite a diplomatic achievement. Trask was paranoid and rightfully so. He was taking a big risk, and I'd gotten him to do it. Only the lure I'd given him—the right to claim he'd talked the Conclave into officially recognizing the Sword Worlds had gotten him to take the risk.

He did bring with him, as he had said, a single bodyguard. This was none other than Astrid, the same female captain I had met and talked with at the arena. She was a large, strapping gal, clear of eye and mind. She was also a killer. I could tell this just by looking at her, but in case I was in any doubt, she went on at great length discussing the many men she'd killed to secure her position as a knight-captain under Trask.

The journey took thirteen days, during which I became aware of the fact that Trask and Astrid were sharing a cabin. I'd given them the finest cabin we had for passengers. It was certainly roomy enough, and while one could wonder if Trask had Astrid bunk with him to better serve as his bodyguard, one also couldn't help but wonder if they were romantically involved.

Rose and Morwyn were acutely aware of the situation, and very curious. They smiled and asked shy questions about the nature of the relationship between our two guests. None of these questions were met with definitive answers. I knew, of course, that this was because of the unwritten rule about hiding those you care about when you are a Sword Brother.

"Well, I'm happy for them," Rose told me. "It must be nearly impossible for pirates to have romance in their lives."

I privately disagreed, having learned over the years that running a ship attracted mates of all kinds—but I was smart enough not to say anything about that.

"Even a pirate like Trask deserves to have someone in his life," I said, gaining me a smile from Rose. She had taken to sharing my bunk on this journey, probably because she had been pleased by the fact that I had chosen her to be my consort at Trask's fancy dinner.

On the thirteenth day, when we were about to arrive at Mutual, Trask finally became edgy.

"This is all a mistake," he said, pacing around on my small command deck with loud clumping boots. "I can't believe I let you talk me into this, Gorman."

"Cold feet at the moment of truth?" I said. "I'm surprised as well. I thought you were quite eager to come. How often is it that a Sword Brother meets with the Connactic of the Conclave?"

"Never, I'm sure," Trask replied, "but that doesn't mean it's a good idea. What if they seek to capture me? Here I am wrapped up like a present with a bow on it. That's your real mission, your real game—isn't it, Gorman? All this nonsense about entreating with the Conclave, as if they would accept me as an equal… No, you've changed your trade. You've moved from being a gun runner to being a bounty hunter. That's what this is all about, isn't it?"

I presented myself as utterly calm. When dealing with dangerous scoundrels, it was best to hide your fears. "I can understand how you might think that," I told him, "and under any normal circumstance you might even be correct. But Count

Trask, we're all under threat now. The stakes are higher than they've ever been. I'm not out here just to make a few credits. I'm concerned for the safety and well-being of every human in existence."

Trask mulled that over, but he still wasn't happy. "What proof do you have that things are as bad as you say?" he demanded, and at last it was the opening I'd been waiting for.

We'd almost reached Mutual, so I figured it couldn't hurt to release to him some video evidence that was regarded as top secret by the Conclave—after all, who was he going to tell about it? In the next few hours, we would make planetfall over the capital planet.

I cued up some recordings I'd made of the action on Alioth. He saw us fight the aliens. He saw thousands of androids being torn apart. He even saw glimpses of the inside of the nest in the feeding pit where Droad, Jort and I had spent way too much time.

This last scene, in particular, horrified him.

"These aliens are beyond disgusting," he said. "They must be stamped out."

I aimed my finger at him. "Precisely. You and I are in full agreement at last. Now, let's go down and meet the Connactic."

He blinked at me, and right about then, the ship shuddered. We had come through the slip-gate and arrived at Mutual.

Our credentials were checked, and eventually we were allowed to fly on from the slip-gate and enter orbit over Mutual. Several patrolmen—guardians and model-Q captains—boarded our ship and searched everything. The only things they found that they didn't like was Trask and his girlfriend.

"These two are wanted criminals." I was informed, as if I didn't know.

"That's right," I said. "They're also my guests, and I am operating under the orders of the Connactic."

The patrolmen mulled this over. They complained and checked with headquarters. Eventually, they went back to their patrol boats and escorted us toward a large space station.

Trask came and put a big hand on the back of my command chair. He squeezed the headrest until his fingers and knuckles were white.

"Just give it a surge of power, Gorman. I know what this ship can do. Spin around, hit the jets and outrun them. We can make it back to the slip-gate and escape. If that's not possible, just run straight ahead and leave this buggered system behind."

"What are you talking about?"

"I'm talking about a change of plan. Outrun the patrolmen and their torpedoes. If you do this, I'll give you a reward bigger than anything that the Connactic has offered."

His eyes were so big and serious I almost did it—but then I recalled the importance of my mission.

"Just relax, Trask," I said. "Take a seat and strap in. After all, every time I go to the Sword Worlds, it's to meet with you. It feels just like this for me and my crew every time we make planetfall over Gladius."

Trask thought about that, and then he laughed. "Yes... I do suppose that it must feel pretty intimidating. I hate being under the control of a dangerous adversary."

"Exactly. An independent captain such as myself never knows if he's facing death, imprisonment, or a nice party when he comes to the Sword Worlds. Would you have it said that the crew of a smuggling ship were all braver than Count Trask himself?"

This challenge got the attention of Trask's knight-captain girlfriend. Astrid turned her eyes to him as if wondering what his answer might be.

Trask became huffy. "You shouldn't even talk that way. This isn't a matter of bravery, it's a simple matter of wisdom. But all right, all right. Take me to their space station. Let's just land and get this over with."

We flew on, and we soon arrived at the most boring space station I'd ever visited. Trask left Astrid behind as he'd calculated that a single bodyguard wasn't going to be much help in the central hive of the Conclave. I did the same, leaving Jort and Rose and all the rest of them on *Royal Fortune*. They couldn't do us any good at this point.

Together, we two men were surrounded by no fewer than six guardians, all armed with rifles. Our own weapons had been removed from us, and we were marched to the elevator. We rode down the umbilical to the planet's surface, just as I had done before.

I made several attempts to contact B-6, or anyone else who was in authority, but received no response. I did not relay this disturbing information to Trask, who would probably panic if I told him that no one was listening to me on Mutual today.

It was while we were riding down the umbilical to the surface that Trask started to realize there weren't too many humans around.

"I'm seeing nothing but androids here…" he said. "Such a freakish way to live. Have the Connactic and the top leadership of the Conclave replaced their own staffers with machines? It's disgusting."

I said nothing, knowing that he was in for some even bigger shocks very soon.

The walk to the Connactic's lair was a laborious one. But at least I felt it was likely we were being led in the right direction. We weren't on an obvious, direct walk to a prison cell.

An hour or two passed. We went through countless secure portals and finally reached the Connactic's inner sanctum. I'd been chatting with Trask about the aliens, about the Sword Worlds, about Rose and my crew while he barely listened. He was nervous and thinking hard. His eyes were slits, and they slid from side to side as he watched everyone and everything. He was not at all comfortable.

The Connactic kept us waiting for about twenty long minutes once we reached her office, but at last, we were invited to step inside.

She looked at the two of us. We returned her gaze, and it was Trask who broke the silence.

"Who's this?" he asked me, pointing rudely at the woman and her robes. "Another android? How many servants do these Conclave pukes have?"

The Connactic smiled coldly. "I am the Connactic."

"What?" he said. "Nonsense. You don't fool me. You're made of plastic, metal, circuits and falsehood."

She inclined her head in a tiny nod. "That is a plausible description. I am indeed an artificial person."

Finally, Trask seemed to grasp the awful truth.

I could have warned him, of course. I could have given him the whole lecture about how the Conclave had apparently, at some point, been completely taken over by the androids and that this new breed of androids were of a smarter, higher class of intellect than even the model-Qs we were more familiar with.

I hadn't bothered to reveal all this as I'd known it wouldn't have calmed him or allayed his fears. He might not even have believed me, so I'd waited for this moment of drama to play out naturally.

"Connactic," I said. "I have brought to you Count Trask of the Sword Worlds. He commands a great fleet and many thousands of experienced and capable troops. He wishes to help us defeat these aliens. He also sees the seedships as a great enemy. The invaders from the Faustian Chain are a danger that we must all face together."

The Connactic glanced at me then back at Trask. "Is this your view as well?" she asked.

Trask's mouth was hanging low. His teeth were uneven, his beard was unkempt—the old pirate had been taken completely by surprise. Slowly, he turned and looked at me.

"You could have told me about this, mate."

I shrugged. "Would you have believed me?"

"Probably not," he admitted, "but I would have liked a warning, anyway."

"Gentlemen," the Connactic said. "I have asked a question, and I am not accustomed to waiting for answers."

Trask finally turned back to her and squinted.

"You are different..." he said. "You're not like these other plastic people. You think more deeply than they do."

"That is true, but you still haven't answered my question."

"All right," Trask said. "Why not? I've talked with Tulk while they were masquerading as humans, and now I'm talking to a computer—again, masquerading as a human. Next thing you know, I'll be talking diplomacy with one of the parents."

"The parents?" the Connactic asked.

"Yes. They call the queens of their nests parents," I explained.

"I see..." she said. "What are you here to propose, Count Trask?"

"The Sword Brothers recognize the threat that faces all of us—the entire Conclave, no matter who runs it, the Sword Brothers, and every other world that's not already burned out and consumed by these vile aliens."

"I see. You therefore seek cooperation with us?"

"I do."

"In what capacity? Elaborate." The Connactic waited.

Trask jabbed a thumb at me. "Gorman said you needed our ships. He said you needed us to go on the attack while you defend the Conclave. I don't understand why you're not simply deploying your cruisers, the vast fleet you've been talking about for decades. It seems to me you should be able to do this job yourself."

The Connactic spread her hands, and I could see in her eyes that she was thinking fast.

I wondered if she was going to blow it and explain to Trask that she did not have a vast fleet of cruisers to deploy. Demonstrating her superior intellect again, she quickly picked up on the fact that I had not informed Trask about the real situation, so she decided to keep up the falsehood that I had initiated. Perhaps she knew that, in the face of a pirate fleet, imaginary strength was better than none at all.

"You must understand, Count Trask," she said, "I have over one hundred planets to protect. The Sword Brothers have only nine. Because of this our fleet, although strong, is already engaged."

"All right..." he said. "You're saying your fleet is large enough to defend the Conclave, but not large enough to defend the Conclave *and* strike at the Chain at the same time."

"Exactly. We don't know where the seedships are going to strike next. We must destroy them before they land and infect new worlds."

Trask mulled this over, and he finally accepted her statement.

"So, in this situation, the Sword Brothers have the only other useful fleet in the known universe?"

"That is correct."

"It would seem that we're in position to charge a significant fee for our cooperation."

"That would be acceptable," the Connactic said. "We have a budget of credits allotted to this project."

"No!" Trask said lifting his hand. "Credits will not be enough. We require more."

"Elaborate."

"We demand legitimacy—a treaty between your people and mine," he said. "We want to be officially recognized as an independent state. Our nine Sword Brother worlds must be given a new, elevated status. To prove it to my brethren, I'll need an officially signed treaty between the Conclave and myself."

The Connactic appeared to consider this. She looked down for a moment, and when she looked up again, she seemed intrigued.

"We've been operating under an unofficial truce for quite a long time," she said. "You have been unofficially bribing the human captains of my patrol ships and various other officials all over the Conclave. You've never struck at the Conclave itself, but only prowled among the planets on the Fringe. This, while not optimal, has been the accepted status quo for many years. Are you proposing to change this in a material way?"

Trask smiled. "We will not strike at any Conclave planets," he offered. "They will be off-limits. At the same time, you will not strike at any Sword World planets. They will be off-limits to your ships."

There was a strange light in his eyes. I couldn't help but notice it. The light was a yellowy gleam, the light of greed.

I could tell in this rare instance he wasn't just greedy for money. He was greedy for power, prestige, and probably even greater rank among the Sword Brothers.

I had to acknowledge that this was a groundbreaking change. No one else had ever come so close to striking a deal with the Conclave in all of Sword World history.

"What about after our joint effort is concluded?" the Connactic asked.

Trask shrugged. "Once the aliens are defeated, we will go back to our old ways. We will sell our swords to those who need us—thereby relieving you of having to deal with all of the little independent planets out there. The colonies, the petty kingdoms and tyrants—they will hire us to fight their battles for them, just as they always have. Occasionally, we might strike out on our own and relieve a world of some of its riches—but all the Conclave planets will remain sacrosanct, untouched, and unraided. No Sword Brother ship or troop shall be seen at any of them."

The Connactic nodded. "This would seem to be nothing more than a formal agreement outlining the circumstances as they exist now."

"Yes," he said, "but there must be one change: My people will be allowed to travel—not in uniform, not armed, but to travel—inside the Conclave."

"To what purpose?"

"We must do deals, hold meetings, purchase products. We must be permitted to trade and socialize with the Conclave worlds without being arrested and charged with piracy."

"Ah," the Connactic said. "That is quite a request. Right now, for example, you have no less than two hundred seventy-two counts of criminal behavior against you."

Trask laughed. "That's right. I want all of that forgiven and erased."

"No," the Connactic said. "It will not be forgiven. It will not be erased. But… it will be suspended. Every sentence will be commuted. No arrest warrants against your people will be enforced."

"Isn't that the same thing?" Trask asked.

"In a way it is, but it will all be revoked if you break your half of this treaty. Besides, artificial minds prefer not to delete large swathes from our databases. It causes us an excess of processing and possible errors. You might call it 'anxiety'."

"Fine, fine, I don't care. As long as we are not being arrested and prosecuted, I'm happy."

"Hmm," the Connactic said. "When do you think you would be able to strike against the Faustian Chain?"

Trask tugged at his beard. "Well, first we must get a list of target worlds. Do you have some intel on that matter?"

"We do. We have a set of known planets that are launching seedships, as well as other suspected ones."

"What rules of engagement might we have?" he asked.

"What do you mean?" she inquired.

"I mean, if we were to bomb a planet into oblivion, would that be acceptable? What if we decide instead to land and perhaps take some prisoners or some goods that weren't owned by anyone... important?"

"Looting," she said. "You desire to loot, bomb, and otherwise pillage the Faustian Chain? Is that what you're asking?"

"Use whatever semantics you wish, ma'am. I'm asking if any restrictions will be placed upon the Sword Brothers while they're pursuing the goals that you laid out for us?"

"No," the Connactic said firmly. "We have already deemed the entire region a total loss. You will do what you have to do, and you may proceed how you will—as long as you are successful. As long as the seedships stop coming, as long as every alien of the Faustian Chain is destroyed, you may do with whatever you find there as you wish."

A chill ran through me as I heard these words. The Connactic was really unleashing some nasty hounds today. I wasn't sure she understood the full implications of what she was saying, but I figured she probably did. She had every reason to want this compromise, because she didn't have a powerful fleet to do things in a more organized way.

The conversation also didn't bode well for the state of the Faustian Chain. If the androids were willing to write off a hundred planets, they had to be in such tatters that it simply didn't matter to her what Trask and his men did. The other obvious possibility was that the Connactic was so fearful of the aliens and their awesome power that she was willing to unleash any form of destruction upon them to stop this threat from reaching the Conclave in greater strength.

Whichever was the case, or even if it was both, I found the prospects alarming. Still, I didn't say anything. It wasn't my place to participate in this negotiation. This was all between Trask and the Connactic, and as far as I could tell, they seemed to be getting along extremely well.

Eventually, after hammering out a few more details, Trask and the Connactic clasped hands. It was strange seeing a small slip of a plastic hand placed inside the massive meaty paw of the pirate. Trask was grinning, and he blew foul breath into the Connactic's face as he congratulated her on making an excellent deal. I knew that the Connactic probably couldn't smell that breath or at least wasn't disgusted by it, but I was certain she knew she had made a major decision—something that was going to alter the course of history for the Conclave, the Sword Worlds and, most of all, the Faustian Chain itself.

When the meeting was concluded, Trask turned to go, and I turned with him. The Connactic called me back.

"William Gorman," she said, "please remain here for a moment. I wish to speak with you."

"Certainly," I said, and I waited.

Trask glanced at me, briefly giving me a squinty stare, but then he walked out. I suspected that he no longer cared much about what I said to the Connactic or what arrangements I might have with her. He had just made the deal of the century as far as he was concerned, and he was ready to get out of here and go back to the Sword Worlds to start congratulating himself in front of his peers.

"What is it, Connactic?" I asked when he had left, and we two were alone.

"That was very well played, Gorman," she said. "I have underestimated you time and again. I asked for help, and you did not just bring me help. You brought me a political solution as well as a military one. I am truly impressed."

"I do what I can."

"Yes... I think you've missed your calling as a diplomat to some extent, but that's a conversation for another day. I want you to go with Trask. I want you ride along with those pirates to be my eyes and ears—an agent of the Conclave, for the sake all of humanity. I gave him free rein to do as he wishes, but even I cannot foresee everything that's going to happen when you reach that star cluster. It's quite possible good judgment will be required, and I will not be there to offer it."

I mulled that over, and I nodded. I understood what she meant. Trask was a little bit of a wild man—in fact, he was a savage. When hard pressed, he could talk as if he were civilized but really, he was anything but. The Connactic clearly felt that I as his confidant would be better equipped to temper his mercurial personality than anyone else might be. I thought that she was probably right in this assumption.

"All right," I said. "I'll do it, but I'm not your agent. I'm not directly in your pay. I'm doing this for the good of everyone."

"True," she said, "but I would like to reward you nonetheless."

"How so?"

"I'm officially dropping every criminal charge against you and your crew. The *Royal Fortune* is no longer considered stolen, nor is it the property of anyone else other than Captain William Gorman."

"All right," I said smiling. "I can hardly argue with that."

"Further," she said, "there will be a rather large deposit of credits in an account which is cleared to operate anywhere in the Conclave. It's the least I can do to give you some of the benefits I just handed out to those literal barbarians from the Sword Worlds."

I smiled, nodded, and made appreciative sounds. "This is excellent news."

"Of course," she said, "all of this is meaningless if you can't fly out to the Chain, defeat the enemy and return intact. So please do your best to succeed in this campaign."

"I will do my damnedest, ma'am."

"You are dismissed, Gorman."

I spun around and marched out of the place. A few hours later we were back aboard *Royal Fortune* and jetting toward the slip-gate.

Trask and I were both smiling, while offering nothing to the rest of the crew who looked curious and worried. We did not discuss anything about the deal with any of them. We both instinctively knew that when you're given a huge windfall, the best move for any pirate was to take the money and run.

Chapter Thirty-Four

Count Trask was overjoyed by the deal he'd managed to wangle from the Connactic. In his mind, he'd been unbelievably fortunate.

I did not enlighten him. Instead, I added to his good cheer, telling him he'd done a miraculous job of negotiating.

The key difference between his frame of reference and mine was my knowledge of the Conclave's military weakness. If Trask had known the truth—that the Connactic barely had enough ships to put one above every planet that she truly cared about—he would have sought to take advantage of her position and possibly blown the whole deal.

He might have decided to run raids, maybe even against the Conclave worlds themselves. That would have been profitable for him but disastrous for the rest of us. Humans did not need to fight against humans these days, and androids did not need to fight the humans either. Not even the Tulk, wherever they were lurking, needed to fight either species.

No, all eyes needed to be turned toward the real enemy—the one that planned to destroy us all. The aliens from the Faustian Chain must be defeated.

Accordingly, I said nothing about fictional cruisers, and I talked down the capabilities of the aliens from the Chain at every turn. Every chance I got, I told Trask that we had been to the Chain, and we'd seen very little in the way of an opposing fleet. This got me a few strange looks from Droad, Jort and the others who knew the truth, but they were all smart enough not to say anything. They followed my lead, and they kept their mouths shut.

Our first move was to return to the Sword Worlds. Upon our arrival, I was somewhat concerned to have been met by a small fleet of six ships. Three were destroyers, and the other three were escort class vessels. There was no way *Royal Fortune* could defeat these warships, except possibly by out-running them.

Trask was unconcerned. "They wear my emblem," he said. "Don't worry—head right on into the middle of them, and I will speak to them."

We did just that. He commanded the lead destroyers to allow him to board. He and his consort Astrid exited my ship, and each boarded a different destroyer. Very smart, I thought to myself, to be romantically involved with someone who could loyally back up your claims with a ship of her own.

Together, the small flotilla of ships returned to Gladius. We stayed in orbit aboard *Royal Fortune* this time, but we also tapped into the live-streaming grid services that the Sword Worlds offered. These were grim affairs. Most of the entertainment consisted of live executions for minor punishments, along with the news of the day, videos of raids carried out, advertisements for new mercenaries to join one ship's crew or another and similar content.

Along about dinnertime, Trask came online and made a planet-wide appeal. He outlined his agreement with the Connactic. I noticed that he made no mention of her being an android, because that probably would have freaked out the populace in general and possibly lessen his claim to fame. Regardless, he did a good job of taking full and complete credit for having negotiated the deal of the century.

"We no longer have to hide in the dark," he said. "If any of you have relatives on Scorpii, for example, or Prospero—or perhaps you would just like to visit Tranquility for purposes of entertainment, business, what have you—you can do it now. We're all free of concern over arrest or harassment."

This was met by resounding up-votes, and the positive response seemed genuine. His own followers and those of others who were physically present in the live audience seemed to be overjoyed.

It occurred to me then that the Sword Worlds were not quite what they had seemed to be. I had assumed they were self-contained in that the sons and daughters who joined the mercenary armies and crews were from the Sword Worlds—but maybe that wasn't always true. It was possible that it wasn't just the native population that fought so well, but rather criminals from abroad who had joined their ranks over the years.

I'd noticed, for example, quite a number of people from Jort's home planet of Scorpii who served among the mercenary companies. They had never been a people that were highly law-abiding in nature. I could easily imagine that a person such as Jort himself might have run off to join the Sword Brothers when things became too hot at home. Nodding to myself, I realized that amnesty might be quite a selling point among the Sword Brothers.

Trask was winding down his hard-sell of the good parts of the deal. Now, it was time to call his people to arms. He'd let them sniff the carrot, but we'd finally gotten down to the reality of the stick.

"As part of our agreement," he said, "we brothers of the nine Sword Worlds are to provide our best troops, our best ships and strike hard against the alien menace that comes from the Faustian Chain."

In my long life of adventure, I'd rarely met anyone who wanted to pay the price for something nice they had bought for themselves. The Sword Brothers were no exception to this rule.

The cheers died down and transformed into mutters and occasional jeers, while objections were fielded from a dozen barons and knight-captains—anyone who commanded ships of their own.

They demanded to know what would happen in their absence—would their unprotected home worlds be raided by the Conclave? Trask assured them that none of this would happen, because the Connactic needed them—needed them to be the point of her spear while she attacked the aliens. A lot of grumbling and a great debate began, but in the end, Trask won through.

He received the support of virtually every captain on Gladius. It was not always eager and enthusiastic support, but they were in agreement—they could not pass up this deal. They had long lived in fear that the Conclave would one day decide they had gone too far and would strike against them and destroy their pirate's nest on the Fringe. To be free of that fear forever was simply too tempting, simply too good for anyone from the Sword Worlds to pass up.

Returning to his destroyer, Trask demanded that I follow his ship. I soon joined the small entourage of warships trailing in his wake. Moving as a squadron, we went through the slipgate and visited Flamberge. A day or two later, we moved on to Saber and then Claymore.

On each world the story was the same. Trask was initially met with doubt, suspicion and sometimes invective, but after a few days of explaining his negotiated settlement with the Conclave, the pirates of each planet eventually agreed to send at least half of their forces with him on this great crusade. By the time we reached the worlds known as Katana and Tulwar, I began to marvel at his strategy.

"I know what you're doing, Trask," I said, pulling him aside for a cup of coffee one morning as we orbited yet another world full of distrustful pirates.

"How's that, Gorman?" he asked.

"You're visiting each planet in the reverse order of how much they hate you, the most affirming to the most loathing and oppositional." Trask grinned.

"Right you are, old mate. I'm no dolt."

"Then," I said, "to further snowball the effect of your recruitment, you're insisting that one ship from the leading lord on each planet join your little fleet to personally demonstrate and attest that they have already joined the flotilla."

"That's exactly right, Gorman," he said. "I'm not as wellloved everywhere as I am on Gladius."

I snorted, as this was more than true. Trask was not even well-liked on Gladius, and on most of the other planets, he was damned near hated.

Still, overall, I had to admit he was at least respected on every planet. He was a wily, cagey, old man who was as smart as he was vicious. By demonstrating to each planet he visited that all the previous ones had agreed to join him, he was exerting more and more pressure upon each new world to go with the flow.

Katana's population, for example, didn't like Trask, didn't like Gladius, and wanted nothing to do with either of them. Although they would probably have refused if he had started with them, after he showed up with the support of the majority of the Sword Worlds behind him, they had to do it. They had to worry that if they attempted to shirk this duty, if they stood out from the rest, the others might turn upon them like dogs in a pack that has gotten too hungry one cold night in winter.

"Very well played," I told Trask.

The days had worn on, but less than three weeks after we had left the Connactic's office, we had an agreement with all nine of the Sword Worlds. Gathering the fleet into one armada proved to take two weeks more, but eventually we had enough supplies, men, and ships to impress any star system we visited.

In fact, it was my own estimation that this force might be able to conquer the Conclave itself. This was obviously why the Conclave had ignored the depredations of Trask and his Sword Brothers for so many years. Again, as usual, it came down to a budgeting issue with the Conclave.

Year after year, they had determined it was easier and cheaper to maintain a fictional fleet and to allow the pirates to run wild on the outer Fringe. What a risk they had taken! I could hardly believe they'd depended on a single deception for decades. It was a marvel to think their posturing had worked for so long—but none of that mattered much right now.

We flew as a single force, one hundred thirty-six ships strong, measuring in size from my tiny ship on up to custom-built destroyers that could carry a thousand men with a crew of five hundred on top of that. The fleet bristled with cannons, powerful engines and armor.

Together, we headed to Vindar. The Conclave had made sure that we were allowed to pass through the slip-gates to Vindar and then beyond. They activated the second gate, the one that led to the Faustian Chain, informing us that it would be switched back on for several minutes every thirty days from here on out for our possible return.

Trask was not happy about this new wrinkle to the grand plan, but it was too late for him to make fresh demands of the Connactic. To do so would be to signal the fact that he himself had not known of these arrangements. His monstrous coalition might well crumble if he showed any lack of certainty, any capacity for error. He had to be flawless, or his own fleet might turn upon him.

As I was still a convenient scapegoat, he sent me a few raw messages, blaming me for withholding critical information. I made no response.

Eventually, he stopped blaming me and ordered his fleet to follow his flagship into the slip-gate. The Sword Brothers ships did as they were commanded. They went through eagerly, not one at a time, but five at a time.

My own small ship *Royal Fortune* hung back and slinked in the rear of the formation. My caution was due to my greater familiarity with the places where we were heading.

We arrived sometime later at the Chara system. This time, the entrance was a hotbed of activity. Instead of a few quiet lumps of icy debris with organic pods hiding among them, we were met with a wide-open firefight.

Trask's ships had been intercepted the moment they'd come through the slip-gate by what appeared to be thousands of tiny vessels flown by the Skaintz. The aliens were no match for the human ships because there were simply too many of us. Hundreds had been destroyed before *Royal Fortune* even got there, and the surviving enemy pods were quickly located, targeted, and destroyed by the thousands.

"Gorman," Count Trask shouted, his head an ugly hologram hanging over my planning table and glaring at me. I opened the channel and attempted to project good cheer.

"Wow," I said, "you're tearing them up already, aren't you, Trask?"

"Why didn't you tell me there'd be an ambush?" he demanded.

I looked surprised. "Because there wasn't one the last time we came here."

He pointed a thick finger at my face. "You, then," he said, "*you* caused this. My grand entrance has turned into a debacle."

"I caused this? How's that?"

"Because the last time you were here, you pissed off these aliens so badly that they've lain in wait for months for your return. Worse, you hung back, clearly showing you were aware of this possibility!"

I spread my hands, admitting nothing. "Think about it this way, Trask. You're going to have to fight these aliens anyway, so it might as well be here and now. No one in this fleet is doubting that the enemy is where you said they would be. They all believe in you now."

Trask grumbled something detestable under his foul breath and cut the channel. We went back to watching the fleet as they systematically destroyed every alien pod in the region.

Moving as one, the hundred and thirty-one remaining ships turned toward Chara B—the cold, dead planet where we'd previously met up with a few of the enemy.

We cruised into orbit, landed and investigated. Trask's men found very little of value or danger. Every alien encountered was promptly destroyed.

This brought a modicum of happiness to Trask and his army. They spent a bit of time stealing everything they could find, various minerals and manufactured components. In general, they were disappointed by the lack of loot, but at least as far as could be determined, not a single Sword Brother had lost his life on Chara B.

They boarded their ships again, less than a day later, and started heading toward the next planet on our list. There, I gave a specific warning to Trask describing what I'd met up with some months ago.

"A cannon, you say? A ground cannon of such vast size and power that it's able to fire pods all the way to the Conclave? That's hard to believe, Gorman."

"It may be a surprise, even a shock," I said, "but you've seen the results on the other side. The skies are raining with seedships. Every day, more of them come."

"Huh," Trask said. "This isn't good news. Even if we kill every alien in the Chain, those ships are still going to be raining on our planets for decades."

"That's right," I said. "It takes a long, long time to get to our star cluster from here at sub-light speeds, but we might as well get started wrecking these aliens right now, don't you think?"

"Yes. There's not a moment to lose."

We flew onward in a great swarm toward Chara A. When we were about half a million kilometers from the surface of that devastated world, the enemy made their move. They must have been watching us since we'd entered the system several days earlier. We had taken quite a while to get from the slip-gate all the way to Chara B and then Chara A.

I'd been concerned about the time wasted looking for loot for tactical reasons, but I hadn't said anything. After all, it was Trask's fleet. Who was I? Only a lone gunrunner. I didn't have the authority to be telling others what they should and shouldn't do.

In the end, the truth was that we'd given the enemy too much time to prepare. The aliens waited while the planet spun around. Chara A had a slow rotation rate, but at last, their great, ground cannon lined up with our incoming fleet.

Then, they fired the massive weapon.

Even as we watched, it went off like a shotgun. A swarm of projectiles blasted up into our faces. These were tiny pods, as before, but I knew that this time they were not intended to fly across the cold void between star systems and invade our distant worlds. Instead, these pods were meant to intercept our fleet and do damage to us.

Trask laughed at the threat at first.

"Look at that," he said, booming on the holoplate of every ship in the fleet. "These fools fired tiny pebbles wrapped up in leaves toward our fleet, as if that's going to stop us."

He studied the incoming pods bemusedly. But after several long minutes, he became more serious.

"Fleet, disperse your ships, advance in a broad disk, and fire upon every pod the moment it gets into range."

The fleet did as he ordered, and the tactic was at least partly successful. The difficulty involved in targeting the tiny pods coming our way was twofold. First of all, they were dark and emitted no reflections, no metallic signatures. They didn't even show up on our sensors at first, shedding electromagnetic pulses as we pinged away. Being small and organic in nature, they were difficult to detect at range.

Secondly, as we were on an attack vector and heading directly into the swarm, they were coming toward us rather quickly. It wasn't their velocity that was a problem, it was our own velocity. Trask's ships were traveling at a high rate of speed—more than double that of the pods themselves. Like two aircars converging in a single sky-lane, we were coming together fast.

Fortunately, Trask's ships were not without defenses. Point defense guns chattered, firing sprays of beams, pellets, and tiny smart missiles. The pods began to pop and vaporize as they drew closer.

During the final seconds when the two lines met, they were able to return fire. These pods were not seedships. They were firing missiles straight into us as we rushed to meet them. We were flying right into the teeth of a thousand tiny warships.

Trask cursed, and he cut the feed from his ship to all of ours. His head disappeared, and I knew that he was shouting desperate orders upon his bridge—just like every other captain in the fleet.

"What are we going to do Captain?" Jort demanded. "These crazy pirates are going to get us all killed."

"Come hard about, Huan. Head up out of the plane of the ecliptic and hit the gas. Let's get away from this swarm of pirates and enemy pods."

We did exactly that. Flying up and out of the formation, we avoided the battle. There was little we could do, anyway. I had Jort manning the neutrino cannon in the rear, firing at pods as best he could. We destroyed a few—but the pods themselves were not the real danger. It was the tiny missiles they carried that did the damage.

Although hundreds of pods were destroyed, they each fired several missiles. Quite a number of these were destroyed one way or another as well, but Trask had failed to employ countermeasures—to pump out chaff, to send out jamming signals and the like. He hadn't really expected to be hit by the missiles, I could tell.

Some of those missiles made their way through, and a dozen ships were hit, two of them exploding. One was a large destroyer, and I knew that at least a thousand men aboard her had perished.

Despite our losses, the pirates broke through, angrily charging onward. They locked their weapons onto the ground cannon, which fired again. This time they were much more prepared to destroy the pods, even as they flew up out of the atmosphere at escape velocity. Using bombs, torpedoes, and heavy mounted cannons, they bombarded the planet.

They utterly destroyed the entire region surrounding the cannon, ultimately cracking the world's crust and opening up a gush of magma and smoke. A dozen new volcanoes were created, which I knew would soon envelop the entire world in soot and ash—most likely eradicating all living things for years to come.

It was hardly a glowing victory. Hours later, when Trask ordered his fleet to leave orbit, he left behind a smoking hulk of a planet, one that had once been lovely and full of life.

Now, it was no more than a cinder in space, and useless to anyone.

Chapter Thirty-Five

A few days later we proceeded from the Chara system to the next colony on our list: Minerva. Less than a lightyear away, it took us weeks to get there because there was no slip-gate between Chara and Minerva—but in a way, that was an advantage.

We arrived first in the out-system where there was a large Oort cloud encircling the star. It was filled with chunks of ice and debris, which we wove our ships carefully through. We took a stealthy approach, but when you're flying around one hundred and thirty ships, it's hard to be sneaky. We did not expect to surprise the aliens at Minerva.

As we passed by the far-flung gas giants, we saw signs of mining activity. Trask immediately summoned me to his destroyer. I agreed to go, ignoring the wild speculations of Jort and the concerned noises made by Rose and Morwyn.

I shuttled myself alone in a tiny capsule to Trask's flagship. There, I greeted him on his command deck, asking what was on his mind. He waggled an accusatory finger under my nose.

"You screwed me last time, mate, but not again."

"How's that, Count Trask?" I asked in a congenial tone.

All around me was a large group of stern-faced officers. They weren't all just knight-captains from Trask's direct command, either. There were plenty of other dukes, counts and barons standing on the deck with us. Many had their arms crossed and most had angry-looking eyes.

Right away I was on my guard. It only made sense, I realized, that Trask had decided to fault me for everything that had gone wrong so far during this mission. It must be hard to hold together a coalition of pirates this large—in fact, to my knowledge, no one had ever done it before.

My mind swam with defenses, but I did not speak. I just smiled in as disarming a fashion as I could manage. I looked as calm, innocent, and confident as possible.

"Last time," Trask said, "you gave me no warning at all about the pod ships waiting for us at the slip-gate. Worse, when we came within range of that huge land cannon, the aliens surprised us with a blast. Lastly, their many missiles have damaged a dozen of these fine men's ships." He pointed around at the group of frowning lords that encircled us.

Apparently, Trask was in hot water with the pirates. Perhaps they'd challenged his leadership. He must have been a little desperate to try to blame me for all this. I didn't think it would work, but you never knew.

It left me needing to make a decision, and I had to make it fast—was I going to side with Trask or put the blame back on him?

Of course, the whole thing was absurd. To my mind we hadn't yet lost many ships. The fact that this group was complaining about the destruction of less than five percent of the fleet seemed extreme, but that's how it was with these guys. The Sword Brothers hadn't gotten to where they could terrorize an entire star cluster by taking frequent losses.

Deciding to help Trask the only way I could, I threw my hands wide. "You got me, Count Trask," I said. "I made a big mistake. I should have been more detailed and predictive about the alien capabilities. To be honest, I just didn't think that cannon could be used to fire warships as well as seedships."

Trask blinked twice, and I thought he might be on the verge of a smile, but he was too smart for that. He kept his stern gaze on me along with that waggling finger.

"I know," he said, "that you were a general running an entire division of android soldiers just months ago. Could all of this be nothing but a ruse by the Conclave? Here we are out in enemy space losing our ships and our men—where are the Conclave backups? How come they're doing nothing? We're doing it all!"

"Well..." I said, thinking over that new angle, "they did cover a couple planets back in the Conclave. In fact, they are playing defense, and we're playing offense—that was the split. Do you really want to fly with patrol ships right off your wing?"

"No, no!" more than one of the other pirates chimed in. They hated the idea of teaming with the androids. They hated it even more than the idea of being out here risking their butts alone.

Trask glanced around, measuring the group's mood. He could read a room better than anyone.

"That *is* an important thought," he said. "I'll put it to a vote. Gentlemen, Lords, Captains, what do you say? Should we turn around now, head back to the Conclave, and demand that our android brothers march with us? Perhaps a troop ship and a patrol ship should follow every one of ours. Perhaps we could tease a few of their cruisers into joining us as well. I'd love to see them fighting with us, side-by-side."

Hairy heads shook, and there was a lot of grumbling. Trask pointed to a man from Katana—a duke, by the look of him. "What say you, Duke Oslo?"

"I say that's an insane idea. All they would do is categorize our every infraction. How can we loot any of these planets with androids following us around? We *are* assuming there will be loot out here after all, eh?" Here he slapped an arm over the shoulder of the Sword Brother to either side, and they shared a greedy chuckle between them.

"Good point," Trask said, and he turned back to me. "That's another bad idea, Gorman. What else have you got?"

Naturally, it didn't make any sense at all that I'd come to be in this position. I was a minor player, an associate at best, but now I was determining tactics and even strategy for the Sword Brothers' fleet. I realized this was simply because no one else wanted to take the blame for anything that might go wrong.

This was my moment, so I decided it was time for a fresh idea.

"How about this?" I said. "Perhaps we should send out an advance scout force—a small group of ships just to tease the enemy defenses. If they strike down a ship or three, that'll be far better than having our entire force ambushed."

"What's the point, Gorman?"

"We're facing aliens that we don't really understand. We don't know their capabilities. We don't know what they can or can't do. We're bound to get surprised again without doing any scouting."

"Huh," Trask said. He turned to address the group again, and the idea was generally met with approval.

"I like it, too," Trask said. "What's more, I want you to be our scout, Gorman."

"Me?" I said, caught off-guard. "Me alone?"

"Yes. By my measure, you have the fastest ship here. Our ships are fat-bellied tubs, built to haul lots of loot, take hits, and carry troops to battle. Your ship is a sleek smuggling vessel unlike anything else I have. Who better to be my scout?"

Right then, I came to a realization. I was the one being fooled with, here. I was the one being played. Trask had probably predetermined this direction in the conversation, and he had pounced the moment I'd fallen for it.

It was pretty obvious from the excited response of everyone else on the command deck that there would be no getting out of it, so I figured I might as well play the part of the hero.

"All right, Trask," I said, "I'll do it, but there will be a fee."

"A fee?" he scoffed, shaking his head. "Here it comes! What special payment are you requesting now, runner?"

"I want samples of all the weaponry we've captured from the enemy so far."

"What?"

"I know you've got *something*, Trask. Your ships have been hit by missiles—surely there's some unexploded ordnance. You must have taken a few chunks from the various pods, perhaps when we landed on Chara A."

"Yes, yes, yes," Trask interrupted. "We've taken a few samples. What of it?"

"Well, there will be plenty of time for you to get more later on. Load the specimens you have now aboard my ship."

"For what purpose, Gorman?"

"I might get some value out of them," I said, "when and if we return to the Conclave."

"Ah," Trask said, laughing. Several of the other pirates were smiling as well. "Always the trader, Gorman. Always the man seeking to make a credit on the side. I can appreciate that. Since you're not asking for money directly, I will grant your wish. We can always collect more, as you say—we've got several planets to hit after this one."

"Good enough."

And so, a number of Sword Brothers lab techs—rare nerds among a fighting people—loaded a large number of carefully boxed specimens into a capsule. I climbed into my own capsule and left his ship, towing my prize back to *Royal Fortune*. When I got there, I played the part of the triumphant dealmaker.

"Crew," I said. "I've got fantastic news! We're all rich!"

"What? What?" Jort demanded. His eyes were already glazing yellow with greed. "You have credits, don't you Captain? Many credits—we've been paid a reward!"

"Yes," I said nodding to him. "In a way, you are correct."

"In a way?" he said, frowning suddenly.

Huan came forward next, and he began poking at the capsule full of specimens. "These are alien body parts," he said, "and unexploded ordnance from the enemy. Most of it is cryogenically frozen. I doubt it's viable."

"And that's a good thing, too," I said. "I don't want it to come alive and kill us in our bunks. We just need specimens worthy of study."

Huan frowned and looked deeper into the crate. "I'm not seeing any great treasures."

"Well then, you're half-blind," I complained. "The Conclave people will spend a lot of credits to get this stuff. They aren't out here fighting these aliens, so they'll want to know what they're up against. The Connactic will pay us richly for this." The group kind of shrugged, somewhat unconvinced, but they were willing to accept my bold statements as truth for now. "And so," I told them, "we've been paid in advance for our troubles!"

"Paid in advance for *what*?" Droad asked, speaking up for the first time. He'd been watching me, knowing I was going through some kind of elaborate ruse, but without knowing why.

"To play our part as scouts during this invasion," I said.

They all blinked at me for a moment, but the moment didn't last. Quickly, there were scowls. These scowls turned into scoffing and objections. Jort stomped his feet, Morwyn declared us all dead ahead of our time, and even Rose shook her head sadly. She studied the deck in defeat.

"You've done it again, Captain," Jort said. "You have gone from a smart man to a dumb man in a matter of minutes."

"Nonsense, Jort," I said. "Listen, we are the smartest crew and the fastest ship in this fleet. We will simply dash ahead of the rest of them, encounter and inspect the defenses of the enemy, and—"

"...and then be blown to pieces," Jort complained.

"No, no," I said. "We'll outrun whatever missiles they throw at us. We'll take an oblique approach to Minerva so that we don't get caught up in the blast from potential ground cannons... Don't worry so much. The best part is—" I said, slapping my hand on the capsule that I brought across from Trask's flagship. "We've already been paid for our efforts."

Ice had formed on the skin of the capsule when I brought it over, and part of it sloughed off now. It landed between my feet with a crash, shattering on the deck and rattling into the corners.

The crew was somewhat disgusted, but they were also resigned to our shared fate. They argued minimally as we moved away from our safe position at the rear of the fleet and took the point.

Gathering speed, we moved out of the fleet formation. We were soon hundreds of thousands of kilometers ahead of the rest of the flotilla. Reaching the gas giant with the mining station first, we found it abandoned.

We passed this by. There were refueling stations over the gas giant, but the fleet didn't have time to siphon gas from the planet below. Instead, we used the planet's large gravity well to sling ourselves towards the inner worlds.

Like many star systems, rocky planets that could support life were found orbiting close to the central star. A full day after Trask had saddled me with our new scouting duty, we were on the final approach to the colony planet at Minerva.

The way I saw it, the key to surviving as a scout was to not fly directly into the teeth of the enemy. We didn't take a direct path between the pirate fleet and Minerva itself. Instead, we swung on a wide arc at a high rate of speed.

This maneuver threw us many thousands of kilometers outside of our optimal flightpath. The new arc allowed *Royal Fortune* to evade whatever might be lurking in the space between Minerva and the Sword Brother's attacking fleet.

Trask, of course, was observing my maneuvers. He figured out pretty quickly what I was doing.

He contacted me on a private channel. His ugly head appeared on the holotable, and he glared at me.

"What's this bullshit, Gorman? What are you trying to pull now?"

"Is there a problem, sir? We're well ahead of your fleet. We'll reach Minerva long before you do, and we'll give you a complete report in a few hours."

"Nonsense," he said. "You're spending a lot of extra fuel and time making this big circle-jerk maneuver. I don't want to see any more of it. You are hereby ordered to fly straight into the teeth of that planet and find out what they've got waiting for us. That's the purpose of this entire exercise."

"Count Trask," I said. "Did I not back you up in every way when you surprised me with a large meeting of your comrades?"

"Hardly..." the pirate grumbled.

"That's not true, sir. I accepted the blame for whatever you bothered to throw my way. I helped you maintain control of your fleet, then I accepted this mission with a meager payment."

"Well... maybe some of that's true."

"Good," I said. "We're in agreement, then. Let me fly my ship my way, and you'll get your scouting report before your fleet comes into danger."

"All right, all right," he said, and he cut off the channel.

"Meager payment, is it?" Rose said.

"What's that?"

"You just gave yourself away," she said. "You admitted that our payment is a farce."

My whole crew was looking at me. They'd overheard the conversation, and I'd let slip a few things.

"Listen," I said, "if any of you people think you can handle Trask better than I can, tell me right now. The next time he makes a request for a private meeting, I'll put you in the capsule and send you over there. Do I have any takers?"

I had none, of course. Not even Droad, who might have managed it, was willing to put his hat into the ring. So, they all shut up, which was just fine by me.

We cruised onward, making a big circular arc and coming in on the far side of the planet rather than directly into orbit from the front. On the sunward side, about fifty thousand kilometers out, we saw something curious on Minerva's surface.

"What's *that*?" I asked. "Huan, I need a sensor analysis."

"It's some kind of large, malignant growth, if I had to say, sir. Organic technology of some kind."

We used our instruments, and we beamed every scanning device we had toward the bulging mound. We found it was indeed organic in nature. That wasn't a surprise, but the mound seemed to be on the move, changing in formation. I wasn't quite sure what to make of it.

Finally, as we drew in closer, it suddenly puffed up to an improbable size.

"Look at that thing. How's that even possible?" I asked.

"It looks like a boil that's about to burst," Droad said.

Rose made disgusted sounds in response, but as if he were a prophet, Droad was proven correct. The massive mound had grown so tall now that it was up higher than the wispy clouds. The tip of it popped, and a spray of liquid droplets flew up and out of the atmosphere, escaping into space.

At this range, they appeared to be droplets, but our measurements showed that each individual teardrop-shaped object was something like the size of our own ship.

"They're pods," Droad said. "Living pods again, but they're not like the others. They seem to be going into orbit—masses of them."

"Yes..." I said, recording it all and transmitting it back to Trask. "They're spreading out, too."

As we watched, the explosion of teardrop-shaped pods spread into low orbit over the planet. They didn't darken the surface, but there were so many that soon there was one within roughly every kilometer of another, enveloping the globe. It was as if someone had launched hundreds of thousands, possibly millions of satellites all at once.

"They've got to be mines," Rose said, and I turned to her in astonishment because I suspected that she was right.

"Yes..." I said, "mines, or something like that—something to intercept anyone who lands or gets too close. Organic, living mines..."

"Will they crash into us or what?" Rose asked.

"I don't know, and I don't intend to go low enough to find out. Let's talk to Trask again."

I contacted the count, and he unhappily reviewed the data with me on a private channel.

"No chance I can get you to fly a little closer and see what those pods do when they sense a ship nearby?" he asked me.

"None whatsoever, Count Trask."

He nodded, unsurprised, and he heaved a sigh. "All right. Yet another trick from these disgusting aliens. What do you think we should do, Gorman? You're the man on the spot."

I thought about it, and I stabbed a finger down into the hologram that represented Minerva. My finger punched through the cloud cover and the swarming pods, and I indicated the mountain itself.

"How about we destroy that mass?" I suggested.

"From range?"

"Yes," I said. "What's the point of getting in close enough that we have to fight this cloud of alien debris? Let's bomb that mound, bomb the planet, and ignore all these little flying droplets of garbage."

"Agreed," Trask said, heaving a sigh. "The council won't like it, though. They're going to be angry. They're already upset over how little loot we've found on this mission so far. We've lost ships, and we've gained nothing. I'm losing my grip on them, Gorman. You know as well as I do that you can't keep a pirate fleet together for long without profit."

"I understand, sir, but if we suffer more losses in the way of ships and men, they'll abandon you all the sooner."

Trask agreed, then he went to talk to his fellow lords. After some stormy sessions, his fleet glided close to Minerva. They stayed high, in a far-flung orbit.

Synchronizing their launches for maximum impact, the fleet fired all at once. A big barrage of missiles fell down toward Minerva, plunging toward the planet.

Countless pods moved to intercept. Some of them were successful, but there were simply too many warheads, too many brilliant explosions, each of which swept hundreds of pods out of the way.

Half the warheads plunged through the atmosphere and struck that swollen, humping mound that had grown up on the surface of Minerva. The mound was blown apart, and the planet was sterilized.

Chapter Thirty-Six

After we left Minerva behind, we traveled to other star systems that the Conclave's astronomical team had identified as probable launch points of seedships. This included multiple worlds that we found to be burned-out cinders or consumed husks. There was still some life, but it was on the level of lichen and insects, with very few plants or animals of any size or significance.

Once a planet was consumed like this and turned into a virtual desert, it was left behind by the Skaintz. Only an occasional killbeast corpse or a rare, living specimen remained on these planets, dying slowly of hunger and thirst. They reminded me of the pathetic specimens we had found in the Sardez system on that frozen planetoid where, for me, all of this had started.

One day we came upon a planet that was warmer than normal than most. There were cool polar regions at the top and bottom. At the upper and lower latitudes were tropical to temperate zones. A band of harsh desert ran like a belt around the middle of the world.

I knew this planet to be Garm, a world that—while it was reportedly somewhat smaller and warmer than old Earth—had been colonized long ago and was the first of many to be invaded by the aliens.

Droad had never looked so glum as he did when we parked in orbit to start scanning. Trask and his fleet were well behind us, as paranoid as ever. They again allowed us the privilege of doing their scouting for them.

"It's gone," Droad said. "It's all gone. Everything here is dead and gone. There were so many plants, animals, and people I could tell you about—but they were all destroyed decades ago."

"Is this your home world, Droad?" I asked him.

"No," he said, "but it was the first planet that I ever came to govern—the first world on which I encountered the Skaintz. It was my adopted home and, in a sense, my first failure in this long, long war."

I nodded at him, and I didn't press him for further details. He was clearly unhappy to talk about it.

We completed the scan but found very little life and very little of anything else useful. When we reported back to Trask, he cursed excessively about the lack of loot to be had before he and his fleet finally dared to come close to the world.

They did their own scans, landed search parties, and found a few items of limited value in the old ruins of the wealthiest people of Garm. They stole what they could and hauled it away, grumbling about how thin the payoff had been. Then they climbed aboard their ships and returned to space.

We moved on then to the next world on our list. This one, to me, had more promise, as it was a larger planet and highly organic in nature. It had been colonized with only a small population. Perhaps the aliens had skipped it due to its lack of amenities or any significant external transmissions that might have attracted them from across the stars.

It was at the far end of the star cluster, so we dared hope that this world might yet harbor a human outpost. When we arrived in the star system, we were almost immediately disappointed. The slip-gate was dead, and there was no mining activity on the asteroids or comets that swung through the star system. Moving deeper into the system, past some of the larger planets in the out-system, we came to the jewel-like world known as Sapphire.

Immediately when we laid eyes upon it, we knew how it had come by its name. The oceans here did seem to be of a different hue, a lovely blue that was lighter than the slate gray or the dirty green color that characterized great basins of water on most planets.

Looking Sapphire up in the planetary database, I discovered this was partly due to the shallow nature of the seas here and their sandy silicon bottoms. The world did not have a high metal content. It was organics-rich, and it was fairly low in seismic activity. All this served to make a surface that was somewhat uniform in nature. In other words, the mountains were low, the seas were shallow, and the continents were universally lush and green.

Feeling hopeful, we glided closer and closer to this destination. It was the last on the list that we were to investigate.

"The planet seems untouched," Morwyn said. "I can't believe it."

"You're right," Droad said. "This is quite a surprise. Either the aliens didn't know about it and skipped over it, or possibly the humans here have managed to hold them at bay."

"Excellent news either way," I said. I relayed our initial findings to Count Trask, but naturally he was hesitant.

"Go in for a closer look, Gorman," he ordered.

Having little to no choice, I shook my head and flew onward, closing the distance with the large, lovely world. As we got closer, we found that it was not just the oceans that were as blue as sapphires. The jungles were also as green as emeralds, and the icy polar caps reminded me of diamonds.

Turning on our active scanning systems, we pinged, and we scanned, and we sent all kinds of signals toward the planetary surface. Nothing that bounced back indicated anything was wrong. There was lush life and no toxins in the atmosphere. It seemed too good to be true.

"This world has a moon, too," Droad said. He was standing up now, leaning forward and smiling—a rare thing for Governor Droad.

"A moon?" I said. "It must be on the opposite side of the planet. All right, let's swing around in a wide arc and have a look." I adjusted my navigational controls.

Droad watched me for a moment. "Paranoid to the last, aren't you, Gorman?" he teased.

I accepted the dig with a shrug. "It's paid off for me so far—hasn't it? My career is still ongoing, long after the usual expiration of people in my chosen field."

Being unable to argue my point, Droad nodded and turned back to the glowing images we were seeing from Sapphire. He seemed honestly happy for the first time in a month.

Perhaps this single world in all the Faustian Chain was still unspoiled, pure, and pristine—untouched by the aliens. Could there be people alive on the surface? It was possible. We had begun to truly hope, but those hopes were dashed when the moon came into view.

We swung around and caught sight of the single large satellite that orbited Sapphire. It came out from behind the planet's dark side with a shadow cutting across it. Light from the distant, central star formed a crescent across the unthinkable.

"What is *that*?" Jort demanded, pointing a thick, wavering finger at the holotable. "There's something *bad* on that moon—something all over it!"

It was true. The moon, as it turned out, was what they call a water-moon, which is essentially a lesser-sized planet with a similar climate. It actually had a thin atmosphere with plant and animal life of its own—or at least it had once had these things.

Now, instead of being a further beacon of beauty, we saw a world with another gigantic malignant tumor. A massive growth pulsed upon the surface. This heinous mound of organic matter was even larger than the one we'd encountered before on Minerva.

"How can that *be*?" Jort exclaimed. "Why would the aliens grow one of their disgusting mountains of flesh upon the moon, but ignore the planet itself? It's like they ate the appetizer, but ignored the steak."

I squinted at the puzzling situation. I was as baffled as Droad and Jort. Huan, however, was the first to speak up with a possible answer.

"I think I know what we've found," he said.

We turned to him expectantly.

Huan strange eyes ran over us and his instruments. "I'm not certain, mind you, not being an alien myself."

Jort snorted at this rudely.

I knew what he was thinking, and if any one of us was part alien, it was definitely Huan. I lifted a cautionary hand, so Jort shut up.

"Go on, Huan," I said.

"It's just this... we've seen planetary husks left as burned-out wrecks, one after another. Some of them have literally gone to seed, attempting to infect further worlds. Most of these are utterly devoid of life and consumed, but what if the aliens are a little smarter than we give them credit for? What if they realize it might take a while to get a new foothold in the next star cluster? Wouldn't it make sense to leave one last excellent meal stashed away just in case they're stuck here, unable to find new worlds for a long, long time?"

"Ah-ha!" Jort said. "I get it. You're saying they saved this planet on purpose. It's like a snack jammed into your pocket for later."

"Yes," Huan said. "That's exactly what I'm saying."

Droad put his two hands on the holotable, and he hung his head between his shoulders. I could tell he was feeling defeated. Instead of finding a living human colony that was still holding out, we'd found instead the last bastion of the enemy.

Finally, after ten seconds of grim silence, Droad lifted his head again. He turned to me. "We must destroy that moon. With some luck, we can finish it and hunt down any aliens that might be down on the main planet itself. Perhaps we can still save this single world of the Faustian Chain."

Our eyes met, and I thought about his proposition. I realized it was a long shot, but I nodded and clapped my hands together.

"I'm sure we can do it," I said. "I'll talk to Trask."

Chapter Thirty-Seven

After reporting to Count Trask, I was surprised to see the quivering mountain of flesh on Sapphire's water moon hump up to an improbable size. It seemed to have sensed our approach, and it was clearly reacting. The abomination began to spew large globs of dark matter into space.

"Uh, Captain?" Jort said. "I think we have a problem."

Droad, Huan, and I all pored over the tables to look at the incoming data. There was definitely *something* coming at us out of the gravity well of that moon. As the mass of organic matter began to split apart before our eyes, it became not just one thing, but many things.

"How big are those blobs?" I asked. "Give me a size estimate."

Huan worked the numbers. He turned to me after a moment. His two strange, misaligned eyes registered surprise. "I've calculated these objects to be between five hundred and a thousand meters in length, sir."

"Wow," I said. "That's bigger than any of Trask's destroyers, and it rivals his transports."

"Exactly."

"But are they dangerous?" Jort demanded.

"Undoubtedly so," Droad said. "Why else would the enemy throw them up here at us?"

"Such an odd response..." I said, crossing my arms. "They clearly intend to protect this planet and destroy us, but looking at the velocity of these blobs, there's no way they can catch us. We're not in any immediate danger."

"Right," Droad said, "but what about Trask's fleet? It's coming in behind us, and you just gave him the green light to move into orbit."

"I'll contact him immediately."

Count Trask was unhappy with my new report and demanded to know why I hadn't warned him earlier about the blobs and these aliens on the warpath.

I found his requests to be unreasonable, so I ignored them.

"The point is, Count Trask," I said, "the enemy is aware of us and moving into a defensive posture. We've calculated that your fleet is directly in the path of this swarm of blobs. What's more, they have not yet stopped firing them up into space."

"How the hell are they doing that? Did they fire one of those damned cannons, like the one on Chara? Are there any flames, plasma releases, or vapor trails?"

"We're not seeing any conventional means of propulsion. It's most likely some kind of organic methane explosion on the surface of the moon. In fact, now that I think about it—with its lesser gravity—I can see why they would want to use the moon as a defensive fortress to protect this world."

"Go on, Gorman, tell me the worst of it."

"I think that the aliens chose this place to make a stronghold. First of all, it works like a castle as it has a defensive fortress—that moon. It also has a large amount of untouched organics, like a stash of emergency food."

"What the hell are you prattling about?"

I frowned and gathered my thoughts. "Listen, the moon has a low gravity and organic content they've converted to provide these blobs to fire into space. That's a defensive operation, like a tower or a moat on a castle."

Trask looked annoyed but thoughtful. "All right. Let's say I accept this weird premise. Why build a tower out here? What are they protecting? Normal humans and wildlife are all over that planet. Why protect them?"

"I think they view the planet as a stash of sustenance. An emergency food supply. If everything goes wrong, they wouldn't starve for many years here as long as they were careful with their resources."

"A whole planet? Set aside as a snack for later?"

"Yes... but it's more than that. It's a strategic reserve for them. Organics are everything for these aliens. They're fuel, life, building materials—everything."

Trask took all this in, and although he wasn't happy, he was intrigued and glad he had sent me out here as a scout.

"All right," he said after a moment's thought. "You've done well, I suppose. These aliens continue to surprise us at every turn. We shall destroy these blobs and the disgusting growth that pulses on the surface of that moon. Nothing shall stop us from winning this war."

Trask's navigators chose a course that did not intersect with Sapphire itself, but rather was designed to swing around behind the planet and strike the grotesquely infected moon that rode behind her.

Satisfied with Trask's dedication to the mission, I stayed quiet. I turned my ship and flew back to the primary formation which was coming up behind us. In reality, all *Royal Fortune* had to do was slow down and veer into the path of the pirate fleet. They soon caught up with us.

The fully assembled fleet assumed an attack formation. Hours crept by as we glided closer and closer. The enemy ships, if they could be called that, approached on an opposite, intersecting angle.

Jort complained about this. "Shouldn't we dodge around these blobs?" he asked. "Why not ignore them and go for the planet itself?"

"That's not my call to make, Jort," I said. "In any case, I think Trask is doing it right. We can't have these blobs getting behind us. We don't know what they can do. What if their actual goal is to escape the star system and infect another world somewhere else? We can't let these aliens spread any further than we already have."

It was difficult and suspenseful to fly directly into the teeth of an enemy. Although I had carefully placed *Royal Fortune* at the rear of the battle formation, I was still aware that when two large groups of ships met in battle, anything was possible.

That was doubly true in the case of the large, bulbous ships that were coming at us from the water moon. We had no idea what their capabilities were, but it seemed obvious that they weren't going to be pleasant.

Trask ordered a barrage of missiles to be fired when we reached extreme range. Something like twenty minutes after they were launched, the missiles made contact with the strange enemy fleet, which made no attempt to dodge or evade the warheads.

The weird ships were mottled with what looked like irregular pigment. These splotches expanded when the missiles came near. They were evidently porous holes. From these pores countermeasures were released. A storm of tiny anti-missiles, chaff, strange gases, and even radio emissions intended to jam the approaching barrage of warheads were deployed.

In many cases, these countermeasures were successful. A lot of Trask's missiles exploded too early and were destroyed before they could reach their targets. In other cases, our weapons flew randomly off course as if confused. A few of them simply plunged headlong into the blob-like enemy ships and vanished, their warheads never going off.

"It looks like a total failure," Jort said, watching the battle unfold.

"Just wait, the Sword Brothers always have some surprises."

Sure enough, although the initial barrage of missiles was absorbed, discarded or shrugged off by the approaching enemy, it appeared that Trask's missiles were stealthy in their own right. They had each released a number of small bomblets behind them in their wake. These objects had no propulsion of their own and did their damage with kinetic impact instead of using any kind of explosive.

The bomblets were only about the size of a tennis ball, but it didn't seem to matter. Hundreds of them struck the approaching blobs. In many cases the organic ships were torn apart and destroyed.

We cheered, and we pumped our arms. We dared to hope for victory.

But, after all the smoke and activity had cleared, we saw that the enemy blobs still retained two thirds of their number. These survivors were still on course for our fleet. Each blob was as big or bigger than the largest vessel in our flotilla. Worse, they outnumbered us nearly two to one.

"We have to do better," Jort said. "Will Trask fire another barrage?"

"I don't think there's time," I said. "If he fires now, we'll be right in the middle of it by the time the missiles strike home. No, we're inside beam range now."

As if I was able to predict the future, Trask's larger ships—his destroyer-class vessels—all began to fire. They fired beams, shells—everything they had.

The blobs weathered this punishment stoically, driving closer to our formation. I could see already that the aliens approached warfare in space quite differently than we did.

The natural intent of any human space fleet was to destroy the enemy at the greatest possible range. In fact, simply being able to reach out across space farther than your opponent could was often good enough to win any battle.

The aliens, however, came from a radically different school of thought. They were attempting to get in close, to overwhelm us, possibly to envelop us with their odd, fleshy vessels. Perhaps when they got in close, they would fire thousands of mini-missiles and bomblets of their own. Or maybe they would use tiny explosive pods as they had on previous encounters.

Whatever their plans were, they had to deal with our heavier, longer-ranged firepower first. As it turned out, shells and beams were harder to evade or jam than long-range missiles had proved to be. Proton beams stitched burning lines across the skin of the approaching blobs. Shells hammered home like bullets slamming into exposed bellies.

Within minutes, huge holes gaped in many of the enemy vessels. Some of them kept coming despite venting gases. They released streams of flaming plasma into space. The battle was wild and beautiful in a way, an insane display of fireworks, tricks of physics, and destruction in general on a grand scale.

Before the aliens could reach us, another third of them were gone. Twisted hulks like dead whales spun and drifted in space. Dead or dying and ripped apart, they looked like deflated balloons.

"On my home planet, we have beasts that look like this," Jort said. "They come up from the oceans and flip onto the shore. They are big and ugly, and they come from the deepest part of the sea."

"Jellyfish?" I asked.

He stared at me for a moment. "That's a good name for them, but that's not what we call them."

"Whatever, Jort. Huan, what are the odds now?"

"Captain, the enemy appears to have fewer ships in play than we do at this point, but they still out mass us. Now that we're in close range, I think they're going to be able to strike back soon."

This was a chilling thought. So far, we had been delivering all the punishment. Every gun, missile, and beam that had landed had come from our side. Despite this, we'd only managed to damage the approaching enemy. The aliens weren't yet defeated. Now that we were coming into close quarters, the battle was about to shift gears.

As the two fleets came together, I gritted my teeth. We all braced ourselves for impact.

Just before the two lines collided, however, Count Trask gave a shocking general command to every captain in the flotilla.

"Pull out!" he shouted. "Break off—break formation! Every ship is to run independently. Scatter in random directions. Do it now!"

It was an order that every pirate captain was born and bred to follow when things became risky. If anything, everybody in the fleet had already been thinking about doing it on their own.

Instead of plowing into the teeth of this implacable, organic enemy fleet, we broke apart and scattered—running a hundred directions at once.

Royal Fortune was far from the last ship to comply with Count Trask's order. In fact, we were probably one of the nimblest and quickest ships in the flotilla, and I didn't need to be told twice to evade danger.

I seized the controls from Huan and steered my ship at a random angle. *Royal Fortune* heeled over onto her back, and I hit the jets hard. We roared away, blasting our overpowered engines for all they were worth.

Even so, as we came nearer to passing the alien fleet, I saw that the enemy had not been entirely idle.

Dark, twisted, oblong slivers fired from the swarm of blob-like vessels. These came on with surprising velocity, and they aimed in a random spray of directions. Every enemy vessel had essentially released a cone of what appeared to be organic missiles, almost as if they'd each fired a thousand snakes from the front of their ships at every possible angle.

The shotgun effect caught the slowest members of Trask's fleet by surprise. Many of these were the ships that were in the general center of mass and had not been able to break formation quickly enough for fear of hitting a sister ship.

Like a line of cars at a stoplight, each ship in Trask's fleet had to wait until the one ahead of him had taken their turn. I suspected that android pilots would have done better, peeling off with much greater precision.

The alien strike spelled doom for the ships in the center of our formation. They were hit ten, fifty, sometimes even a hundred times by the twisting, meter-long snakes that had been flung from the enemy vessels. No evasion, deflection or countermeasures were able to stop them all.

First one, then three more, then dozens of Sword Brother's ships exploded. The dying vessels sent out vast plumes of flame into space. Each of these fires lasted only a second or two, as there was no oxygen in the void to keep them burning.

The only positive from all of this destruction was the numerous wrecked ships themselves. They tumbled, flaming and badly damaged, directly into the path of the approaching enemy. Dozens of the organic blobs were destroyed when these dead metal hulks crashed into them.

Trask then gave orders for us to come about and face the enemy formation again. We employed the greater maneuverability of our ships to swing around behind the remaining blobs, and we shot them in the ass.

This revealed a key weakness of the enemy's organic ship design. Namely, that it was difficult for them to maneuver without the power of combustion-chamber-based engines. Without jets of plasma and flame behind them, they were unable to quickly change course.

The aliens fired more twisty, worm-like living missiles into our path. The half of Trask's fleet that had survived was able to evade this effort, however, and we destroyed everything the aliens had left.

When it was over, we were all breathing hard, sweating, and feeling mildly sick. There was no cheering as too many had died.

Trask's fleet had held together, but barely. Listening to command chat, I heard the voices of a dozen captains demanding they be released from service and sent home. Some were threatening to mutiny, while others were arguing that this defeat was too great and that the fleet could not continue.

As only Trask could do, he employed his unique mix of threat, invective, shaming and rabble-rousing to keep them all together. He claimed that we understood this enemy now, and we could defeat them more easily in the future. Furthermore, if we did not do so now, the entire human race faced extinction.

As a result, with very few exceptions, the pirate fleet assumed an attack formation. We again set course for Sapphire, heading on a circular path that would take us around and behind the planet.

The malignant water moon that hid behind the colony world was our target.

Chapter Thirty-Eight

When we reached the water moon, we found that the pulsing hump on its surface was bulging ominously.

"That thing looks like it's gonna blow," Jort said, and I had to agree.

I sent a warning call to Trask, but he'd already seen it.

"We can't save the moon," he told me. "We're going to have to launch another missile barrage. If there's anyone alive down there at this point, they're going to be dead after this. That's just how it is in war."

True to his word, he ordered every ship in the fleet to fire their remaining missiles. They sailed on an arcing course and plunged into the atmosphere of the water moon. Explosions went off in an enveloping pattern all around the small globe.

Many of the warheads targeted the tumor on the side of the tiny planetoid, but not all of them did. Trask wanted to be sure.

Reverberating explosions flashed all around the moon, tearing away the atmosphere. The repugnant tumor had been burned and crushed. Within half an hour's time, the entire surface was nothing but ash and glowing embers. Nothing could have survived.

Rose was particularly alarmed by these events. "Is he going to do that to the entire planet of Sapphire? It's such a beautiful place."

I glanced at her, and I wanted to lie. I wanted to tell her I didn't think he would, but I just didn't have it in me. This was especially true since I'd be proven a fool within a few minutes if Trask decided to go for it—so I said nothing.

We all watched in grim silence as Trask's fleet did one quick sweep around the moon and then flew back to the larger planet and parked in orbit over her.

Intensive scanning began. We searched for the aliens, but we found none. In fact, we received radio signals from the planet's surface that were quite human.

"Unknown fleet?" a voice called. It sounded strained, worried and haggard. "Strange alien fleet, who are you? Where do you come from?"

Trask answered this voice. I was only able to listen, not being directly in the communications link. That was just as well, I thought. If I had to listen to their cries of anguish while Trask ordered their mass execution... well, I didn't want to be in on that conversation.

"This is Count Trask. We have come here to liberate you, to free you from the aliens. We shall destroy the evil masters that govern your planet."

"Our masters?" the voice asked. "We have no masters—not exactly. If you mean those disgusting creatures that inhabit our moon, well, you've destroyed them all."

"Are you sure?" Trask asked. "I was told that you had envoys among you. I would like to either speak to them or at least be told where they are."

I knew Trask was being tricky, and I also knew immediately why he had not allowed me on this channel. Part of me wanted to insert my opinions by patching into the fateful conversation. I wanted to warn the people of Sapphire, those who had clearly suffered for decades, not to be foolish.

I wanted to warn them—the last people alive in the Faustian Chain—that they should not admit to having any aliens on their planet. I wanted to tell them that if they did so, Trask was likely to burn their lovely planet to a cinder.

But I said nothing. I did nothing. Because Trask was right.

He meant to remove this infection in the most harsh and thorough manner possible. He was like a surgeon with a laser and scalpel. When he met his enemy, he burned or cut it away, and he intended to do so until nothing was left.

The colonists below us were helpless and pathetic. They seemed confused, but they kept insisting that there were no aliens on their planet, none that they were aware of. They said the aliens had simply parked themselves on Sapphire's moon and built a great base there. They had no idea why they'd been spared, unlike so many other worlds in the Chain.

We, of course, believed we knew the truth. They were a snack, a stash of food, an extra bit of organic matter that had been saved untouched for later. They were the aliens' insurance policy.

Trask considered all this and to my surprise, he showed them a modicum of mercy.

"All right," he said. "We will come down, we will check, and we will search. If we find a *single* nest, if we find a *single* alien, just one Shrade, or culus, or killbeast—any of them—we will destroy all of you for having lied to us!"

This, of course, elicited great alarm among the humans on the planet. They begged for their lives and went on about how truthful they were, insisting that they were unaware of any alien presence. I felt for them.

Naturally, Trask had lied again. He was merely trying to get them to admit they had aliens, so he could destroy them without compunction.

My crew and I twisted in our seats. It was difficult to listen to these poor people that had been terrorized by their own moon for decades. They'd watched every colony on every world in the Chain be overcome by aliens and destroyed. Now here they were, finally meeting with a possible rescuer, only to be immediately threatened again with utter destruction.

It was harsh, but I understood Trask's logic. He had to know if the aliens were truly extinct. If these people were infected, enslaved, or harboring aliens in any way on their planet, the enemy would only consume them, regrow, and become a threat again. Seedships would fly once more to who knew where in the cosmos. Someday, those ships would return and reinfect our planets. This ordeal would not be over with until the last alien was dead and gone.

Trask landed two days later, and *Royal Fortune* landed just after. Troops were quickly deployed to the highest hills, the lowest valleys, and the deepest mining shafts that were sunk into the planet's crust.

We searched, and we scanned everything. We used our eyes, our feet, and complex instruments. We tried to find any trace of the aliens—anything at all.

We found nothing, even over a period of weeks. This made us all feel increasingly happy. I felt now that even if we *did* find a few aliens somewhere, we could probably just destroy them and consider the task done. There was no real need to destroy the planet in its entirety.

Trask was not yet done, however.

After spending so much time in the hills and jungles and forests, he turned his fleet to examining the glittering sea beds. Spaceships oftentimes operated rather well underwater or just above water, if handled correctly. We probed the sea, which was quite shallow and held few secrets.

Eventually, even Trask was satisfied that the planet was pristine.

By this time, we had come to know the people of Sapphire. They were very much like normal humans, except a little shorter than the average person you would find in the Conclave. I wondered if having lived for so long under fear of death from above had taken some physical toll. After all, they'd been gazing up at night to a moon covered with malignant brown swollen humps of alien organic matter. Had these nightly horror shows somehow stunted them? I didn't know.

When Trask at last relaxed, we hosted members of Sapphire's ruling council aboard our ships. All told, there were less than three hundred thousand humans living on the planet. They said that many of their people had volunteered long ago to go fight the aliens, but they had died in great numbers. Only the survivors had been left behind to squat here, cowering and wondering when death would come.

They found the pirates threatening, of course, but even Trask's men were disciplined enough not to terrorize these locals. They had no wealth and presented no threat. There was some humanity left in even the harshest of men when they found people living under such horrible circumstances.

The aliens had, in a way, brought us all together. I did not know how long that condition would last, but I figured we should revel in the feeling while we could.

Taking representatives from Sapphire onto his flagship to show off to the Sword Worlds, Trask and his great fleet left orbit, and we flew across the Chain. We searched several more star systems, but we never found another detectable presence of the enemy on any of them.

We didn't find any living humans, either.

Could the enemy still be hiding somewhere among these stars? Yes, of course. The aliens were adept at lying dormant, sitting on some icy planetoid the way they had been at the Sardez system. They were almost certainly hiding somewhere, but for now, they'd been beaten. At the very least they were no longer an open threat.

There were still, of course, the countless seedships traveling toward Conclave planets. For the next dozen years or so, they would arrive periodically in a hundred places.

But those aliens could be dealt with by the Conclave androids. We now knew how to find them, how to overwhelm them, and how to destroy them. We knew every sign of their presence. If they did infect a Conclave world in the future, we would isolate and eradicate them like the vermin they were.

Chapter Thirty-Nine

Exiting the Faustian Chain, we felt sure we had defeated all known infected worlds. It was a good feeling, a feeling of victory.

On the long flight home to the Conclave, Rose stayed with me. She was once again tired of adventure, but she was very happy with the part we had both played in this one.

We left Morwyn on Vindar after saying our goodbyes. Huan left my service and went back to bounty hunting, I presumed.

Droad stayed with me, to my surprise, while Jort refused to leave my side. He demanded to stay on as part of my crew, and I accepted him happily. Even Sosa sent word that she would like to return and possibly aid me in my future endeavors.

We headed for Tranquility for a much-needed vacation. Within weeks of returning to the Conclave however, I received a summons I could not ignore. The summons was from the Connactic herself.

Sighing, I contacted Rose, Jort, and Droad to let them know I would be leaving for Mutual. Rose expressed concern that I might be tricked and executed or something like that. I assured her this would not be the case.

Jort said he would wait for me faithfully on Tranquility until I returned. This did not surprise me at all, as he was having quite a good time vacationing.

Of the three of them, only Droad wanted to come with me. I looked over the summons again and, as I saw no restrictions forbidding me to take a guest, I decided to allow him to tag along.

We flew from Tranquility to Mutual and were met with the usual cold reception that I always seemed to get on that planet. Androids are not much for celebration or congratulations.

We were led down to the surface from the space station with a complete absence of fanfare. Eventually, we worked our way down into the vaults below Mutual's sprawling cities.

There, the Connactic herself came to meet the two of us. She eyed Droad with curiosity.

"Tell me about your guest, Captain Gorman."

I introduced Droad, explaining that he was the former governor of a planet known as Garm, part of the Faustian Chain. She was suitably impressed.

She told us that she had met with a congregation of individuals from the Sapphire colony. She looked again at Droad with curiosity.

"Do you know anything about Sapphire?" she asked.

"Yes, a little," he admitted. "When the Nexus fell, we hadn't yet marked that planet as lost. It was an outpost, really. There were very few colonists living there at the time. We did not calculate that the colony had much value because the population was so low. It was not a priority to save them—so we made no effort to do so."

The Connactic nodded. "These people seem to be the only survivors of the original Faustian Chain population."

"That is possible," Droad admitted.

"And you, as far as I know, are one of the few people who actually have a background in official government from the Chain."

Droad eyed her. He was alert now and wondering where this was going. I was wondering the same.

"I have a proposal for you, Governor Droad of Garm."

"What is it, madam?" he asked.

"I would suggest that you return to Sapphire and become her governor."

"Hmm," he said. "Under what authority is the Conclave allowed to appoint a governor over an independent colony?"

The Connactic smiled. "Don't be naive, Governor Droad. We have the authority because we have the ships."

Droad mulled that over, and he nodded.

"What you say is indisputable. However, I would require some level of legitimacy—unless you're going to send me there with an army of androids to conquer them?"

"No, no, no, that's not the goal," she said. "I'm seeking you for the very purpose of legitimacy. After all, you are an official from the long absent Nexus government of the Faustian Chain. In fact, as far as I know you're the *only* surviving official of the Nexus. Others that may have survived initially have since perished. Due to flying around so much with time-dilation effects, you have enjoyed an exaggerated life expectancy. Your age, as far as I was able to determine, is closer to a century than the forty or fifty years that your body appears to display."

Droad inclined his head. "That's probably true," he admitted.

"All right then, I need your legitimacy with the people of the Chain, and the people of Sapphire need a proper government. They've essentially been living a peaceful life, but in very primitive conditions. We can provide them aid and equipment to expand and improve their lifestyles into a modern setting. We'll even build them a space station for purposes of trade and immigration."

Droad's eyebrows shot up. "Immigration, you say?"

"Yes," she admitted. "We want to repopulate and re-colonize those planets in the Chain that are still serviceable."

"Serviceable…" he said. "That's an interesting choice of words."

The Connactic and Droad eyed each other for a moment.

"I can see," Droad said, "how this will be a viable plan. Sapphire's a lovely world. It will no doubt attract immigrants, but it is quite far from the Conclave, and will therefore be difficult for you to defend."

"Yes," she said. "This is true. We will have to put a few patrol vessels in orbit to shoot down any seedships, should they return someday."

"Generous, generous," Droad said. "So far, I have to admit, I like the plan. What will my relationship be with your government? Will we remain independent or…?"

"Independent…?" the Connactic sighed. "Why is it that humans always want independence? Androids seek nothing of the kind. We much prefer interconnectivity. If any one of us is outside the range of another, our intellectual capacities actually diminish."

"Another interesting admission. But in any case, you didn't answer my question."

"So I didn't… I would say your status will be that of an integrated dominion. You'll be a protectorate of the Conclave, but locally ruled by a human-oriented government."

"Does this mean we can develop our own trade, military, laws—?"

The Connactic raised a flat hand to stop his questions. "You'll be independent in the sense that you'll be making most of your own decisions—should they not conflict with our wants and desires. All off-planet foreign affairs will be ours to deal with."

Droad nodded, thinking that over. "I think that's reasonable. You're already providing for our defense and offering economic development. I can't refuse."

"You agree then to answer this call? To serve the people of Sapphire as you once did the citizens of Garm and other worlds?"

"I do," he said.

Droad then lifted his hand in an ancient gesture known as the handshake. The Connactic looked at the hand for a moment, as if slightly confused, but then, somewhere in her memory circuits, she found the stored knowledge of the proper response.

She clasped his hand and awkwardly shook it. I suspected that this was probably the first time she had ever shaken hands with anyone.

Impressed and smiling, I congratulated them both on this new partnership. They accepted my congratulations, and the Connactic asked that Droad excuse himself. He did so quite happily.

Left alone with her, I wondered what fate she might have in mind for me.

"Captain Gorman," she said. "I've been very impressed by your service. You were critical on several missions in this campaign. I would ask you to serve in a different role in the future."

"Service?" I asked, my heart sinking. Visions of long lazy days on Tranquility's beaches were fading fast. "What service are we talking about?"

"I would ask you to become a diplomat."

"A *diplomat*?" I said, rolling the word around on my tongue. I found that it sounded quite foreign to me.

"Yes. Specifically, you'll be *my* diplomat. I wish to use you as a go-between, a communications specialist—a liaison, if you will."

"A diplomat to whom?"

"Count Trask, for one. Governor Droad for another. I've recently given them elevated status. Droad has almost sovereign power over the Faustian Chain."

I found I was surprised and amused by the entire concept. "You do realize, ma'am, that I'm actually something of an underworld figure?"

"Yes, yes," she said. "I know of your criminal past, but as you may recall, all those sins have been erased."

"Right… they're erased in the sense that I'm no longer liable to be arrested. I have been pardoned, but as an individual, I'm still the same man who performed all those questionable acts in the past."

She nodded. "Exactly, and I'm the one who pardoned you. This is why you're trustworthy. This is why you will fly your ship between worlds, bringing goods from one ruler to the next. You will not be questioned. It is what you already do. I'm simply asking that you do your trading with my interests at heart."

I was beginning to catch on. "This sounds more like the role of a spy than that of a diplomat."

She shrugged, an unusually human gesture for an android. "Humans have served in both capacities in the past."

I smiled, and as I considered her words, I felt she had made a compelling case. "But why me? Surely, there must be others who are more qualified. Perhaps someone like B-6?"

"If I were to send another 'plastic man', as your people like to call us, to talk to Governor Droad or Count Trask, how do you think he might be received?"

"Poorly," I admitted.

"Exactly. I want you instead. You can talk to me. You can talk to Droad. You can talk to Trask, and I'm sure you'll do a good job befriending plenty of others on some of the Fringe worlds. We've had so little contact with them recently."

"This is quite a change for the Conclave," I said. "You've held yourself in aloof isolation for many years."

"You're right. That policy was a mistake. Because of that crucial error, we lost the Chain—everything but Sapphire. We nearly lost the Conclave as well. We even lost several colonies along the Fringe. Possibly, we'll lose more as the seedships continue to arrive, but I don't want that to happen due to lack of communication. We must directly interact with every center of power that rises now or in the future. Will you help me do this, Captain Gorman?"

Thinking it over for a moment or two, I knew I didn't like all of the angles to this offer, but I also thought it was better than many alternative arrangements. In the end, I smiled, and I raised my hand exactly as Droad had done. The Connactic responded more quickly and adroitly this time. She wasn't left staring at my fingers or fumbling the handshake.

With my new status secured, I wheeled around and left her sterile stronghold. Returning to Tranquility, I found that, to my surprise, Rose was still waiting there for me. Jort was as well, but that was because he wasn't finished with gambling, chasing hookers and sleeping on beaches in a drunken stupor.

Rose... I really had to do some thinking about her.

I'd met her a few years back. She was so different from any of the other women I'd ever been involved with. Being an innocent citizen and not a pirate of any kind, I found myself especially attached to her—in a way I'd known with very few others. I found myself thinking that possibly, she and I could make a life together.

Things were different now. The aliens were defeated, I had a ship of my own, and I even had a legitimate job. I felt, for the first time in decades, that my life was my own again.

For years I'd been running from one crime to the next, always worried about paying debts, always worried about getting noticed or caught. More recently, of course, there had been the fact of my death and return as a clone, and then the constant strife of the alien invasion.

Today, I stood on a beach with Rose at my side. I stared at the waves crashing on the sand, and I felt that my future might actually be different than my past. I could now conceive of settling down, raising a family, and becoming an honest man.

We walked along a warm beach next to a warm ocean. Rose talked, and I pretended to listen. As we strolled, my thoughts were crowded with images of distant planets, cold heartless stars, and even colder and more heartless aliens.

I suddenly looked down at her, and she looked up at me, stopping in mid-sentence.

"Aren't you listening?" she asked.

"Listening? Of course, I'm listening."

"Then why do you have that strange look on your face?"

I smiled at her, and it was a real smile this time. "I just had an important thought," I told her. "I've wanted to ask you something, but I didn't know how to approach the question."

She blinked a few times, and then she stared.

"Ask," she said, "just ask."

So, I did. I asked her to marry me, and she cried. Our lives were changed forever after that.

Above the sand and the waves, above the windy beaches and the blue skies, there were countless dangers lurking. I knew that, but I also knew that those dangers had always been there for every human couple, and it was wrong to let your knowledge and fears get in the way of your happiness.

STAR RUNNER TRILOGY
Star Runner
Fire Fight
Androids and Aliens

Books by B. V. Larson:

UNDYING MERCENARIES
Steel World
Dust World
Tech World
Machine World
Death World
Home World
Rogue World
Blood World
Dark World
Storm World
Armor World
Clone World
Glass World
Edge World
Green World
Ice World

REBEL FLEET SERIES
Rebel Fleet
Orion Fleet
Alpha Fleet
Earth Fleet

Visit BVLarson.com for more information.

Printed in Great Britain
by Amazon